The
ALIBI

Published by Magpie Creative Media

ISBN 978-0-6484406-7-3

NIKKI LEE
TAYLOR

The
ALIBI

Magpie
CREATIVE MEDIA

Dedicated to the place I love most.
My hometown; Newcastle.
Then. Now. And Always.

Chapter One
ELLE

The call crackled in over a police scanner hidden on my desk somewhere beneath a mountain of council reports and old newspaper editions.

All units. Human remains found in the south dunes of Stockton Beach. Access via Waterboard Road. Ambulance and emergency services are en route.

I glanced over my shoulder, then leaned in and turned down the volume. If I was lucky, maybe the other reporters hadn't heard it. I glanced across to the centre cubicles, all allocated to senior reporters, and saw that my nemesis, Willamina Fraser, was not at her desk. With as little fanfare as possible, I slipped off my glasses and rose from my seat.

At the end of the newsroom stood the glass-walled office of our Editor-In-Chief, Henry Walters. He was a gruff bear of a man who loved three things—the Newcastle Knights football team, a beer at his local pub, and shattering the dreams of reporters like me.

I was a metre from his door when I caught sight of her heading in my direction. *Goddamn it.*

I'd been given the role of lead crime reporter while Willamina was on sabbatical at the *Sydney Morning Herald* for the past three months. Now she was back and clearly thought her shit didn't stink even more than she had before.

When we reached Walters' door, I was half a step in front.

"I want it," I announced, trying to elbow her out of the way. "Technically, I'm here first and if it's the body of Isabelle Summers, then I deserve to cover it. It was my piece when she went missing."

Compared to Willamina's statuesque frame, I felt like a pipsqueak but I wasn't going to let her latitude, or my lack thereof, get in the way of being the lead reporter on what was surely going to be a front-page story—especially if the body turned out to be my missing person.

"You've got to be kidding, Nolan?" she scoffed, tossing back her mane of black hair and immediately reminding me of Cruella De Vil. "You filled in for a few months and didn't fuck it up. Good for you. Now go back to your council meetings and wait your turn. Having a famous father doesn't count for shit in the newsroom." Certain I was firmly back in my place, she looked over my head toward our editor. "Boss, I've got this. I'll grab a clicker and head out. Call you when I'm on the ground."

Walters nodded and looked back down at his sandwich, its filling spilling out across the paper bag on his desk. Fraser turned to leave. It was now or never.

Newcastle might be the sixth largest city in Australia, but dead bodies on the beach didn't come about all that often. Isabelle Summers had been missing for three months, and technically, it was my story. If I could follow it through to the end, maybe it would be enough to get me off the council round—a job that, for so many reasons, I needed out of.

"Wait," I announced. "Everyone, just wait a minute."

To my surprise, Willamina stopped and stared at me. Walters froze mid-chew. "I think I deserve to be considered. This is my story. I've been on it since she went missing."

Willamina snorted, tucked her pen back behind her ear, and planted her fists against her hips. "And I appreciate you filling in, Nolan. But like I said, I'll take it from here." She turned her attention back to Walters. "I'm heading out."

Again, he just nodded and looked back at his lunch.

"Seriously, boss? Not even a response?" I asked when she was gone.

"She's the senior crime reporter and you have a story on your desk that I'm waiting on," he said in a bland tone. "Besides, there's nothing to prove it's the body of that missing girl. Could be a shark attack or a drowning. We don't have any details. Don't get so wound up, Nolan."

"But if it is her— "

"Then Fraser will handle it."

I would not let myself cry in front of Walters, but the rest of what I wanted to say was stuck beneath a giant lump in my throat.

Sensing my struggle, he pushed the air out of his nose, put down the sandwich, and pulled some tissues from a battered-up cardboard box that had seen better days. "You need one of these?"

I shook my head defiantly, not trusting my own voice.

"Look, Nolan," he said with a sigh. "You did a great job while Fraser was away, but she won the Walkley Award last year. I know you want the crime round and I have no doubt you were up all night listening to true crime podcasts, but you're a kick-arse council reporter. You really have a knack for digging deep and your relationships are strong, especially with the Lord Mayor. Take a piece of advice from an old hack. Stay in your lane, at least for now."

I steadied myself until I was confident my voice would not crack. "I need out of the council round, boss, and I do want crime, but I'm open to other suggestions. Anything. Just not council."

"Have you read the report I gave you?" he asked, completely ignoring my last response.

"I did. Makes for a great sedative."

"Well... it might have legs."

Despite my disappointment, I almost laughed. "Newcastle City Council is never going to approve a flashy Gold Coast style beach resort at sleepy Stockton. It's a residential village and you know how Andrew... the Lord Mayor... feels about keeping it that way. He grew up there. Trust me, boss, it's not going to happen."

"Good yarn, though."

"Is it?" I asked with a frustrated sigh. "The rezoning application will get knocked on the head at the next council meeting. That land will be carved up for residential development. Trust me, the story is a dead end."

Walters scrunched up the tissue and attempted to volley it into the bin. He missed by a mile.

"I've been where you are and I get it, Nolan," he sighed. "But for now, can you just read the damned Ridgemont Capitol report and write the story? I've got it penciled in for tomorrow's edition and online tonight if you can get it done in time."

I turned to leave, but then stopped and looked back. "Anne Rule."

"What?"

"I was up all night reading Anne Rule," I sighed. "She wrote *The Stranger Beside Me*. You know, Ted Bundy? I'm not much for the podcasts."

"'Course you were," he said, rolling his eyes. "Now just go write the damned council piece, please."

Back at my desk, I turned off the police scanner and let out a long, frustrated breath. I couldn't bear to hear any more calls about the dead body I wanted to cover. I'd worked my arse off while Willamina was out making a name for herself in Sydney. I made contacts and had insight into angles even she wouldn't have got, and for what? The minute she stepped her stupid black high-heeled boot back into the office, all my hard work went out the window. Reluctantly, I picked up the council report as my mobile phone buzzed with a text message.

David: *You covering Stockton?*

Me: *No, but I wanted to*

I held onto the phone, knowing it wouldn't take long for him to respond.

David: *Fraser?*

Even seeing her name on the screen made my chest tighten. Not only because she was on the story I wanted but also because she was just a bitch in general.

Me: *Afraid so*

David: *Makes you feel any better there's just a leg. No body. Female though*

Before I could digest the information, another text buzzed through from David with a photo of the crime scene. The dunes were already swarming with police, SES, and ambulance crew.

Me: *TV crews there?*

David: *Local crews are being held up at the gate. Metro has a bird in the air. There's a marquee over the leg so they won't get much*

David Hammond was my source. He was also a friend. We completed our communications degree together at the University of Newcastle and crossed paths five years later at a press conference outside the Newcastle Local Area Command. By then, his career had taken a left turn and he was Unit Commander in the local arm of the NSW State Emergency Service. I was a reporter at the Newcastle Tribune. He'd been a huge help in Isabelle's missing persons case and even though we hadn't found her, David provided me with exclusive video and content as he and his team searched the Glenrock State Conservation Area where she was last seen.

Me: *You think the leg belongs to Isabelle?*

David: *Hard to say*

Elle: *I know it's weird but I really want to be there*

David: *Not weird. You're a journo. You're supposed to want to be here*

Despite the fact I wouldn't classify myself as attractive, mostly due to my oversized arse, squinty eyes, and mop of mousy brown hair that refused to grow past my collarbone, I always got the feeling David had a crush on me. It made no sense because he was a handsome guy, and I didn't understand what he could possibly see in me. If he did have feelings, it definitely wasn't appropriate for me to take advantage just to get inside information, especially when my heart was somewhere else. But, I also wanted to be a great journalist.

I put the phone down and gazed into the side pocket of my tote bag. Staring back was a tempting array of colourfully wrapped chocolate bars. To anyone else, *eating your feelings* was a natural reaction to disappointment. If I were to unwrap one of those chocolate bars and eat it in commiseration, for most people, it wouldn't be any big deal. But I wasn't most people. For me, after one chocolate bar would come another, and then another, until there was nothing left. Knowing I'd already let myself down, I'd follow up with McDonald's, a tub of ice cream, an entire packet of biscuits, then whatever else was in the house until I felt the repulsive waves of oil and sugar coursing along the inside of my skin.

I was a binge eater. And it sucked.

In times of stress, I would gorge myself until I could barely stand. Then, hunched from the strain of an almost bursting stomach, I would stumble into the bathroom and force myself to purge everything I ate. My throat would burn and tears would sting the rims of my eyes. I wasn't sure if the shame of it made me cry or if the tears were just my body's reaction to the heaving—but I hated it. Afterward, there was a small window of relief when my stomach was empty and I would delight in the hollow ache inside. In the week that followed a binge, I would relentlessly try to outrun my demons on the treadmill, but only in my living room, never at a gym where people might figure out my secret. As I ran, guilt and anger would chase me, nipping at my heels like starving shadows. Faster and harder, they would push until every remaining calorie, real or imagined, was either sweated out or burned into oblivion. It was a relentless and exhausting cycle. And one that had been going on since university.

I glanced back down at the phone and bit my lip. What I was about to do next would no doubt start the cycle all over again, but making your way in a newsroom was cut-throat. If I didn't grab hold of every opportunity, *I would never reach my full potential.* And everyone knew that was to become a famous crime writer like my father. It had been that way since a novella I wrote during the first year of my degree, *The Nine Lives of Kitty Kramburger* won The Patricia Wrightson Prize for fiction. Since then, everyone expected me to carry on his legacy, but so far I was yet to deliver.

I pulled my eyes away from the stash of chocolate and started typing a message back to David.

Me: Any chance we could meet for a drink later?

David: You got it.

Under David's leadership, over the next few hours, or maybe even days, the SES team would continue searching for more body parts. If the leg belonged to Isabelle Summers and they found evidence to confirm her identity, I wanted to know before Willamina. If I could get in front of it, maybe Walters would let me take over the story, and if I did a good job, there was every chance he might promote me from the council round. And I needed an escape. Sooner rather than later. The rest of my career depended on it.

Chapter Two
ANDREW

"They're still out looking," Stella said as their golden cocker spaniel Gucci ran ahead like a cork just popped from the bottle.

Andrew nodded and held up a hand to shield his eyes from the slowly setting sun. It was four-thirty in the afternoon and the dunes were still crawling with SES and police.

"Who do you think it belonged to?" she asked. "The leg, I mean. Do you think it could be that woman who went missing a few months back?"

Andrew pondered whether to tell his wife everything he knew or just stick to repeating today's news headlines. He settled with, "That's their job to figure out, I guess."

"But what do *you* think?" she asked, a sharp tone in her voice. "You're the Lord Mayor, for Christ's sake. You must know more than the news."

He briefly met her eye and considered how to answer. "What I think, Stell... is that it's sad no matter who the leg belongs to."

Clearly frustrated, she shook her head and took two strides ahead. It wasn't unusual for Andrew's wife to be unimpressed with his response, or with most things he did, but after nine years in a miserable marriage, he was getting pretty used to that.

"Stella..." She stopped but didn't bother turning back. "Look, I do know something," he said, jogging to catch up. "But I don't want you making a big fuss of it, alright?"

She turned to face him, her smile big enough to devour whatever was left of the fading sunlight. "Tell me immediately."

"You can't tell the other women. You have to swear."

"Andrew, do you think I share everything with the girls?" she asked, readjusting the Tiffany necklace she bought for him to give her last Christmas. "Just because we lunch together doesn't mean I disclose everything I know."

He nodded, but knew better. "I don't think the leg belongs to the missing woman."

"And why not?"

Andrew scanned his wife from head to toe. Blonde hair that was impossibly sleek given they were out on the beach, a full face of make-up, and Camilla clothing from head to toe. The outfit must have cost him at least $800. "I think I saw her a few days back, standing up there on the south dunes."

"The missing woman from the news?"

"No, a different woman. She had blonde hair. Isabelle Summers' hair was dark." He stopped walking and stared out at the sea. "I saw her standing up there when I was walking Gucci. I was too far away to see her face, but she was there. It struck me because it's a long walk back to the road and it was such a shitty day. I thought any moment it was going to pour rain. I actually turned and headed straight back to the house myself because I didn't want to end up getting soaked."

Stella came in close, leaving him no choice but to tear his eyes away from the ocean and look at her. "Why haven't you told the police? Andrew, you're the Lord Mayor."

"Exactly. I'm the Lord Mayor. Do you think I want to be personally involved in a case where they found a woman's leg in the dunes just metres from where we live?"

Stella rolled her eyes. "Jesus, it's not like you had anything to do with it. All you did was see her."

He nodded and stared over at the ant's nest of emergency service workers crawling over the dunes.

"That said," she continued, "you need to tell them. There are hundreds of juvenile white sharks out there. She might have gone swimming and been attacked."

"She didn't."

Andrew could feel his wife's eyes on him. He knew she wanted to ask how he could be so sure, but that was the thing about Stella. She might be annoying as hell, but she knew when to stop asking questions.

Chapter Three
STELLA

Stella often wondered whether her husband thought she was stupid. After twenty-seven years of marriage, did Andrew really think he could hide something from her? Maybe if he paid a little more attention, he would realise she knew every one of his secrets. Including the one about *her*.

When he got a few steps in front, Stella stared at the back of his head. She hated the stupid shape of his skull. Often, on their afternoon walks along the beach, she would try to get out in front just so she didn't have to look at it stacked upon his neck like a Halloween pumpkin. Andrew was a handsome man—from the front. But the back of his head, the way it morphed out into the shape of a guitar pick, made her crazy.

As they drew closer to the flurry of police and SES covering the dunes, Andrew scooped Gucci up and under his arm. "Ready to head back?"

"So, you're really not going to tell them what you saw?"

The sun was moments from setting. Around them, the wind collected drops of cold sea water in its arms.

"Stella, just drop it, alright?" he said with a sigh. "I'm certain they'll figure out who the remains belong to. That's what they do. There's really no need."

She studied him as he kicked at sand that was quickly becoming frigid beneath their feet. Something was off and it was annoying her. "You have a civic duty to tell them what you saw."

"Oh bullshit, Stella. Don't give me that crap," he snapped.

"You're the Lord Mayor."

"Correct, and that's exactly why I don't want to get involved."

A hot rush of frustration spread out across her chest despite the cold air. "You're not making any sense."

"Just drop it."

Stella marched over and snatched Gucci from his arms. "Now you listen to me, Andrew. I don't care if you're the Lord Mayor or the Fairy fucking Godmother, you are going to tell them because if it turns out that leg does belong to the girl you saw, and they find out you withheld information, there'll be a media shit storm outside the house. I don't care how you seem to be so sure she wasn't attacked by a shark, but we have two teenage boys living at home, and I for one, will not be explaining why their father lied to the police when it's all over the news."

Andrew's face tightened, and his jaw clenched the way he always did when things weren't going how he wanted. At six-foot-two, he towered over his wife, but he was kidding himself if he thought she was going to back down. As they stood toe-to-toe, staring each other down, Gucci barked and Stella turned to see a female police officer making her way toward them, her feet sinking into the soft sand. Senior Sergeant Lucy Dickson. Despite her petite figure and delicate features, Stella knew the other detectives referred to her as 'Dicks'—a name she was sure the Senior Sergeant had tried to discourage.

"Lucy, hello," Andrew nodded when she reached them. "Any updates on the case?"

The Senior Sergeant glanced briefly at Stella, a shadow of discomfort falling over her face. "Yes sir, we've found more remains."

"Really?"

Stella looked at her husband expectantly, waiting for him to tell the Senior Sergeant what he'd seen. He didn't.

"And are the remains *significant*?"

"Yes, sir."

Another uncomfortable glance at Stella, and it was clear the Senior Sergeant was weighing up how much to say in front of a civilian.

"Well, spit it out," Stella snapped. "What did you find?"

"Sir, I think it would be best to discuss this at tomorrow's briefing," Senior Sergeant Dickson said, casting her eye over Stella one last time. "We all good here?"

Stella pulled Gucci back even further under her arm. "What's that supposed to mean?"

"Means I'm just checking in with you guys. I heard raised voices."

"You've got to be kidding."

"Not kidding, ma'am, and I don't mean any disrespect," she said, her tone flat and unemotional. "Just doing my job."

"Your job is over there." Stella flung her free arm toward the dunes where SES crews were setting up lights powered by the hum of a generator. "Not sticking your nose into our conversations."

"Stella, for Christ's sake," Andrew said and sighed out loud.

"No, Andrew, she's being extremely disrespectful. You're the—"

"Lord Mayor. Yes, I'm aware."

"Sir?" Senior Sergeant Dickson asked.

"We're fine, Lucy, thank you."

The Senior Sergeant nodded and turned to leave, her heavy boots once again sinking with each step.

"Wait!" Stella called out. "Senior Sergeant Dickson..."

"Don't even think about it," Andrew hissed.

Stella pointed her finger into her husband's chest and looked him deep in the eye. "You never have my back. That woman humiliated me, and you just stood there. Besides, I'm not taking any chances on them finding out you saw some girl and didn't say so."

"Yes, ma'am?" Senior Sergeant Dickson was back in front of her, an expectant look on her face.

"My husband forgot to mention that he saw a young woman." Stella cast her eye over Andrew and then back to the Sergeant. "Apparently, she was standing up on the dunes last week. I just thought it might be important."

"You did, sir?"

Senior Sergeant Dickson shifted her gaze to Andrew and pulled a small notepad out from the inside of her navy windbreaker.

Andrew shifted his weight from one foot to the other. "It was hard to tell, really," he said eventually. "There could have been. But as I told my wife, I can't be certain."

The Senior Sergeant nodded and raised her pen, ready to take notes. "And when was this?"

Andrew took a deep breath and stared out at the sea as though he was trying to recall. "I couldn't say for sure."

"It must have been Monday because you were home early, remember?" Stella said. "We had the plumber coming, and I was in Sydney."

"Right," he nodded. "Monday."

She scribbled something in her notebook and glanced over toward the house. "That's your place, right?"

Andrew glanced back at the stark two-storey white residence overlooking the beach. It had been their dream house. "Yes, that's where we live."

"And you were out here on the beach when you saw her?"

He leaned in and scratched Gucci on the head. "Yes, walking the dog."

"Of course," she nodded. "And what time was this?"

"Maybe around 4:30 p.m."

"Great." Senior Sergeant Dickson flipped the notepad closed and slipped it back into her pocket. "We'll be briefing you in the morning when we know what we've got."

Andrew nodded and then he and Stella stood in silence, staring after Senior Sergeant Dickson as she turned and trudged back toward the dunes.

Chapter Four

LUCY

"**D**icks! Get your shit together, it's time for the briefing,"

Yieldon's booming voice echoed across the bullpen, and as always, Lucy Dickson cringed. She hated the name, but giving him a reaction only made things worse.

"Ready, sir," she called back. "I'm good to go."

They would hold a private police briefing to update city officials on the human remains found at Stockton Beach, followed by a public press conference for the media. The *presser*, as it was known, would no doubt turn into a shit fight of questions and angles from reporters hoping the remains belonged to missing woman Isabelle Summers.

Lucy gathered up her notes and waited as her superior, in rank only, Inspector Chris Yieldon to made his way toward her desk. He was a buffoon, to say the least. His passion for beer and cricket far outweighed his dedication to police work. But while ever he held rank over her, he was in charge. That's just the way it worked.

"This should be interesting," she said, as they climbed into the patrol car and headed for City Hall. "What do you make of the information I received yesterday about the Lord Mayor seeing a girl up on the dunes?"

He popped a mint into his mouth and looked out the window. "Hard to say. Could be nothing."

"But it could be something."

He shrugged and turned his attention back to the road. "Best leave that one alone, Dicks. That's what I make of it."

Lucy bit her bottom lip and silently repeated the mantra she had come to know by heart. *I move through stress with a steady calm. I move through stress with a steady calm. I move through stress with a steady calm.*

"You hear me, Dicks?"

She quickly shook it off and nodded. "Yes, sir."

"If it was anything of note, Andrew would have let me know. That bitch of a wife was probably just trying to stir up drama by telling you that."

Lucy didn't know the Lord Mayor well enough to decide whether *that bitch of a wife was probably just trying to stir up drama,* or if perhaps there was a deeper reason he hadn't mentioned seeing the woman at yesterday's briefing. Either way, it wasn't sitting well with her.

"Andrew and I go way back, you know that," Yieldon continued, reminding Lucy of her place. "If there was anything I needed to know, trust me, he would have told me personally."

"Of course, sir," she nodded. "I have no doubt."

The thing was, Lucy had plenty of doubt and every intention of finding out why the Lord Mayor had kept potentially vital information about the case to himself. But she would have to be careful. The last thing she needed was Yieldon on a warpath. If he started looking for ways to make an example of her, he might find more than he was bargaining for.

As they headed along Church Street and past the towering Christchurch Cathedral, Lucy looked over and said a quiet prayer not to fuck this up. Despite her catholic upbringing and three generations of Christian guilt, she didn't believe in God. But if she found dirt on Newcastle's beloved Lord Mayor, she was going to need all the help she could get.

They climbed the stairs to City Hall, an elaborate building designed by a theatre architect in the late 1920s. The irony never failed to amuse her that the building, which also housed Newcastle City Council's monthly meetings, had been designed by someone with a theatrical flair. As far as she was concerned, the building was a perfect reflection of the drama that usually took place inside.

When they entered the designated meeting room housed in the east wing of the building, their audience was already there—a polyester huddle of suit jackets and blazers gathered around a table decorated with muffins and fruit platters.

"Morning everyone," Yieldon announced, as he strode toward a wooden lectern, his arm curled around a pile of unnecessary but official-looking folders.

"Good morning, Inspector," the Lord Mayor replied, quickly taking a seat in the front. "Welcome, and on behalf of everyone here, thank you for coming to brief us on this most unsettling situation."

Lucy took her place beside Yieldon and surveyed the room. In addition to the Lord Mayor, the General Manager of Newcastle City Council Wendy Donahue was in attendance, along with Ward One Councillor Charlie Johnson who represented the residents of Stockton, SES Unit Commander David Hammond and a few of his volunteers, a blonde pinched looking woman sitting by Wendy who she placed as Council's Communications Director, the Head of Hunter New England Health Dr Bart Hastings, and a few other suits she failed to recognise.

"Okay, I'll get right to it," Yieldon began. "Last night, David Hammond and his SES team found additional female remains in dunes to the north of the original site. Medical teams are of the belief that all the remains belong to one victim and it is not missing woman, Isabelle Summers."

"And we're certain of that?" Cr Johnson asked.

"Dr Hastings, do you want to respond to that question?" Yieldon asked.

All eyes turned to the doctor, and he shifted in his seat. "Look, there's no easy way to say this, so I'll just come out with it. The remains are too *fresh* to belong to someone who went missing three months ago. It is the medical team's determination that the victim's body was placed into the water no more than a week ago."

"Is it possible she was being held captive somewhere until then?" Wendy asked.

"We don't believe that's the case," Yieldon answered for him. "There's no evidence or intelligence that I'm aware of to place Ms Summers anywhere near the area and she was last seen in dense bushland more than twenty kilometres south. The tides don't match up, so we are all but ruling out that line of enquiry. If, and I am saying, *if*, Isabelle Summers came to harm at the hands of a perpetrator, there's plenty of places around the Glenrock Conservation Area where she was last seen to stash a body. There'd be no need to dump her so far away. But forensics will be able to confirm that when we get a positive ID."

"Do we have any idea who the remains belong to then?" Wendy paused and took a deep breath. "Is there anything *identifiable*?"

Yieldon nodded and opened one of the folders he'd placed on the lectern. "Since the first remains were discovered in the dunes yesterday by a surfer at ten o' three am, SES search teams and police have uncovered an additional partial leg with the foot still attached, a partial forearm, and section of torso. Nothing overtly identifiable, however."

Despite the emotionless delivery of the information, everyone in the room either shifted in their seat or closed their eyes. It was a gruesome list and for the average person, the thought of decomposing body parts didn't sit well with breakfast muffins and fruit platters.

"Shark?" one of the men asked, but Lucy didn't catch who.

"We believe so," Yieldon said. "However, there is something you need to know which we will not be disclosing at the press conference. This is highly confidential information, so please treat it accordingly."

Together, everyone leaned forward.

"We have found evidence to suggest the body was weighted before predation took place."

Lucy trained her eyes on the Lord Mayor as Yieldon provided the information everyone had been waiting to hear.

"So, you're confirming this was a homicide?" the Lord Mayor asked.

Despite being in his late forties, Andrew Ashley was still in great shape. A former reserve grade NRL football player, the Lord Mayor could be physically capable of carrying a woman's dead weight into the ocean if the swell was low. Lucy opened her notepad and scribbled a reminder to double check the tide and swell.

"Senior Sergeant Dickson?"

She heard her name and snapped the notepad closed. "I'm sorry, could you repeat the question, Lord Mayor?"

"I said you were out on the dunes yesterday. Did you find any identifying belongings like a handbag or purse?"

"Not at this stage, sir, no."

"So, it would make sense that her body was brought there after she was killed," he stated.

"Not necessarily. Could be her belongings were taken or perhaps she didn't bring a purse with her, especially if she and someone were simply walking along the beach and things turned ugly." *Just like they did yesterday with you and your wife.*

"I see," he nodded. "So, we don't know anything about who she is or... was?"

"Once forensics are back, we'll know more," Yieldon concluded. "What we know for sure at this stage is that a woman was placed into the water with what we believe to be a weighted object attached to her right leg. Predation took place in the time that lapsed between her body entering the water and her remains being washed onto the shore on Wednesday night's high tide which reached its peak at around three am. The remains show signs of significant trauma in line with shark predation but also abrasions, which could be a result of bottom dragging due to the strength of the current. We believe she was placed into the water on Monday evening. It's the end of spring but the water is still cold, so it may have been earlier but we don't believe so at this stage. There were no items of clothing or materials attached to the remains, and with the extreme state of predation, it's difficult to tell, but we are working off the belief she was naked at the time of entry into the water. At this stage, the entire stretch of Stockton Beach is a crime scene and must remain closed to the public."

Yieldon closed the folder and looked over at SES Unit Commander David Hammond. "David, is there anything you'd like to add?"

Lucy broke her gaze and looked over at David. His eyes were red, his hair was dishevelled, and despite only being in his early thirties, his shoulders hung low, as though they were being dragged down by an invisible weight.

"Nothing at this stage other than the fact my teams are obviously working tirelessly to assist in the search. We expect to find further remains today and possibly in the days to come," he said. "These types of cases have a great emotional and psychological impact on the team, so we will be keeping a close eye out for anyone who isn't coping well and switching them out. It's a process that does widen the knowledge circle, but I'll be reminding them of the need for confidentiality at all times."

Everyone nodded, and Lucy imagined they were all grateful not to be the ones out looking for more decomposing, shark-ravaged body parts.

"Okay, thanks everyone," Yieldon said.

As everyone filed out of the room, the Lord Mayor hung back. "Sir, is there something further we can help you with?" she asked as he stood awkwardly by the lectern.

"I just wanted to apologise for yesterday," he said, mostly to Lucy. "My wife can be a handful, but she means well."

But before she could respond, Yieldon jumped in over the top. "No need to apologise, Andrew. If anything comes of your sighting, I'll give you a call but honestly just forget it. We've all had our romps out in the dunes, am I right? I mean, Christ, the place is known for it. The woman you saw could have been anyone."

"Right," the Lord Mayor nodded. "That's what I told Stella, but she wanted to make sure we were doing all we could to help. If there's anything more I can do, please let me know. I'll make myself available for whatever you need."

"I appreciate that, Andrew, but I don't expect we'll be following that line of enquiry. Right, Senior Sergeant Dickson?"

Lucy cast her eye from the Lord Mayor to Yieldon and back again. "No, not at this stage. There was one thing I wanted to ask you though."

Yieldon turned, his frame towering over her.

"How did she seem to you?" I asked.

"How did who seem?"

"The woman you saw. Was she standing up tall or was she hunched over?"

"I really couldn't say. Like I already told you, she was too far away. Why? Does it make a difference?"

"Goes to state of mind. Helps us determine if the woman you saw really was having a happy romp in the dunes like the Inspector said or if maybe things weren't going so well."

"But as I said," Yieldon jumped in again, "we won't be actively following that line of enquiry."

The Lord Mayor nodded and held out his hand to Yieldon. "I appreciate all your hard work, Chris."

She noted their handshake was firm—trusting.

"You too, Senior Sergeant Dickson," Andrew added, casting his attention back to her.

"Of course, sir, and you can rest easy knowing I'll be doing all I can to solve this case. You have my word on that. Whatever it takes."

Chapter Five
ELLE

When it became clear last night that David was standing me up, I had paid my drinks bill and left. It was a different version of the traditional walk of shame, but making your way down Darby Street alone, surrounded by happy couples enjoying a night out on eat street wasn't the best feeling in the world. So much for the allure of an oversized arse and squinty eyes.

As I got settled at my desk, an apology text dropped—about thirteen hours too late.

David: *Sorry for last night. Got stuck onsite, but should have called. No excuses. IOU one*

Had it been a date, I would have been furious, but given I only planned to squeeze him for information, I just felt disappointed. And maybe a little ego burned.

Me: *No prob. You missed a couple of good cocktails and you do owe me. $40 to be exact lol*

David: *That's fair. Sorry again*

Whatever he could have told me would be public information in about fifteen minutes when the presser got underway outside City Hall. The location meant police had already briefed the Lord Mayor and other officials first thing this morning. That pointed to one thing.

Me: *You found more remains?*

David: *We did*

Elle: *Is it Isabelle?*

David: *No*

Elle: *You're sure?*

David: *100% gotta run. Got the presser soon*

I wasn't sure how I felt. Relieved that Isabelle might still be alive. Curious to find out who the body parts on the beach belonged to. And maybe a little less frustrated that Willamina Fraser might be stealing my story. The legend of Bloody Mary quickly came to mind when, not a second after thinking of her, Willamina appeared before my eyes.

"So, apparently you're coming to the presser," she stated flatly.

"I am?"

"Boss says so. He wants you to go talk to the Lord Mayor about some report while I interview the police. Said he already set it up."

"Oh," I replied. "Okay, let me get my stuff."

When we arrived outside City Hall, Inspector Chris Yieldon and Senior Sergeant Lucy Dickson were already standing on the step, a half-moon of reporters curved out around them. In addition to the local television and radio crews, I also recognised metro reporters from channels Seven, Nine, and Ten in Sydney. The story was heating up.

As Willamina stepped in to take her place at the front of the media scrum, she glanced back at me. "I don't have all day. Once I'm done here, I want to get back and file the story, so make it snappy. I'm not waiting around for you."

When I arrived at the executive floor, I fake smiled at the Lord Mayor's gatekeeper Jackie, otherwise known as his executive assistant.

"My editor called ahead to set up a quick chat with Andrew." I told her.

Jackie reminded me of a hawk or a falcon. I wasn't sure which, but it was definitely a small bird of prey. She had a hook nose, sleek stature, and eyes that never missed a trick. She also scared the bejesus out of any little mouse who dared try to sneak their way into the Lord Mayor's office without her permission.

"Go on in, Elle, he's waiting," she said. "But he only has ten minutes."

"That's fine," I told her. "Apparently so do I."

I knocked gently and when he called me in, I took a deep breath and stepped inside the lavish office. "Good morning, Lord Mayor."

"Elle, come in, come in. Close the door, would you?"

I nodded and pulled the door closed as hawk-eye Jackie watched closely from her perch outside.

When we were alone, he rose from his desk and came toward me. He smelled like a mix of soap and cedarwood. The soft scent against his strong physique was hard to resist.

Andrew was twelve years older than me and the Lord Mayor of Newcastle. He was also married and handsome as hell. We'd been crossing the line with stolen kisses and flirtatious texts, but in the past few weeks he had become distant, almost cold. After the heated nature of some of our exchanges, his sudden change of pace was making things awkward, and I just wanted off the round.

"It's nice to see you," I began. "Walters, set this up. I didn't... I mean, I... he told me to come."

Andrew gave my arm a quick, almost friendly squeeze, then limped over to a couch beneath the window.

"Andrew, are you hurt?"

"I'm fine. Just a collision at soccer last night. The guys can get pretty heated, considering it's just a local game."

I smiled and followed him over to the couch. "So long as you're alright."

"I'm fine. Listen, Elle, I'd love to sit and catch up, but I have a lot on my plate right now. It's nothing personal. I just don't have a lot of time."

His tone was tight, almost agitated. I had no idea what changed between us, but it was obvious something was wrong.

"Are you sure everything's alright?" I asked. "I'm here if you need to talk. Is it Stella?"

He rolled his eyes and grinned. "It's always Stella. But no, not specifically. Just work."

I nodded, but wasn't convinced. "Alright, well... speaking of work, I need to ask you a couple of questions about the Ridgemont Capitol development."

He squared himself in the seat. We were back to business. "Sure. What do you want to know?"

I took out my phone and placed it on the desk. "Can I record?"

With a sweeping motion of his hand, he indicated that I could proceed, and I hit the red record button. "Lord Mayor, you have long been an advocate for keeping the seaside village of Stockton just that, so you can't be in favour of the rezoning application that if approved would see a sprawling Gold Coast-style holiday resort one step closer to being built right on the beach?"

He nodded and thought for a second before answering. "I have always been in favour of keeping big developments out of Stockton, but inevitably it is up to council staff to determine the merit of any development application."

His answer threw me off guard, and I looked up. "That's certainly a change of tact compared to your outspoken opinions on developing Stockton in the past. What's changed?"

"Nothing's changed, Elle. It's always been our process that whenever we have development applications, including those for the rezoning of land, council staff review the application and put forward a recommendation based on its merits. Then our twelve councillors vote to determine the final outcome. So, it really doesn't matter how I feel personally. Due process must be adhered to with these kinds of things."

I didn't miss his sideways glance at my recorder or the way he shifted in his seat. Something was off and it had nothing to do with soccer or a busy schedule. "So, you won't try to oppose the application?"

"I won't be voting for it. But as I said, at the end of the day, it's not up to me."

I nodded and watched him for a moment before leaning over and switching off my recorder. "Andrew, what aren't you telling me?"

"Nothing, Elle, but I really have to go," he said, getting to his feet. "I have another appointment, so that's all I can give you for now."

I stood and gathered my things. "I don't mean to press the issue, Andrew, but I feel like you're not yourself. You're being very short with me."

The slightest hint of a shadow fell over his face, but just as quickly, he brushed it off and smiled. "Sometimes even the Lord Mayor has a shitty morning, Elle. Everything is fine."

I studied him a moment longer, then nodded. "Okay then. So long as you're sure."

He gave me a tight smile and stepped toward the door. "I'll speak to you soon."

And that was all I got.

Chapter Six

LUCY

By 4 p.m, police search-and-rescue officers and SES teams had located the rest of the woman's remains. By 9:15 p.m, they had a name—Lauren Ellis. And for Lucy, that's when things got really interesting.

It was unusual for her to stay at work longer than the usual eight-hour shift, but today was an exception. Identification of the remains had opened a can of worms and the station was buzzing. There was no chance she was going to make it home tonight. Lucy picked up her phone and made the call.

"Hey, it's me," she said when James picked up on the first ring.

"Let me guess. You're stuck at work?"

"You have no idea what's going on down here," she told her husband. "It's a shit storm. Can you feed and bath the girls?"

Mia was their four-year-old whirlwind of a child. She was a tireless Tasmanian devil who never wanted to go to bed, while Miranda, at age seven, was a quiet, thoughtful girl who Lucy felt sure was going to become a scientist or maybe a poet when she grew up.

"Course," he replied. "They'll miss you, though. I will too."

She smiled into the phone. "Same. And thanks. I have no idea when I'll be able to get out of here."

Even though Lucy couldn't see him, she knew he was nodding.

"You got an ID on the remains by the sounds."

"We did."

"And?"

There was a time when Lucy wouldn't have hesitated to confide in James, but that was before the Marshall case, and before she let her emotions get the

better of her. When she hesitated and silence found its way between them,
Lucy knew the moment was lost.

"Yeah, okay," James said eventually, his tone deflated. "We're still doing
that, I guess."

"James..." She wanted to tell him everything, bring an end the silent and
awkward pauses. She just didn't know how.

"Forget it, Lucy. I'll take care of the girls," he said eventually. "You do your
job."

The warmth was gone from his voice, and they were back to matter of
fact—to two people co-parenting as best they could.

"Okay. Thanks, James. I appreciate it."

"Yep. See you tomorrow."

He wouldn't be waiting up. And after that conversation, she wouldn't be
rushing home.

Lucy put down the phone and took a breath as Yieldon bellowed her name
across the bullpen. He was the last person she felt like dealing with, and now
she would be stuck by his side all night. Before she had time to answer, he
appeared beside her desk.

"Before we get any deeper into this, I want to make myself clear. You
do not, and will not, follow any specific leads without my approval. Is that
clear?"

Yieldon wasn't an ugly man, but it was obvious from the pockmarks on his
skin that he had endured severe acne in his younger years. Given his height,
he probably would have been gangly as well. Lucy wondered as he stood there
barking orders at her, if girls had rejected him as a teenager and that's what
turned him into such a chauvinist. It was hard to know for sure and there
were so many things she longed to ask him. Things like, did her five-foot-two
stature make him think she was incapable of doing her job? Did her ethnicity
get under his skin? The fact her father was a Torres Strait Islander, and
it showed in her dark eyes and black wavy hair. Was he threatened by her
successful close rate, or ability to read people's body language—a skill passed

down by her poker-loving grandmother? Or was it none of those things and something as simple as he just didn't like women?

"Sir, this ID changes everything, especially given what Ashley's wife told me on the beach yesterday. You can't expect me not to follow up?"

Yieldon rubbed at his chin and gave it some thought. After a moment, he motioned to her notepad and cap sitting on her desk. "Get your things."

"Sir?"

"You can ask some preliminary questions, but I'm coming with you."

"Sir, that's not the usual—"

But he cut her off. "Andrew Asley is the Lord Mayor. *Usual procedure* no longer applies. Let's go."

Chapter Seven
ANDREW

Andrew's first thought when he saw Inspector Yieldon and Senior Sergeant Dickson standing at his front door was that Stella might be the most predictable woman he had ever met. When he told her about seeing a woman standing up on the dunes, he'd known that somehow, someway, she would manage to spill the beans. Now it was 9:30 p.m. on a Friday night and the police were at their door.

"Andrew," Yieldon said, his hand outstretched. "I apologise for the intrusion, especially at this hour."

"No problem," he said with an easy smile. "Please, come in. Senior Sergeant Dickson, it's good to see you again."

"Lord Mayor," she nodded.

As they settled in the living room, the irony of their expansive view over the beach was not lost on Andrew. There was only one reason the police would come to his home at this hour—they had more questions about whatever took place out on the dunes.

"Can I get anyone a drink?" Stella asked as she appeared, having changed from the pink silk pyjamas she had on to some form of designer active wear. "Coffee or tea?"

Both Yieldon and Dickson shook their heads, and Stella took her place beside Andrew on the couch.

"Andrew, I'll get right to it," Yieldon began. "We've received a positive ID on the remains."

"That was fast."

"Well, science moves quickly these days. I'm sure I don't need to tell you that."

As he nodded, Andrew could feel Dickson's eyes watching his every move.

"The victim is Lauren Ellis, a twenty-nine-year-old—"

"Did you say Lauren Ellis?" Andrew repeated, interrupting him.

"Yes, you may be familiar with her. She is an employee of Newcastle City Council."

Andrew turned to Stella and patted her on the knee. "You know, I will take a coffee if you don't mind."

She seared him with a look, but got to her feet anyway. "Anyone else changed their mind?" she asked tightly.

Both officers politely declined, and Yieldon continued. "We wanted you to be the first to know, given your connection to her."

Andrew got to his feet and padded over to the floor-to-ceiling glass windows that stretched the length of their living room. Outside, the dark rise and fall of the dunes flowed like an ocean of sand. Behind him, Yieldon and Dickson turned in their seats.

"Did you know that Stockton Beach is thirty-three kilometres long?" Andrew asked quietly, without turning around.

"No, I didn't," Yieldon replied. "Used to come surfing over here a lot when I was a kid though. Couple of good breaks."

"The northern end is home to the largest dunes in the southern hemisphere."

It took a few seconds for Yieldon to respond, and Andrew assumed he and Dickson were exchanging confused looks, wondering what the hell he was going on about.

"Nope, didn't know that either," Yieldon said eventually.

"My point is," Andrew said, turning back to face them, "that kind of expanse offers a hell of a lot of places to dump a body. Why do it so close to the community? Did they want her to be found?"

"That's a tough question, Andrew," Yieldon replied. "But the body was weighted. If he wanted her found, he could have just left her where she was.

My guess is it was more of an access issue at the northern end. The dunes can be hard to get in and out of up there if you don't have a four-wheel drive. You'd need to be experienced at driving on sand, especially if it was dark."

"He? So, you have a suspect?"

"Not at this stage. We're just going off the fact she would have been heavy to carry down to the water."

"I see. So, you think she was killed elsewhere and brought here at night?"

Stella handed Andrew the cup of coffee before returning to the couch where she sat and leaned in, clearly desperate to catch up on whatever she missed.

"We don't know at this stage," Dickson answered. "But we are hoping you can shed some light on what kind of person she was. Did you know her well?"

"I couldn't help overhearing," Stella added. "I Googled her while I was out in the kitchen. Attractive girl."

At that, both Yieldon and Dickson turned toward Andrew, clearly waiting for a response.

"She worked in our Sustainability Department. She was an Environmental Impact Officer," he said, ignoring his wife's observation.

"And that means?" Yieldon asked.

"She worked mostly surveying land earmarked for development. She would carry out research to investigate the possible presence of sensitive flora or fauna that may impact the outcome of development applications."

"That's a job?" Stella asked.

"Yes, it's a job," Andrew said tightly. "It's a vital element in assessing the potential environmental impacts of land clearing."

Dickson wrote notes in a small pad, the same one she pulled out the evening he and Stella and had been arguing on the beach. "Did you work closely with her?"

"Closely?" he repeated. "No, I wouldn't say that."

"But you saw her frequently?"

"On occasion. Council does a lot of media stories on environmental initiatives, so Lauren usually... well, she used to... brief me before interviews."

"And yet you didn't recognise if it was her standing up on the dunes that afternoon?"

Andrew took a sip of coffee and winced. Stella had failed to add any sugar. He glanced over at his wife, but she didn't meet his eye. "Like I said, she was a long way off. At least one hundred metres, maybe more. The afternoon sun was in my eyes, and—"

"Our reports say the day she went missing, the day you saw a woman we now think may have been Lauren Ellis, the sky was overcast. In fact, it rained not long after you saw her. You mentioned it was about 4:30 p.m?"

"Maybe I'm getting mixed up with the days," Andrew said with a shake of his head. "I try to walk Gucci most afternoons. It helps me de-stress from work."

"And you were looking north?" Dickson pushed.

"Yes. Why is that important?"

"Dotting the Is and crossing the Ts. It's just procedure, Lord Mayor, nothing to be concerned about."

Not convinced, Andrew placed his cup down on the glass coffee table and looked at Yieldon. "I can't believe I'm about to ask this, Chris, but am I a suspect?"

"Of course not," Yieldon replied with a wave of his hand. "We're just trying to piece this thing together." He paused, then inched closer toward the edge of his seat. "I do have to ask, though. Do you have any insight into whether she was in a romantic relationship?"

Andrew shook his head and unconsciously moved back as Yieldon leaned in even further.

"We think the cause of death was either strangulation or blunt force trauma," he continued. "Hard to tell for sure given the state of the remains, but both are common forms of assault in domestic violence situations. Sometimes death is accidental, other times intentional. There is an intimacy to the act though, so we're thinking there were probably strong emotions connected to the killing. Love, passion, hate. That kind of thing."

"No, I didn't know anything about her personal life."

Yieldon and Dickson glanced at each other momentarily and then got to their feet. "Thank you for your time, Lord Mayor," Dickson said. "You've been most helpful and apologies again for the intrusion on a Friday night."

"No problem at all," Andrew said, standing to walk them out. "If there's anything else, just let me know."

"We trust you understand the identification is delicate information and extremely confidential at this time," Yieldon added. "There will be an official briefing tomorrow."

"I'll make myself available."

Andrew watched them walk down to the road and when the lights of their patrol car flicked on, he closed the door and turned to his wife. "I'm going to take a shower."

When he was certain Stella wasn't going to follow him into the bathroom, Andrew leaned against the dark wood vanity and finally let out a long breath. He had underestimated Dickson. She was clearly on a mission, and it wouldn't take long for her to figure out that he had just lied.

Chapter Eight
ELLE

When Andrew called out of the blue on a Saturday afternoon, emotionally, I was not in a good place. Losing the human remains story to Willamina, being left sitting alone with a limp straw at the Coal & Cedar bar the night before, and the angst of what to do about my love life, had all become too much. So, like anyone with an eating disorder, I was stuffing my face.

What most people don't know is that binge eating is not a random act. When an episode strikes, instead of mindlessly eating anything in sight, I succumb to it in a regimented order—which I have concluded is a very stupid way of fooling myself that I'm still in control.

Nonetheless, my routine goes something like this. Stage One: I order a large Big Mac Meal with a soft drink and apple pie from one of the delivery apps on my phone. Stage Two: After my order arrives and I whet my appetite, I drive to the McDonalds three streets away and get the second burger that I was too embarrassed to order the first time and eat it in the car. Stage Three: I head over to pick up two large pepperoni pizzas from a quaint little restaurant a few blocks away. I eat one pizza in the car on my way home, which can get pretty messy, and the other I pretend I'll keep for *later*. Stage Four: I go to the supermarket grab a frozen chocolate cake which I leave out to defrost in a particular place on my kitchen sink that gets just the right amount of sun but not too much, a barbecue chicken for something healthy to nibble on, *because that's important*, a large bag of plain crisps, and a family block of chocolate. Just the plain one because for some reason I think anything else would be overdoing it. *As if. Stage Five:* Once I'm home,

I close the doors, pull the blinds half down, turn on Netflix, and wallow in an unhealthy mix of reality television and my own self-loathing until it's time to hit the bathroom and purge.

So when the pressure of the past forty-eight hours triggered an undeniable urge to start my routine, I gave myself the typical self-imposed one hour of contemplation. Out on the back veranda, I tried to overcome the compulsion to numb my pain by putting food in my mouth, and then, as usual, justified all the reasons it wouldn't be the end of the world when I did.

When Andrew called, I had already completed Stage One and my car keys were in my hand.

"Can I see you?" was the first thing he asked.

"Umm..." I looked down at my keys. "Is everything okay?"

"Not really," he sighed.

My feelings for him were strong enough to have pushed me over the edge and into the routine, and yet interrupting it for him was going to be a challenge. It had never been clearer that I needed to get some help.

"Sure," I replied, willing myself to be stronger than the urge. "When?"

"I'll be at your place in thirty minutes."

I glanced across the living area of my two-storey townhouse and winced. Dust was littered across the floorboards, there were dishes in the sink, and my striped pyjamas were crumpled on the couch from when I got changed by the drying rack. At least one daddy long legs had taken up residence in the corner of the ceiling, and the kitchen smelled like grease. Andrew had never been inside my home and now I had exactly thirty minutes to make it worthy of a visit from a man who was both the object of my affection and the Lord Mayor of Newcastle.

When he knocked on the door, despite a residual bead of sweat on my brow, I proudly stepped back, knowing every room smelled like ocean mist and not a speck of dirt was to be found anywhere. But to my surprise, instead of breezing in as I expected, he just stood there, hands shoved in his pockets and looking uncomfortable.

"Andrew? Is everything okay?" His hair was wet, and he smelled like soap.

"Can you come with me?" he asked. "There's something I want to show you."

I glanced behind me at all the hard work I had put into cleaning up and sighed. When he called, my first thought had been that he needed me. The second was of us cuddled up on the couch, finally able to spend some quiet time alone and in private to see what this really was. But instead, as I followed him out toward the shiny black sedan, I found myself searching the street to make sure no one was watching. Because that's the thing about spending time with someone you shouldn't. You can never just relax and enjoy the moment. You can't just reach for their hand or linger at their side. And if you don't keep your wits about you, who you wish you were, and who you really are, can become painfully blurred.

"So where are we off to?" I asked once we were in the car and turning left onto Darby Street.

"Home." I shot him a quizzical look, but before I could ask any questions, he simply said, "You'll see."

As we headed out of Newcastle and over Stockton Bridge, I wondered if he was taking me to his house. Maybe his wife was away, but that didn't seem like Andrew. He may have a broken marriage, but he wasn't a disrespectful man. Not that I had seen, anyway.

We turned off the bridge and a cluster of abandoned hospital buildings, officially called the Stockton Centre, loomed ahead. The eighty-four-hectare site, known to locals born before the 1980s as the old Stockton mental hospital, was the land Ridgemont Capitol had purchased from the NSW State Government for its proposed five-star beachside resort development.

"You really think the rezoning application is going to get up?" I asked, as we continued past a vast tangle of scrub creeping up on each side of the old buildings.

"I hope not," he replied. "But it concerns me that Ridgemont is also in talks with the Department of Defence about purchasing the vacant land on either side of the site. If they purchase the old rifle range on the left and the Fort Wallace site on the right, that makes for a damn big footprint."

I watched out the window and tried to imagine a sprawling Versace-style resort stretching its bejewelled arms out across the land. As quickly as it came, I erased the thought from my mind. It would be a blight on the landscape and a crime against a generational community that had known nothing other than a village lifestyle since the 1700s. I glanced at Andrew and wondered if he was thinking the same thing.

Eventually, we turned off the main drag of Fullerton Street and weaved our way through a maze of narrow roads until Andrew pulled over outside a small bungalow-style home with a tidy yard in Roxburgh Street. He switched off the engine and sat back against the leather seat.

I wanted to ask what we were doing, but sensed he wasn't quite ready to explain just yet. As I waited for him to speak, his proximity became intoxicating. He was so close, and the car was so quiet that I could hear him breathing. Just for a moment, I wondered if it were possible for two hearts to fall into the same rhythm.

"I spent most of my childhood in that house," he said eventually. "Mum and Dad lived there all their lives until they passed."

I looked over at the pretty blue cottage decorated with white trim and imagined Andrew as a small boy, a face full of freckles, playing in the front yard. A smile tugged at the corner of my lip and the urge to reach over and touch his leg pulled at my heart.

"That must have been a nice way to grow up," I said softly.

"It was. Once they had found me."

I tucked my legs up under me and turned so I was facing him. "Once who found you?"

"My parents. Well, my adopted parents."

It suddenly dawned on me how little I really knew about Andrew. When someone is a public figure, it can be easy to form a false sense of familiarity, even more so when they pull you into a romantic embrace. But for all our late-night texts and stolen moments, I knew nothing about his life before he became the Lord Mayor.

"Not many people know this about me, Elle," he began. "But I was born in Sydney. My mother was a heroin addict. I was in the system by the time I was two years old."

A soft light fell across his face as he spoke, and I reached for his hand. "Andrew, I'm so sorry."

"I had a tough time," he sighed. "My memories are blurry in some parts, but in others..." He trailed off, and I tried to stop myself from imagining the worst. "But then Majorie and Greg took me in as foster parents and eventually adopted me." He laced his fingers tighter with mine and smiled. "I remember the day they came to get me like it was yesterday. She was wearing this yellow skirt, and it reminded me of the sun. As we turned onto the freeway and headed north, away from Sydney, I looked out the window and swore I would never live in a big city again. Not for anything."

"How old were you?"

"I was seven when they came to get me."

I nodded and let everything he said settle between us. "Why did you share this with me, Andrew?" I asked eventually. "I mean, I appreciate it. But why?"

He started the car, and I silently cursed myself for having spoiled the moment, but my disappointment was short-lived.

"If this development goes ahead, it will change the landscape of a place that has always felt like a sanctuary to me," Andrew began. "After Majorie and Greg came to get me, I was blessed with the kind of childhood that is quickly becoming all but extinct. I got to play with my friends out in the street and ride our bikes to the beach. Mrs Williams at the corner store knew my name, and on summer afternoons, all our neighbours would take turns hosting barbecues in the street. Those memories and all the moments that came after were what made me choose a career in politics. It was never about having a profile or people knowing my name, although that's always been the attraction for Stella. It was about giving back, about making sure Newcastle never lost its identity."

"That's certainly a worthwhile way to spend your life," I replied. "I would never want to get in the way of that."

"I know you wouldn't, Elle, and the fact that you are nothing like my wife is one of the things that draws me to you most of all. I just wanted you to know who I am. It's important to me."

"That means a lot," I told him. "Thank you."

He nodded and reached for my hand. "You're important to me, Elle. Please don't ever forget that."

As we made our way out of Stockton and back toward the city, I knew Andrew and I had reached a turning point. I could accept what little he had to offer me, or our moment, just like the river below, would become water beneath the bridge.

Chapter Nine
STELLA

When Jackson got home that afternoon, Stella was relieved that their younger son, Levi, was away for the weekend on a camping trip with his mates. Andrew was out, and they had the house to ourselves.

"We need to talk," she told him, as he dumped his soccer bag onto the kitchen floor, flecks of mud dropping onto the cream tiles. He was eighteen and already pushing six-foot-tall with his father's green eyes and her olive skin.

"What's up?" he asked, his head disappearing inside the fridge.

"The police were here last night."

Instead of pulling out his usual array of cold cuts, day-old pizza, and last night's leftovers, Jackson closed the stainless-steel door and sat down at the island bench empty handed. "What did they say?"

Stella leaned in and focused on keeping her tone as calm and even as possible. "They identified the victim in the dunes as Lauren Ellis."

"Fuck." He immediately climbed off the stool and began pacing the length of the kitchen. "Do they know?"

"No, Jackson," she told him. "They don't know."

He stopped where he was and raked his fingers through his mess of shoulder-length hair. "Will they find out?"

Stella wanted to tell her son, "No, they wouldn't find out," but that would be a lie, and she had never lied to her sons. So, she told him the truth. "I don't know."

"Christ," he swore. "What do we do now?"

She walked over and rested her hands gently on his shoulders. "Nothing. You hear me? We don't do anything."

"But—"

"No buts." She looked him dead in the eye. "What happened was a mistake, but trust me, Jackson, I'm your mum and I won't let anything happen to you."

He momentarily held her gaze before taking a deep breath. When Stella sensed he had composed himself, she let go of his shoulders.

"Do they have a suspect?" he asked.

She hated herself for having allowed him to get so tangled up in all of this. When Jackson confessed to over hearing his father talking to another woman on the phone late at night, she should have reassured him it was probably just a work thing. Instead, Stella had let him see her reaction and without realising it, inextricably pulled him into their mess. But despite whatever drama lay ahead, the only thing that mattered was making sure Andrew was not charged with murder. And from the way Senior Sergeant Lucy Dickson had been staring at him, Stella had a terrible feeling they may be in for a fight.

"Mum, do they have a suspect?" Jackson asked again, this time with more urgency.

"They do," she replied, fear finally finding its place in her voice. "And I have a nagging feeling it's your father."

Chapter Ten

ANDREW

Andrew followed Elle inside her townhouse and tried to calm his nerves. Everything he told her in the car was true and yet he still felt like a fraud. She deserved so much better than this, but what choice did he have? Chris was onside for now, but it wouldn't be long before the evidence started piling up. The secret meetings alone would be enough for he and Senior Sergeant Dickson to conclude that they had been having an affair. It was already in their heads that the killer was someone she had been intimately involved with. He expected them back at his house any day now, asking more questions.

Elle closed the door, and Andrew looked around her home. It was cosy, eclectic, a lot like her, and a far cry from the cold perfection of the beach house. The red and burgundy couches were mismatched but still managed to complement each other. There were mustard throw rugs, loose magazines, and on the wall hung a framed image of Virginia Wolfe's *To the Lighthouse*.

"Sorry, it's a bit of a mess," she said quietly.

"It's fine," he told her, with a wave of his hand. "It's nice. I like it."

She laughed politely and dropped her bag down next to a folder marked Ridgemont Capitol.

"Bringing your work home with you?" he asked.

Without missing a beat, she looked right at him and said, "Clearly. You're here."

Andrew loved her dry sense of humour, and a chill ran through him as he thought about why he was really there.

"Drink?" she asked.

"No, I'm fine."

She nodded and laughed nervously. "Andrew I—"

"Come here."

She tucked her hair back behind one ear in a gesture he guessed came from being nervous. When she was close enough, he pulled her in and ran his finger along the length of her cheek. "There's nothing to be nervous about, Elle," he whispered. "This has been a long time coming."

"I know," she told him. "It's just..."

"What?"

"You're *you*. You're Andrew Ashley. I'm just... me."

If only she knew, he thought as he pulled her even closer. To her it would have felt like an intimate embrace, but the truth was, Andrew just didn't want her to see his face and the upheaval this was causing him.

"So, do you want to see the bedroom?" she whispered, and he knew it was time.

With each step, Andrew searched his mind for any option other than dragging Elle into this. He genuinely liked her, but when this started, he had been a different man. Six months ago, he had been a bored and disgruntled husband who was grateful for a career he loved and stimulated by a flirtatious relationship with the local journalist. They shared a kiss now and then and a few steamy text messages, but that was the extent of it. Before everything happened, he probably would have relished the idea of sleeping with Elle, but not like this. Not when it felt like a transaction that she had no idea she was making.

When they stepped into the bedroom, it was dark, and Andrew was grateful. The last thing he wanted was for Elle to see the reluctance in his eyes and think it had something to do with her. When she folded her arms around his neck, he closed his eyes and silently apologised for what he was about to do.

"I can't believe this is actually happening," she whispered, her body pressing against his.

"Why not? You're a smart, beautiful woman."

She let out a small laugh and turned away. "What, Elle? You are."

"Come on, Andrew," she whispered. "I'm not beautiful."

He pulled back and looked at her closely. "Why would you say that?"

"Because..." She unravelled her arms and moved to sit on the edge of the bed. "I'm just not, and to be honest..."

He sat down beside her. "And to be honest, what?"

She fidgeted and refused to meet his eye. "I was all for you coming up here in the moment, but now I'm kinda scared for you to see me naked."

Her response caught Andrew off guard. She always seemed so confident, and hearing she was self-conscious only made him feel worse. "Don't be," he whispered. "I've wanted to be here with you since the day we met, Elle. I need you to believe that."

Guilt weighed heavily on him as he looked at her, knowing what was about to happen, and wondering if he could actually go through with it. It wasn't right. Sex shouldn't be strategic. It should be about passion and desire, but there was also a part of him that wanted her so much. He pushed the thoughts away and leaned in and kissed her. Slowly and gently, until an urgency began to grow, and she moved in closer. When he felt the time was right, Andrew broke away and removed his clothes. Elle watched his every move until he pulled her to her feet and slipped the pink jumper she wore up and over her head. Beneath her bra, Elle's breasts were just as he had imagined. Generous with perfect nipples that he suddenly longed to close his lips around. She laughed and wiggled from side to side as he peeled down her jeans. He noticed right away she wore black lace underwear, not a thong, but briefs that were sexy as hell.

"You are gorgeous," he whispered honestly, kneeling to slide down her underwear.

"Andrew—"

"Shh," he told her. "Just lay down and let me prove it to you."

Andrew took his time and slowly kissed and touched every part of her, allowing himself to let go of his fears and become lost in the moment. When he moved further down her body, she arched her back and a warm rush coursed through him, knowing she was allowing herself to let go. But as he moved inside her, despite the warmth of her body and the delighted sounds that escaped her lips, demons began to whisper in his ear. He wanted to stay lost in Elle, to let her steal away his guilt and fear and sadness, but it wasn't enough. Andrew was a liar and a fraud, and soon everyone would know.

Afterward, Elle wrapped her legs around him and tucked her head in under his shoulder. "I'm so glad we did this," she whispered.

"Me too. If things were different..." he trailed off, unsure how to finish the sentence. It was the most honest answer he could manage. *If only they could be.*

She took a moment, then propped herself up on one elbow and gazed at him. "Andrew, I know this is going to be hard for us, but I really care about you. What you shared with me today over at Stockton... it really made me feel like I matter to you."

Andrew's heart shrivelled beneath his ribs. Looking at her flushed cheeks and hopeful eyes was almost enough to make him tell her the truth, but he couldn't. Instead, he told her the next closest thing. "You do matter to me, Elle. You matter more to me than anyone ever has."

And it was true. No one had ever been more important to Andrew than Elle, because very soon she was going to be the only person who could save him from spending the rest of his life behind bars.

Chapter Eleven

LUCY

"Jesus, Lucy!" James swore, as he scooped Mia up into his arms as though she might break. "She was reaching for you."

Lucy searched her husband's face, trying to figure out if he was angry, disappointed, or just confused. He clearly had no idea why she refused to pick up a red-faced screaming Mia after their boisterous golden retriever knocked her over as he ran wildly through the kitchen. Technically, James hadn't asked a question, but from the look on his face, he expected an answer.

"You swooped in before I had a chance to pick her up," she lied, knowing he would immediately call her on it.

"Bullshit," he hissed, quickly checking if their other daughter, Miranda, who was old enough to understand curse words, was listening. "I heard her screaming from our ensuite and by the time I got out here to the kitchen, you still hadn't picked her up."

He gave Lucy one last scathing look, then focused all of his attention on cradling Mia's head against his shoulder. "Can you at least get her some of the children's Panadol from the top cabinet? She hit her head when she fell."

Lucy turned and opened the cupboard above the pantry where they kept the medicines. She wanted to reach out and take her daughter in her arms, to hold her close and tell her she was loved more than anything in the world. But instead, she robotically measured out a dose of painkiller and held it up for James to decide who was going to administer it.

"Just give it to me," he said with a sigh. "I'll take the day and stay home instead of sending her to daycare."

"You're sure?"

"Why?" he snapped. "Are you going to do it?"

The way his hand rested over Mia's forehead reminded Lucy of how he used to gently stroke her bulging tummy, the excitement of a new life kicking inside. "James..."

"Are you?" he demanded, quickly pushing her memory back into the past.

"I can't," she told him flatly. "The case is—"

"The *case*," he repeated. "This is our family, Lucy, and lately it seems like you've just checked out."

"That's not fair," she told him. "Do you even know what day it is?"

"It's Tuesday, so what?"

"It's not Tuesday," she told him softly. "It's *her* day."

Lucy could tell by the way her husband's face instantly slackened and the tension fell away from his forehead that he understood. It was the anniversary of her sister Libby's death. The day a drunk driver lost control of his car and hit her while they were walking home from the shops. It had been her ninth birthday.

"Lucy..." he began. "I'm sorry. With everything going on, it slipped my mind."

Standing there in their messy kitchen with its grape patterned tiles and a gaping hole where a new dishwasher should go, Lucy nodded and waited for the tears to sting, but none came. "It's fine, James. Forget about it."

With Mia tucked up under one arm, he stepped over and pulled me in close. "I'm sorry, Luce, really."

He was warm, and it would have been easy to melt into his reassuring scent of sleep and home. She wanted so much to give in, to feel all the things tearing at her heart, but she couldn't. It was too dangerous. After a beat, Lucy stepped away and leaned in to kiss Mia gently on the forehead. "I'm sorry too, James, but I have to go."

As she walked out of the kitchen, Lucy ached to look back and take in the perfect picture of her husband and child, the loves of her life, together in their cosy ramshackle kitchen. But instead, she forced herself to grab the keys and find Miranda.

"Mum, are you okay?" her daughter asked, as Lucy hovered awkwardly in the doorway. She was lying on the bed, propped up on her elbows and engrossed in her iPad.

"Course, I am sweetheart," she managed. "Why would you ask that?"

"I don't know," Miranda shrugged, finally tearing her eyes away from the screen. "You just seem weird lately."

Lucy swallowed hard and wondered if her internal anguish had become so obvious that even their seven-year-old daughter had noticed. "Well, I'm sorry if I made you feel like that. I don't mean to be *weird*."

"It's just, you used to always hug us. Now you never do." Miranda finally met Lucy's eye, and it felt like all the air was being sucked out of her lungs.

"Oh no, sweetheart, that's not true at all." Lucy dropped her bag and jacket and rushed in, pulling her daughter so hard against her chest that she gasped.

"Too much, Mum," she coughed. "Let go, it's too much."

Lucy immediately let go and stepped away. "I'm sorry, Miranda, I have to go, but I want to talk to you about this when I get home. And of course, I love you. Don't ever think otherwise. I'll see you tonight, alright?"

As she headed for the door, for the second time that morning, Lucy longed to turn and see her beautiful little girl sitting pretty in her perfectly decorated bedroom. She missed them. They were right there, sharing her home, but she longed to have them share her heart again. No, she quickly reminded herself quickly as she stepped out into the crisp morning air. It was too dangerous. If she let them in, she'd only let them down. It was what she did. So, without looking back, Lucy pulled the door closed behind and hurried down the path, her eyes fixed on the road ahead.

At her desk, Lucy sat and opened a black folder marked *Crime Scene Photos*. Looking at decomposed body parts before ten in the morning wasn't her idea of an ideal way to start the day, but if there was something, anything, that would help nail Andrew Ashley for the murder of Lauren Ellis, then it was worthwhile taking another look. And it would distract her from dwelling on what happened back at the house.

As she studied each image, Lucy made a concerted effort to make sure she was looking at the scene strategically and not emotionally. She had to distance herself from any thoughts of Lauren as a person. What she liked to eat, how she had her morning coffee, or what her favourite song might have been. Those personal details fueled her to solve the case, but she had to tuck them away in her subconscious, otherwise, the cruelty of what people could do to each other would overwhelm her with sadness.

"Dicks, where are you with the crime scene photos? You find anything new?" Yieldon was suddenly hovering over her desk and waiting for a response.

"Just got started," she said. "Hope to have something for you soon."

"Right, well, in the meantime, I have an Internal Affairs matter to attend to. I trust I can leave this with you for the morning?"

Lucy looked up from the photos and tried to steady her breathing. "Internal Affairs?"

He gave nothing away as he stared back at her. "The Marshall case. I'll let you know if you're needed."

Without elaborating further, Yieldon marched off, leaving Lucy to wonder how long before they called her in for questioning. *The Marshall case,* she thought. *They must have figured it out.*

After a few minutes of trying and failing to concentrate on the Lauren Ellis' crime scene photos, Lucy picked up her phone and scrolled through the contacts until she found the name *Sarah Marshall*. Her thumb hovered over the call button as she considered what to do. If she made the call and Internal Affairs went through her phone records, the timing alone would be a nail in her coffin.

A creeping headache pulled at the back of her neck and she leaned on one elbow to rub at it. Lucy had been fearing this moment every day for the past nine months. Back then, she had let her emotions get the better of her and now it might cost her everything—her career, her reputation, maybe even her freedom. She imagined being handcuffed and led out of the dock in front of James and the girls. She imagined lying awake at night in a cold cell, longing to pull her family close and breathe in the smell of their hair. The thought caused her to shiver and shift in her seat.

As Lucy considered her fate, a voice in her head screamed, *what the hell were you thinking?* But she knew exactly what she had been thinking—that she was saving Libby. Because in that moment, Sarah Marshall's daughter and her sister had been one and the same.

Chapter Twelve
ELLE

The two-seater couch was hard and uncomfortable. The back was too straight, and I felt mocked by the empty space beside me where a support person would sit—if I had one. It was an undeniable reminder that I didn't have a significant other to come with me, to hold my hand and reassure me that everything was going to be alright. Instead, I had a married man who was probably at home with his wife, hoping to God there were no telltale signs he had been in my bed just days before.

When the therapist came in, I noticed right away that she looked like someone who had their shit together. Her hair was sleek and creamy blonde. She was probably in her mid-forties with a perfect figure and it wasn't a stretch to imagine she left work every night and went straight to the gym. She probably ate a plant-based diet, had well-behaved children, and a husband who coached Little League.

"Good morning, Eleanore," she beamed. "It's lovely to meet you."

"It's just Elle," I told her. "Thanks for seeing me."

The idea of telling this woman with gym-toned legs and perfect hair that I was a binge-eater instantly created a whole new level of self-loathing. Instead of being on her couch, all I wanted was to lose myself in Andrew's embrace, to be taken back to those incredible moments when, for the first time in my life, I forgot how I looked and instead focused on how I felt. Like maybe, at least to him, I was beautiful.

"I'm Doctor Kathy Simms," she continued. "Why don't we start with what's brought you in today, Elle?"

I shifted in my seat and pushed feelings that I hated to admit were jealousy back down into the dark. I needed help, and hating her for being perfect would not be conducive to a speedy recovery. "I have some issues with food that I need some assistance with."

"Okay." She nodded and wrote some notes on her pad. "Tell me more about your relationship with food."

I looked her over one more time and rubbed at my temple. She was the kind of woman I could imagine Andrew being tempted by. She was his equal. I was a mess, and not even a hot one.

"Elle?"

"I'm a binge eater," I told her. "It happens sometimes, when I'm stressed or upset."

"Alright." She wrote more notes, then paused before looking back at me. "Elle, you seem reluctant. Does talking about this make you uncomfortable?"

"Yes," I told her. "It makes me extremely uncomfortable, but..."

"But?"

"I want to stop," I said. "I have to. It makes me hate myself."

Dr Simms put down her pen and looked right at me. "Why don't you tell me something you like about yourself?"

"What?" The idea of liking anything about myself was as foreign as suddenly speaking Chinese.

"Tell me something you like about yourself," she repeated. "It doesn't have to be related to your appearance. It can be a character trait or an achievement. Whatever comes to mind."

I mentally listed my character traits. Insecure, inadequate, lack of self-control. Was cheater a character trait, I wondered? Probably more of a behaviour.

"Elle," she said, interrupting my thoughts. "How about you tell me about work, then? What do you do?"

"I'm a journalist," I told her. "At the *Newcastle Tribune*."

"Well, that must be interesting."

"It can be."

"And what do you report on?"

"Council mainly," I said. "Sometimes crime when I get the chance."

"That sounds like something you'd like to do more of."

Despite my extreme discomfort, a smile found its way onto my lips. "Yes, it is."

"And is there a reason for that?"

I took my time to make sure emotions didn't get the better of me. "My Dad. He's a crime writer," I told her eventually. "You may have heard of him. William Nolan."

Dr Simms sat back in her seat and I could see she was impressed, but that was nothing new—everyone was impressed by my father. Everyone except my mother.

"It must have been interesting to grow up with a father who spent his days chasing down serial killers and crime lords?"

I shrugged and let my eyes fall to the ground. "Not so much interesting as..."

"As?"

"Sad, really."

She crossed her legs and leaned in closer. "Tell me why it made you sad."

I thought back to my childhood and how my dad was always disappearing for months at a time or coming home to announce we had to move for a story. "It never felt like we were a family. I think if you asked him now, he'd say Mum and I's lives were just collateral damage."

"I see," she said softly. "And he was a news reporter here in Australia before he became an author? He wrote for at least three different national newspapers, correct?"

"That's right."

"And the books he later wrote, they were often about serial killers in the USA?"

"Yes."

She looked thoughtful, and I could tell she was counting back in her head. I decided to save her the trouble. "I was too young to remember the first three times we moved," I began. "It wasn't until I was old enough to feel the upheaval of having to leave schools and friends that I started counting. We moved eleven times before I turned fifteen, twice overseas, five times interstate here in Australia, the rest around New South Wales."

"That must have been hard for you."

I clenched my teeth to stop from crying. "It wasn't fun. Not for me or my mum."

"Are you close with your mother?"

A tear escaped and rolled down my cheek. "She was the only thing that kept me sane when I was a kid."

"And how did she do that?"

I thought back to the sadness that would engulf me every time I had to leave a new set of friends or a place I just managed to think of as home. "She'd take me somewhere special, just the two of us."

Dr Simms smiled and nodded. "Tell me about some of the places you would go together."

Images of brightly coloured cafes and fast-food restaurants filled my mind. "Despite what you may think, chasing criminals doesn't make you rich, so we never had a lot of money," I told her. "Mum would take me places that just made us feel better. We'd sit together side by side in a booth and she'd let me order anything I wanted no matter what time of the day it was."

"And that made things better?"

I wiped at another tear and met her eye for the first time. "No, but while we were there, it filled the empty space of losing everything all the time."

She leaned in, even closer than before, and smiled at me, not mocking or smug, but caring. "Think about that, Elle. I'm sure your mother had the best of intentions, but whenever you felt like you were losing something or your father was unavailable to you emotionally, she comforted you with food."

It was so obvious and yet I had never connected the dots. "You're right," I told her. "That makes sense."

She sat back in her seat and wrote more notes. "Elle, I think we have more to unpack here, especially around the relationship with your father. Is that something you'd be willing to explore?"

I let out a breath and tucked my hair back behind my ear. "We could try that."

"Good," she said with a warm smile. "And just before we wrap up for today, I'm curious to know about your intimate relationships. Do you have a partner?"

I thought of Andrew, and how it had felt being in his arms. "Nothing serious," I told her, although my heart said differently.

"I think it's important going forward that we focus on more than just your relationship with food," she said. "I'd like to talk about whether you are having any issues with allowing yourself to be loved by a partner."

I sat up straighter in my seat. "How do you mean?"

"I'd like to look at whether there's a pattern of choosing partners who, for whatever reason, are unwilling or unable to love you openly and uncondi- tionally. You see, sometimes when a father has been absent or withholding of parental love for a child, particularly a daughter, it's not uncommon for her to look for familiar patterns when it comes to intimate relationships."

"But why would I want to feel like that again? It was awful."

"You don't, Elle, and that's why those kinds of relationships may trigger your eating patterns. But our reptilian brain, or primal brain, as it's some- times called, is conditioned to tell us that what's familiar is safe, even when the opposite is true."

My mind was spinning. Andrew was older, he was successful, and emo- tionally unavailable. "This is a lot to take in," I managed. "But thank you."

"You're welcome, Elle, and please know that if you're willing to do the work, I am confident we can get the results you're looking for. It will just take some time."

I nodded and stood, hoping my legs would hold me.

"You can make your next appointment on your way out. I'll look forward to seeing you again."

"Thank you," I mumbled on my way out. "I will."

I set up another appointment for a date that immediately got lost amid the jumble of my thoughts. My relationship with my father was strained at best, and the very idea I would want to replicate it in my personal life was absurd. And yet everything she said made perfect sense.

As I walked back to my car, I asked myself over and over again if my feelings for Andrew were real or if he was just another version of my father. My thoughts were interrupted when my phone rang, causing me to jump. It was Andrew.

"Elle, I'm so sorry," he began. "I know we were supposed to have dinner at your place this evening, but I'm not going to make it."

My heart sunk. I had been looking forward to it all day. "That's okay," I told him, trying to hide the disappointment in my voice. "I understand."

"It's work. And Stella. I just can't get away tonight. I'm so sorry, Elle."

I nodded and felt a tear sting in the corner of my eye.

"Elle, are you there?"

"I'm here," I said. "It's fine. I'll speak to you tomorrow."

I hung up the phone and quickly reminded myself that choosing work and Stella over keeping our plans was a reasonable thing to do. He was the Lord Mayor, and she was his wife. They had to be his priorities. But as I dropped the phone back into my bag, I couldn't deny that his absence created an ache in my heart that felt painfully familiar.

Chapter Thirteen
STELLA

W hen Stella was sixteen, to everyone around her, it seemed like the world was hers to rule. With blonde hair that fell in thick natural waves to her breasts, and a gaggle of pretty girls who wanted nothing more than to be her best friend, she had been the envy of almost every other girl at school. At least that's how it looked on the outside.

But the reality of Stella's childhood was a different story. She and her mother had spent many nights sleeping in their battered-up hatchback with cramps biting at their legs and goose bumps covering their skin. Krissy had tried to be a good mother, but some nights the local shelters were full and so her tiny Datsun 120Y had to suffice. There in the dark, she would make Stella promise to marry someone who would take care of her, to not make the same mistakes she had. Krissy didn't have a drug problem, and she didn't gamble or drink—she just chose the wrong men. Men who beat her, men who cheated on her, and worst of all, men who promised the world, then just walked away. Stella couldn't pinpoint the exact moment her mother gave up, but one day the light was gone from her eyes and she knew something inside her was irreversibly broken.

But the day Stella ran out to the car and told her mother she was dating Andrew Ashley, the most popular and handsome boy at Adamstown High School, everything changed. A tiny glimmer of hope flashed across her mother's face. Stella had a chance. The chance at a future that was full of possibility and promise—the kind of life she had envisioned for herself once, before the world devoured her dreams. Back then, Andrew had been the tallest boy in Stella's year, with a mess of chestnut hair and a father who owned one of the area's largest construction companies. It was no secret that at sixteen, the next five years of Andrew's life were already squared away. He would play football for the Newcastle Knights, win a premiership, then take it from there. The world was his oyster—theirs if Stella could pull it off.

They were married just after Stella's twenty-second birthday, and with Andrew's blessing and his family's financing, the first thing she did was to move Krissy into a lovely little two-bedroom home out by the lake. Her mother had always wanted to live somewhere she could watch the sunset over Lake Macquarie and go for walks first the thing in the morning. Seeing her there in her own home, with food in the fridge and clothes in her closet, more than made up for Stella's sacrifice of marrying Andrew.

There was a time, before Stella inevitably surrendered to her new life, when she would stay up all night secretly planning her escape. She told herself she would start a secret savings account and when there was enough money, she'd wait for Andrew to go to work and then take the train to Sydney and book a flight to Morocco or Iceland, or anywhere girls like her never had the guts to go. She told herself she would become a photographer and travel the length and breadth of Africa. She'd hold photo exhibitions and write books about her adventures. She imagined letting let men fall in love with her, then leaving them in pieces on the floor as she strode out, the billowing silk of vintage Chanel catching in the breeze.

But none of those things happened. On Stella's twenty-third birthday, a year after they were married, she found out she was pregnant. Andrew was already the youngest Deputy Mayor in the history of Newcastle City Council, and it was only a matter of time until he was sworn into the top job, his beautiful wife and child by his side. Less than two years later, all of Andrew's, and her mother's dreams would come true when the Mayoral Chains were placed around his neck, the weight of them slowly drowning Stella. By the time she was twenty-five years old, she had never been further than Sydney.

The ocean air whipped at Stella's hair as she tucked her Louis Vuitton tote higher up on her shoulder. Her mother's nursing home was just a few blocks from the house, so most days she preferred to walk. Krissy would be sixty-five soon, much too young to be in the state she was in, but that's what heartache can do. It slowly eats away at your mind and soul until eventually your body crumbles under the pressure. Three years ago, when the doctors diagnosed her with early onset dementia, Stella's first thought had been, *would it really be so terrible to forget a life that caused nothing but pain?*

At the nursing home, Stella greeted each nurse and doctor by name as she made her way along the halls. People, even strangers, always acted as though they loved her, but she was no fool. It was Andrew they loved. Andrew, with his wholesome smile and rugged jawline. Andrew, with his perfect speeches, the words always peppered with just the right amount of passion and conviction. Andrew, who loved his hometown more than life itself and who had dedicated his career to saving it from becoming a soulless haven of development and progress.

To the people who remembered Newcastle before the cranes and developers came to town, Andrew was the embodiment of everything that was slowly slipping away. He spoke of salt air that had clung to their skin as children. He reminded them of the old days, fishing off wooden wharves that had since been demolished to make way for a piazza of stylish restaurants and developers' offices. He shared their memories of long-haired, rebellious rock bands that played on every corner, and carefree nights spent wandering freely from one nightspot to another before restrictions and curfews were imposed. But most of all, he represented a simpler time when a can of beer and a great song sung on a Sunday afternoon in the sun were all they needed. Life had been simple then. Easier. To those people, Andrew was a beacon of hope that maybe someday their lives would be simple again.

Stella hovered in the door to her mother's suite. Krissy was sitting by a window that overlooked the garden. Beside her was a small coffee table with a half-completed jigsaw puzzle and a cup of coffee that looked like it went cold a long time ago. She had her back to the door, and a soft morning light fell over her, lighting the back of her hair.

Krissy had loved Andrew for the same reasons as everyone else, but just like the city he was so desperately trying to save, right before Stella's eyes, her mother was slipping away. Sensing her presence, Krissy turned around.

"Hi Mum," she said. "How are you feeling today?"

The woman stared at Stella for a moment, a shadow of confusion falling over her brow. "Are you the new nurse?"

"No Mum," Stella managed, her voice ready to break. "It's me, Stella."

"Stella?" Her face was jaunt, her cheek bones overstated on her tiny, shrinking face. "I had a daughter called Stella," she said. "But I haven't seen her in a long time."

Stella nodded and tried to swallow the lump in her throat. "Well, I'm sure she loves you very much."

Her mother stared out across the room, then slowly turned back to the window.

"I'll come back tomorrow," Stella whispered, even though she knew her mother was no longer listening. "Maybe you'll feel better then."

When there was no response, she turned and made her way back down the hall. Nothing was forever and no amount of love or passion or speeches would ever change that. Stella's mother was dying and the world around them was changing. All that mattered now was making sure Andrew started to change with it because if he didn't, Stella knew eventually they were all going to pay the price.

Chapter Fourteen
ANDREW

T he flames licked higher, singeing the night sky, as any papers that proved there had ever been a relationship between Andrew and Lauren burned in the outdoor fire pit.

Cancelling dinner with Elle had been difficult. Andrew could hear the disappointment in her voice and the strength it took for her to try to hide it. He didn't want to lie to her, but she couldn't know the truth. If she knew how close he and Lauren had become in the weeks before her death, it would make her uneasy. Worse, it would make her untrusting, and he needed her onside.

Tonight was the only opportunity Andrew had when everyone was out of the house to take a match to anything that might incriminate him. After the police came to the house, he spent hours deleting any email or text correspondence with Lauren. In total, there had been fifty-three text messages and forty-eight emails over the past month. There was nothing he could do about the phone records and the police could get the text messages if they really considered him a suspect, but he was hoping it wouldn't come to that.

Lauren Ellis.

He had trusted her. She had trusted him. Now she was dead.

Andrew closed his eyes and let the heat from the fire warm his face.

At the time, it felt right, like it was he and Lauren against the world. He had never met anyone like her. She was incredibly clever with a light that shone so brightly it was impossible not to feel the luminance that came just from being near her. She was the kind of woman who could mesmerize a man, have him completely lose his mind, and reduce him to nothing more than a string of bad decisions.

He opened his eyes and looked up at the velvety sky above. "I'm so sorry, Lauren," he whispered to the brightest star he could find. "If I could take it back, I would. You have to believe me. I never wanted this."

"What the hell are you doing?" Stella's voice barked from behind him. "Who are you talking to?"

Andrew spun around, his heart racing as he stared at the outline of his wife standing in the shadows.

"I said, who were you talking to?" she demanded.

"No one," he mumbled, the vast night sky shrinking at the sound of her voice.

"Not no one," she said, walking over to him. "It was someone."

He turned to face her and threw his arms open. "Look around, Stella. Do you see anyone else here?"

She stood by the fire and tilted toward the flames. "I know there's no one else here."

"Then what?"

"Then my question, Andrew... is why my husband is standing out here burning documents and apologising to ghosts."

He let out a long breath and rubbed at his forehead. "I thought you were out to dinner with the girls?"

"I was. Now I'm here and I'm asking you a question."

On Wednesday nights, Stella and her friends had a standing reservation at The Junction Hotel, a boutique bar and restaurant that catered to local politicians, decision makers, and socialites. In the past five years, she had never been home on a Wednesday night before midnight. He pulled the phone from his pocket and glanced at the screen. It was 10:03 p.m.

"Andrew—"

"I wasn't talking to anyone, Stella," he said with a sigh, before she could ask the same question again. "Just drop it."

He shook his head and turned to walk back toward the house, but she stepped in front. Warm light danced across her face and just for a moment, Andrew thought he caught a glimpse of the girl he fell in love with—the girl he thought fell in love with him.

"I know who you're out here whispering to," she hissed.

The accusation caught him off guard, and he took a step back.

"That's right," she continued. "I know about you and Lauren."

Without laying a hand on him, Andrew's wife managed to knock the air from his lungs. *It wasn't possible*, he thought. Stella was not the type of woman to turn a blind eye. If she thought he and Lauren had been having an affair, there was no way she would stand back and let it happen. He knew his wife. She would have been out for blood. "What are you talking about?" he asked, trying to stall while he figured out what to do next.

"I'm talking, Andrew, about you and Lauren Ellis."

Her eyes narrowed, and finally he could see it. The rage buried deep inside. "Stella—"

"You lied to the police."

He broke her gaze and turned to stare into the flames. "You're right, I did. But so did you."

"Did I?" she quipped. "How do you figure?"

Andrew had no idea what his wife was playing at, but he needed to find out—fast. "When the police were here, you said you Googled Lauren while you were out in the kitchen making coffee."

"So?"

"So, if you thought I was having an affair with her, I know you, Stella. You would have found out everything about her long before she turned up dead on the beach."

"Maybe," she shrugged.

"Not maybe," he said, fixing her with a gaze. "So, what are you playing at?"

"Lauren came here. Did you know that?" she asked. "Just days before they started finding pieces of her scattered all over the beach."

For the second time that night, Andrew felt like the air had been ripped from his lungs. "Bullshit," he challenged, hoping she was bluffing.

"It's true." Stella turned and calmly walked around to the other side of the fire. "The boys were here. It was Jackson who answered the door."

"Jackson?" he quickly imagined his eighteen-year-old son's reaction to a woman like Lauren standing at the door. "And?"

"He knew, Andrew."

"He knew what?"

"About your late-night phone calls. About a week before she turned up here, Jackson overheard you talking to her."

"What the hell are you talking about, Stella?" Andrew wasn't sure if the fire was getting hotter or panic was sending sparks through his body.

"Let's just say it didn't go well." Despite the heat coming off the fire, Stella hugged her arms around herself. "She shouldn't have come here."

Andrew shifted his weight from one foot to the other and tried not to let panic take over. "What the hell happened?"

"At some point, Jackson is going to get caught up in this."

Andrew's mind was spinning. How could it be possible that Jackson had suddenly become tangled up in Lauren's death? "That's not possible," he told her. "It can't be."

"It is possible, Andrew," she repeated. "And it's all your fault."

Chapter Fifteen
ELLE

O nly a month remained until council would vote on Ridgemont Capitol's application to change the zoning of the land they intended to
use for their holiday resort. If council approved the application, the company
would undoubtedly move to purchase the land on either side and apply for
State Government approval to build all the way down to the sand. It wasn't
a stretch to think the next thing would be another campaign by the Port of
Newcastle, half owned by the Chinese, to develop an international cruise
terminal adjacent to the city.

"Nolan, my office," Walters shouted from half-way across the room. "I got
somethin' for you."

When I reached his office, Walters motioned for me to sit down, then
closed the door behind me.

"I had a think about what you said," he began. "About the Mayor's
attitude toward Stockton and how he'd never endorse a development like
Ridgemont."

"And?"

"You might be onto something."

I leaned in and waited for whatever he would say next. Walters was a
complex man, almost an enigma. He had made his career by writing words
on a page and yet he used them so sparingly in verbal conversations that when
he actually spoke, there was a decent chance it was going to be something
worth hearing.

"Something about it doesn't sit right."

"Doesn't sit right?" I repeated. "What do you mean?"

"It's Andrew, he's not..."

I held my breath. If Walters thought Andrew was being shady, my next job was going to be uncovering dirt on him, and that was not something that sat right with me. "He's not what?" I dared.

"I went back through every comment and statement he's ever made about development in Stockton, all the way back to his campaign speeches before he was elected. He's always taken a hard line against over developing Newcastle in general, but when it comes to Stockton, he's been ferocious. Right up until three weeks ago."

I thought back to the recent interview I did with him at City Hall. I did notice a change in his attitude, but with everything that happened between him and I, I'd put it on the back-burner. "What are you thinking, boss?"

"I'm thinking something changed. Something big."

I swallowed hard, knowing what would come next. "Check it out, Nolan. Usually my money would be on a financial transaction between developer and politician, but I don't know with him. That kind of thing doesn't feel right."

I told Walters I would get right on it, then walked slowly back to my desk in no hurry to start digging dirt on the man I was falling in love with. If Andrew found out, to him it would be a betrayal. But if I didn't do what Walters wanted, it could be the end of my career. Either way, it seemed like I was headed for a fall.

I sat at my desk and stared out into the space around me. Every part of me screamed to tear open a chocolate bar, and then another, and then another, but as I reached into my bag, Dr Simms' words rang through my mind. *You're easing your fear with food.* I knew she was right, but it was like my arm was operating independently from my mind. Before I knew it, I had ripped open the wrapper and taken my first bite.

As the smooth texture of the chocolate fill my senses, I waited for the rush. I would savour the taste and feel a tinge of excitement, knowing I had given myself permission to shed all responsibility and soothe any pain I was feeling in the comforting arms of endless food. But something was wrong. Instead of calming me, the chocolate tasted bitter, and I was over aware that I didn't feel hungry. My chewing felt forced, and I was smothered in guilt. I knew better now. I understood what I was doing. Thanks to Doctor Simms, my honeymoon with food had abruptly come to an end. I looked down at the chocolate bar, and to my surprise, I was suddenly overcome with rage. Anger coursed through me and my face flushed. I wanted to scream, but I didn't know why. And then I felt it—fear. The realisation that I could no longer find ignorant relief in my affliction. For as long as I could remember, it had been my coping mechanism, my escape, and now suddenly I felt vulnerable and exposed, like I was falling and there was nothing to grab a hold of. Despite longer wanting the chocolate bar, I forced it down my throat, then opened another, and another after that, desperate for the solace I had found there since I was a child. But instead, all I felt was guilt and shame. Disgusted with myself, I got up from my desk and walked quickly to the bathroom, where I closed the cubicle door, leaned against the wall and cried until there were no tears left.

"Hey, you okay in there?" Willamina's deep voice echoed through the empty bathroom and I caught my breath.

"I'm fine."

"Bullshit. Open up." She rapped on the door, and I knew I had no choice but to open it.

"I'm fine," I told her as I emerged, red faced and puffy eyed.

"Yeah, you look it," she quipped. "What's up?"

At the basin, I splashed water on my face and tried to think of something to tell her. "Nothing, I'm just overtired."

She was dressed in black from head to toe. Black pants, black shirt, black blazer, and a pen was stashed behind her ear. If Johnny Cash had been a female journalist, I thought as I took it all in, he would have looked exactly like Willamina.

"Nolan, stop bullshitting," she sighed. "You crying over the council round?"

"No," I snapped. "Of course not."

"Because that would be pretty lame."

I met her eye in the mirror, and she smirked. "I'm not crying over the council round, okay? It's just..."

"Not where you want to be?"

Technically, she was right, so I agreed. "No, it's not."

Willamina leaned back against the sink beside me. "I'll tell you what Nolan, I wouldn't normally do this, but you're a good journo, so I'll throw you a bone. I'm going to look into the relationship between the Lord Mayor and the Stockton victim Lauren Ellis. Since you're close with him, how about we work it together? I'll even give you a by-line next to mine if it pans out."

The angle caught me unawares. It was the first I had heard of any connection between Andrew and Lauren, other than the fact she worked at council. "What relationship?" I asked, fighting hard to keep my resolve.

"There are rumours," she told me. "Enough to take a closer look."

My stomach clenched, and a voice in my head said not to ask, but I did. "What kind of rumours?"

"That they were having an affair."

"Andrew and Lauren?"

"Why? Does that surprise you?"

Her eyes locked onto mine and I swore she could read my mind. "No, it just doesn't seem like him."

"Here's a tip, Nolan," she said, turning and fixing her hair in the mirror. "It's like all of them. Don't be naïve and get your stuff. We're going to see him."

"Now?"

There was no time to warn him. Worse still, there was no time to fix my make-up or make peace with the mini eating frenzy I had given in to just minutes before. We were going exactly as I was. Exposed, unhinged, and unprepared. What could possibly go wrong?

Chapter Sixteen
LAUREN

I *didn't make a habit of answering private numbers, but I'd just finished dinner and was home alone with nothing better to do. When he said his name, I was so surprised I almost dropped the phone.*

"I'm sorry to call you after hours, Lauren, but there's something confidential that I need to discuss with you. Could we meet before work tomorrow morning?"

I'd always had a good relationship with the Lord Mayor. I regularly advised him on environmental issues and worked closely with Council's communications team to make sure his comments and lines were on point, but he'd never called me directly and especially not after hours.

"Sure," I replied. "Your office?"

"No, let's meet somewhere else. Are you familiar with the café in the lobby of Crowne Plaza?"

I agreed to meet him there at eight o'clock the next morning. It would mean missing my spin class, but there was something about his tone that suggested I didn't have much of a choice. For the rest of the night, I wandered around the house pondering what the Lord Mayor could possibly want to discuss. The only project of any interest that I was working on was the Ridgemont Capitol environmental report, and so far, it hadn't turned up much at all—except the birds.

I knew the Lord Mayor wasn't an advocate for development and just yesterday, I had submitted a preliminary report on my findings around the potential presence of a rare species called Gemini Birds on the site. They were a protected species in NSW due to their rapid decline in numbers. My report had been clear there was only circumstantial evidence to suggest the ground-nesting birds could be present, but I had asked for more time to investigate.

I flopped back onto the couch and flicked through all my streaming services, but when nothing jumped out at me, I decided to Google Andrew Ashley. I had never given him a lot of thought other than the fact he was the Lord Mayor and extremely handsome. I knew he had been married to a woman named Stella for most of his adult life and was passionate about stopping Newcastle from turning into a city comparable to Sydney, but that was about it.

I scrolled through his official Facebook and Instagram platforms but there was nothing much to learn there. I googled his name in the News category and read all the stories on him that had been posted in the past twelve months. In his photos he always stood so proud, his well-fitting grey suits a perfect contrast to those piercing green eyes, and with the stature of a front row footballer, I suddenly wondered why I hadn't paid more attention to him in the past.

Andrew Ashley.

Handsome, passionate, successful and suddenly on my radar.

Chapter Seventeen
LUCY

When Yieldon came marching toward Lucy's desk, she felt as though her heart was in her throat. "How did you go with Internal Affairs?" she asked, as casually as possible.

At first, he didn't answer, and Lucy thought he was trying to find the words to verbalise his shock and utter disappointment at what she'd had done.

"Yieldon?"

"My office, Dicks. We need to talk."

As she followed him toward his office, Lucy tried to think of anything she could say that might explain what she'd done, that would justify her actions. But when she came up empty-handed, Lucy quickly resigned herself to the fact she would just have to tell him the truth.

Yieldon sat down behind his desk and let out a long breath.

"Before you say anything—" she began, but he cut her off.

"I'm not sure how to say this, Dicks, but they're leaning toward Andrew Ashley as the main suspect in the Lauren Ellis case."

As Lucy's shoulders fell forward with relief, she realised she hadn't taken a breath since they sat down. "So, you finally think he's good for it?"

"No, I don't," he snapped. "I've known Andrew a long time, Dicks. I don't see it."

"I don't know, boss. He lied to us at the house the other night."

Yieldon nodded and looked away. "I know. I just don't understand why."

"Sometimes under pressure people do things that are out of character, things they wouldn't normally do," she said, the Marshall case filling her mind. "No one is so perfect they never make a mistake."

"I'm not suggesting he's perfect, Dicks, and I don't have a boner for him. I'm just saying that murdering a woman then weighing her body down in the ocean is a fair reach of the bow."

"You know the stats, sir. It's far more likely she was killed by someone she was intimate with than a stranger, and the likelihood they were having an affair is getting higher by the minute."

"Yeah, I know. I just don't think it was him."

"Don't think, or don't want to think?"

He sighed and rubbed at his forehead. "We'll need to go back and talk with him again. If he's not forthcoming with more information, we'll have to bring him in, but let's do all we can to avoid that. Once the media gets hold of it, he'll be tarnished by this melodrama for the rest of his career. Guilty or not."

Lucy nodded and gathered her things. "You good to go then?"

But instead of ordering her out to the car like he usually would, Yieldon hesitated.

"I know it's not my place to say," she began, "but you can't let your emotions dictate your decisions. I know he's a friend, but he very likely killed that woman."

Lucy expected Yieldon to bite her head off, but instead he leaned in close. "I think you've got enough to worry about without deciding what I should and shouldn't be doing, Dicks. I covered your arse with IA, but at some point, we need to talk about the Marshall case. In the meantime, you'll follow my lead when it comes to Andrew. You got it? Otherwise, you might have some problems of your own to deal with." He stepped back and straightened his shirt. "We're not going to see him today. We'll go when I say we go. Not a minute before."

Lucy nodded quickly and averted her gaze. "Of course, sir."

"That's it. You can go."

Yieldon knew. He knew about the Marshall case and was going to use it as leverage to make her back off Andrew Ashley. It was bad enough that what she did was interfering with her personal life, but now it might be the loophole that allowed a man to get away with murder.

She glanced down at the childish watch on her wrist. It had a cartoon dog's face, its whiskers acting as the hands, and a pastel pink plastic band—a birthday gift from Miranda two years ago. On the morning of her birthday, her daughter had been quick to say she chose it herself, her face beaming with pride. As Lucy put it on, she and James had exchanged a glance, a mix of resignation and pure unconditional love. Right now, the dog's whiskers told her it was almost noon. She pushed back in her chair and grabbed her wallet and keys. This had to stop.

In the underground carpark, Lucy unlocked her personal car and pulled a plain black sweater out from the backseat. It was covered in dog hair, but she couldn't go in uniform. It would cause too much attention. She unhooked her utility belt, walked around to the back of the car, and locked both it and her gun safely in the boot. Then, with clammy palms and a racing heart, she started the car.

The Marshall place was a Department of Housing property at Mayfield that had seen better days. The yard was a ramshackle of weeds and broken toys. Sections of paint were missing from the outside walls and a discarded tricycle was tipped onto on its side by the front steps. After two knocks, the door opened and Lucy steeled herself. Sarah Marshall was wrapped in a light blue terry cloth dressing gown, a half-smoked cigarette hanging from her nicotine-stained fingers.

"Senior Sergeant Dickson," Sarah said with a grin, as though she knew something Lucy didn't. "What brings you here?"

"Can I come in? We need to talk."

Sarah stepped aside and motioned for her to go in. Inside, Lucy noted the house was much the same as it was the last time she was there. A colourful crocheted rug bunched in the corner of a worn-out brown couch, a wooden coffee table covered in cup rings, the TV on, and the tang of tobacco smoke hanging in the air. She didn't sit and instead stood awkwardly in the centre of the room.

"No uniform," Sarah stated. "Must be this is a personal call, then, is it?"

She was a former meth addict, and it showed. She looked a decade older than her forty-three years. She was frail and had skin that looked like it had been pickled. When she opened her mouth, her teeth reminded Lucy of tiny pegs, and she never stayed still. She was also the mother of a nine-year-old girl named Minty.

"How's your daughter?" Lucy asked. "Is she here?"

"She's out back. She's got a cat now. Won't stop shitting in the damned bath."

"She good?"

Sarah took a long drag of her cigarette, then stubbed it out in an ashtray. "Thanks to you, she is."

"About that..." Lucy hesitated, trying to find the right words. "Internal Affairs is looking into the case. At some point, they're going to question me."

Sarah smiled, her tiny peg teeth on full display. "So, you're here because you want to know if I'm good to back-up your story. Well, I got you Senior Sergeant Dickson. Just tell me what I need to say."

Lucy shifted uncomfortably. "It's not that, Sarah. I think I'm going to have to tell them what I did, and I just wanted you to know first. Give you time to figure out what you want to do."

She stared at Lucy for a moment, then twirled a strand of brassy hair around her finger and stuck it into her mouth.

"Don't do that, Sarah. You'll be okay."

She stopped chewing her hair, then leaned over and pulled another cigarette out of the packet. As she lit it, Lucy noticed her hand was shaking. "So, they'll be letting him out, then? That what you're saying?"

"I don't know."

"You know what he did to her. And to me."

"I do."

Sarah sucked on the cigarette, then stepped in close and blew the smoke straight into Lucy's face. "Thought you had our backs, *Dicks*."

"It was a mistake Sarah, you know that." Suddenly exhausted, Lucy sat down on the dilapidated couch and sighed. "I know he hit Minty, and you, more than once."

"More than once," Sarah scoffed. "If it was once, it was a thousand times. Put my kid in the hospital twice. You remember?"

"Of course, I do."

"Then why you gotta go an be a rat now? It's only cause of you my kid's finally getting back to normal."

"I let my emotions get the better of me that day," Lucy sighed. "Coming out here time after time and knowing he was beating her. After the last time we came up to the hospital, I promised myself I wouldn't let it happen again. But I shouldn't have... done what I did."

"He's a bastard."

"Then you have to take Minty and get away from here before this all comes out, Sarah," Lucy pleaded. "Please, promise me you will."

Sarah threw out her arms and raised her brow to the sky. "What do you think? I'm made of money? Where the hell am I supposed to go?"

"There are shelters and ways of getting help."

"He's her father. He'll find us. Always does."

Lucy stood up and willed herself to be strong. "I planted evidence, Sarah. I knew he was dealing, and I planted enough meth to make sure he went away. I did it to give you and Minty a chance to start over. So please, make the most of it."

"I'm not using. She's got a cat. That's about as good as it gets for people like us," she said. "But you go do what you gotta do. He comes back, we'll deal with it."

"How? How will you deal with it?"

"Like always, I suspect."

"Lucy!" From the back of the house, Minty, with her unruly black hair and wide brown eyes, came running toward me. Before I could stop her, she flung her arms around my waist and squeezed.

"Hi, sweetheart," I managed, willing myself not to cry. "How are you?"

"I got a cat!"

"You did!"

She nodded and smiled so big I had no choice but to smile back. She was so much like my sister that it pulled at my heart. "Well, that's great, and it's so good to see you."

She let go, and Sarah pulled her away by the sleeve. "Senior Sergeant Dickson has to go now," Sarah told her daughter, although her eyes never left mine. "She's got important things to do."

Lucy held her gaze, and Sarah arched her brow, challenging her to disagree.

"It was good to see you both," she said. "Sarah, please think about what we discussed."

She clicked her tongue and nodded. "Right back at you, Senior Sergeant."

Lucy took one last look at Minty and swallowed the lump in her throat. If she confessed, Sarah's husband would be released and the first thing he would do was come back to the house, get drunk, and beat them. But if she didn't, Yieldon was going to pull her around like a dog on a leash until he found a way to help Andrew Ashley get away with murder.

Either way, she was screwed.

Chapter Eighteen
ELLE

"I wasn't expecting to see you today," Andrew said, as I closed the door to his office.

"I appreciate you seeing me on short notice. I know you must be really busy."

He smiled warmly, and made his way toward me. "Never too busy for you, Elle."

I longed to embrace him, to smell his scent and hold him close. Instead, I heard myself say, "Well, *never* isn't exactly true."

His outstretched arms dropped, and he looked at me closely. "I apologised for having to cancel our dinner the other night, but sometimes that's going to happen. It's just the way it is."

I looked away and chastised myself for having sounded like a jealous girl-friend. "I know, and it's fine. There was actually another reason I came to see you."

He motioned for me to take a seat on a deep blue velvet couch beneath the window. As I made my way over, I hoped he wouldn't notice my puffy red eyes. "The other day when I was here asking you about the Ridgemont Capitol development application, you seemed almost resigned to the fact it might go ahead," I began. "Has something changed in regard to how you feel about it?"

He stood beside the couch, hands in his pockets, staring out the window. The bright sunlight only highlighted his perfect skin and the angle of his jaw. "That depends, Elle. Am I talking to my girlfriend or a reporter?"

The word *girlfriend* sent a warm tingle pulsing through my entire body. With every fibre of my professional being, I reminded myself that I was in fact a grown woman researching a story. That I had a job to do. "I was asked to come here by my editor," I managed eventually.

"So, the reporter," he said with a sigh. "In that case, my response is that personally I am not in favour of a resort-style development being constructed at Stockton. However, I am confident our staff will assess the application on its merits."

"Says the Lord Mayor."

"To the reporter," he quipped.

"Touché." I smiled and let my eyes wander out across his office.

"Elle, I can see you've been crying," he said after a moment. "What's wrong?"

I looked back and tried to come up with something, anything, that wouldn't sound lame. Willamina, my colleague and an award-winning reporter, already thought I was crying over the council round. Having Andrew know the truth, that I was crying over chocolate bars, was scraping the bottom of the barrel. "Depends who's asking," I said, trying to sound sassy but instead making myself cringe.

He sat down beside me and reached for my hand. "Someone who cares about you."

His hand was warm and reassuring. Knowing he had beaten me at my own game, I threaded my fingers through his and looked up to meet his eye. "Just some personal stuff I'm working through. Nothing to do with you."

"Well, I hope not," he said. "The last thing I want to do is make you cry."

"Well, then... what *do* you want to do?" I asked, a cheeky smile finding its way to my lips.

His eyes dropped across my body, and he grinned. "You have no idea."

I shifted in my seat and re-crossed my legs, memories of Andrew's weight quickly getting under my skin. I thought again of Willamina downstairs asking questions about him and Lauren, and guilt got the better of me.

Telling him was unprofessional, but we had made love. Every part of his body had been naked against mine. He trusted me.

"Andrew, you should know Willamina is downstairs in the Development Department asking questions about your relationship with Lauren Ellis," I said. "I thought you should know."

He immediately pulled his hand away and stared at me. "What kind of questions?"

"About whether the two of you were having an affair."

He got to his feet and marched over to his desk, where he snatched up the phone and ordered someone to immediately escort Willamina from the building.

"I'm sorry," I began. "I—"

"What was this then?" he snapped, pointing to where we had been sitting together. "A rouse to distract me? Did you tell her about us?"

"What?" I jumped to my feet. "No, to both of those questions. Andrew, no."

"Well, it seems awfully convenient, Elle, that you're here keeping me busy while she's down there asking questions."

"I was here to ask about the development, that's all."

He turned his back and shoved his hands into his trouser pockets. "You should go."

"Andrew, you're overreacting," I tried. "I would never betray you. That's why I told you, and besides, what's the big deal if she asks a few questions? It's not like the two of you actually were having an affair."

When he didn't respond, my stomach folded in on itself. "Andrew?"

"Just go, Elle."

"Andrew, were you sleeping with her?"

A thousand thoughts ran through my mind. If he was sleeping with her, did that mean I was just one on a list of girls he had been intimate with behind his wife's back? Worse still, was it actually possible he might have killed Lauren? The thought sent me reeling. "Andrew?"

He slowly turned to face me, his shoulders slack. "It's complicated, alright?"

"How? Explain it to me," I said. "What was going on between the two of you?"

"Lauren was..." he gazed out across the room, clearly remembering her. "It's hard to find the words."

"Were you in love with her?" I breathed, my heart sinking.

"No, Elle," he said, shaking his head. "I wasn't in love with her and I'm not getting into this right now. I'm furious that you came up here and didn't tell me right away about that journalist being downstairs. And Willamina of all people. Christ, she's like a dog with a bone."

"I did tell you," I tried again.

"Not soon enough. Are you trying to impress her or something?"

"Impress her? What does that even mean?"

"Nothing," he sighed. "It upset me, is all. I'm sure you can understand."

I quickly pulled my bag up over my shoulder and looked him dead in the eye. "No, Andrew, I don't. But what I do understand is that I risked my job to tell you about Willamina being downstairs and you won't tell me a damned thing in return. Not about why you suddenly don't care about the development and not about Lauren, either."

When he didn't respond, I turned and stormed out of the office, every step proving a battle not to rush back and apologise. My head was racing and my heart was breaking. When I got outside, Willamina was waiting on the footpath.

"What the actual fuck, Nolan?" she demanded. "You told him?"

"No," I lied, not knowing what else to say. "Someone called up from Development while I was interviewing him. They must have told him you were there asking questions. How did you get in there, anyway?"

"Bastards," she swore. "And you're not the only one with contacts at council, you know. Anyway, doesn't matter. I think I got something before they kicked me out." A wide grin broke out across her face as she waited for me to ask what. When I didn't, she went ahead and told me anyway. "Seems the Lord Mayor and Lauren were seen leaving the Crowne Plaza Hotel together by one of the Development staffers, and on more than one occasion."

"Really," I managed, my voice threatening to break. "Could have just been a meeting?"

"Before eight in the morning."

"Oh," I sighed, tears stinging the back of my eyes. "Looks like you'll get your story, then."

"Looks like," she agreed. "Say, it's almost knock off time. You need to go back to the office?"

I shook my head.

"Go on home then. You can catch me up on what slime ball Ashley said about the development in the morning." She turned to leave, but then stopped and looked back. "Can you believe that guy? Married for twenty-seven years and he's fucking some staffer. I don't know about you, Nolan, but I'm starting to think we might have found our murderer and hot damn, what a headline!"

I nodded, not trusting my own voice.

"This is what it's all about, Nolan," she beamed. "This is what it's all about. I'll catch you tomorrow."

I waited until Willamina was out of sight and then let myself fall into a heap on a park bench outside City Hall. Andrew had been in love with Lauren. It was written all over his face. I thought back to the images we ran of her in the Tribune. Tall, tanned, and slim. Everything I wasn't. As I fought back the tears, my phone buzzed, and I pulled it out of my bag.

David: *Managed to scoop Fraser on the Ellis case yet?*

Me: *Nah, been bogged down with council bullshit*

David: *Sounds like you need a drink*

I had been planning to go home and eat myself into oblivion, but once again, Dr Simms' words ran through my head. *You've been consoling yourself with food.* She was right. It was unhealthy and definitely time for a change. This evening I would instead console myself with alcohol.

Me: *Just tell me where*

I saw David as soon as I walked into The Junction Hotel. Despite the venue being just blocks from my townhouse, I had never been inside and was surprised at the glamourous décor and beautiful water feature that took up an entire wall. "Wow, fancy," I said as I sat down.

"It sounded like you needed a little pick-me-up. Plus, I owe you, remember?"

I nodded and made myself comfortable in a booth he had chosen in the back. "Yeah, the council crap is starting to get me down. Your timing was perfect, actually."

A waitress placed a glass of merlot in front of me, then handed a Peroni to David. "You still drink red, I hope?"

I smiled and nodded. "I do, and wow, good memory."

"Can't blame you for needing a break," he said, as I took my first mouthful. "Having to deal with Andrew Ashley every day is enough to turn anyone to drink."

Once again, the voice in my head, the one tasked with protecting my heart from smashing into a thousand tiny pieces, screamed not to ask. But once again, I did. "What makes you say that?"

"Can't stand the guy," he said, screwing up his face. "He's a sleaze. Come on, Elle, everyone knows that. I'm sure he's hit on you once or twice when you've been alone in his office."

"I... no... I hadn't heard that about him. He's always been fine to me," I said, not knowing whether it was Andrew I was trying to protect or my pride.

"Well, that's good," he said with a smile. "I'd hate to see you become one of Andrew's *girls*. Anyway, here's cheers to you finally kicking Willamina's arse on the Ellis case."

I took a long mouthful, trying to stop my pounding heart from crashing into my ribcage. I had never felt like such an idiot.

"Did you not read what I wrote in my text?" I said, after draining the rest of my glass in one hit. "I'm not on the Ellis case. I'm stuck on stupid c-o-u-n-c-i-l."

He swallowed his beer, then feigned an exaggerated sigh of contentment. "Well, as of tomorrow, you will be on the Ellis case."

"Oh yeah? And how do you suppose that's going to happen?"

He looked both ways to make sure no one was listening, then leaned across the table toward me. "Because little magpie, I'm about to tell you who killed her."

Chapter Nineteen
STELLA

S tella unpacked the dishwasher, padded over to the window and stared out at the ocean.

If Andrew was charged with Lauren's murder, their lives would be ruined. She had no accomplishments to her name other than being the wife of the Lord Mayor and even though they had savings, it would not be enough to keep their home or continue paying for her mother's care. Add to that the shame and humiliation of Andrew being a murderer and a cheater, and what was left? The only thing worse was the idea of her son going to jail.

Noises in the kitchen caused her to turn, and she saw Jackson sitting on a stool by the island bench. His head hung low and his shoulders were hunched.

"Mum, what are we going to do?" he asked, his voice trembling. "The police are going to come for me."

She walked over and pulled out the stool beside her son. Deep down, she wanted to hold him close and stroke his hair, but he was too old for that and would only pull away. "It's going to be okay, Jackson. I promise."

"But how is it?

Stella took him in. His almost six-foot lanky frame that was yet to grow into and tangle of light brown hair. He had grown inside her, every cell and membrane formed by her own body. When he was born, he came out screaming bloody murder, and she had instantly loved every inch of him. He was her blood, her baby, and nothing was going to come between them—especially not some girl who had wanted to ruin her marriage.

Jackson traced his finger along the flowing marble swirls of the bench. "Mum, there's something I haven't told you about Lauren."

Stella's throat tightened. She leaned in close and placed her hand on his arm, quietly reminding herself that no matter what he said next, she had to remain calm. "What is it, Jackson?"

"I met her before."

"Before she came to the house?"

He nodded, and Stella braced herself for what might come next.

"It was about six weeks ago, up in the dunes. I was walking Gucci one day and there she was, like, out of nowhere."

"Okay... and what happened between the two of you?"

He shrugged and looked uncomfortable. "Nothing much at first. I said hi, she said hi back. I asked what she was doing, and she said she was working, looking for some kind of birds."

"And then?" When he refused to meet Stella's eye, she knew the story was going somewhere she wouldn't like. "Jackson, listen to me. You need to tell me the truth. I won't be mad, but I can't help you if I don't know what happened."

He sighed and shook his head. "She was so pretty, Mum, it was like... I'd never seen a girl like that before in real life."

The comment stung. Knowing her husband had been intimate with a woman Jackson thought was the prettiest girl he had ever seen was a hard pill to swallow. Images of Lauren and Andrew tangled up and naked pushed into her mind, but she quickly re-focused her attention back to her son. "So, you met her out in the dunes..."

"I went back the next day. And the day after that, hoping to see her again. It took a week or so but eventually she was there. I tried to make it look like a coincidence, but I think she knew."

"Did something happen between the two of you?" He hesitated and Stella prayed to God that her son and husband hadn't both slept with the same woman.

"I tried," he said eventually. "She said I could follow her on Instagram if I was interested in conservation and stuff. That was her job. I messaged her a few times after that."

"And the messages, were they... intimate?"

"I told her I really liked her," he admitted, a blush creeping up from the neck of his T-shirt. "I asked her out, but she never answered anymore."

Then, to Stella's surprise, he pounded his fist on the counter and swore. "Fuck! I feel like such a fucking idiot now."

"Why? Because you liked her?"

"No, Mum," he snapped. "Because the whole time she was fucking my dad."

Stella swallowed hard and reminded herself this was about her son, not her husband, and his betrayal. She reminded herself that it had been a long time since she and Andrew had been intimate and that it was she who hadn't wanted to be touched. She thought about the fact she never really loved Andrew and how he had always been the one trying to fix things between them. But despite all that, it burned to realise he clearly no longer loved her—that she had ceased to be the object of his affection.

"Jackson, we don't actually know that your dad was romantically involved with Lauren. I know you heard him on the phone, but—"

"I saw them."

Until that moment, Stella never knew that words alone could pull the air from your chest. That without even being touched, you could feel as though your lungs were nothing more than two shrivelling balloons.

"You... what?" she stammered.

"Lauren never answered my message when I asked her about going out. I knew she was older than me, but I couldn't stop thinking about her. So, I went looking for her again to ask why she never answered. I was heading up one of the dunes when I heard two people. They were... you know..."

Stella was instantly torn between hating her husband more than she had ever hated anyone in her life and being paralysed by the realisation that he really had fallen in love with someone else. Since she was sixteen, Stella had foolishly believed Andrew was so in love with her that it was enough for the both of them. To know that was no longer true spun her entire world on its axis. She was the Lord Mayor's wife. More than that, she was the love of his life—the only woman he had been with since they were teenagers. Or so she thought. Until now, their lives were undeniably and irreversibly intertwined and yet someone had found their way in.

"And you're certain it was them?" she asked, bracing herself against the island bench. "*Together*?"

"Well, I saw her," he managed, looking more uncomfortable than Stella could ever remember. "I crawled up toward the top of the dune and she was down there, you know, on top of him. She was facing me, but he was lying down and I could only see the back of his head and chest, so I didn't know at first that it was Dad. She was naked and... I should have just left."

"Jackson—"

"I was so bummed," he spat. "I mean, it sucked that she was with someone. I was going to leave, but then I saw Dad's Council windbreaker on the ground. That's when it hit me that *my* Lauren was the same girl I heard him talking to on the phone."

"Jackson," Stella began, her grip on the bench easing. "Hundreds of staff have the same windbreaker. It could have been anyone."

But her son shook his head. "No, Dad's has a rip by the back of the collar. Remember, Gucci tore at it when she was a pup. It was that day we had the barbecue out the back. He said he didn't want a new one because it reminded him of how great the day was."

Stella thought back and could hear Andrew saying those exact words. With a sinking feeling, she realised her son was right. "Okay, alright," she breathed. "So, you watched them have sex, and then what?"

"I didn't *watch them* have sex," he said, instantly recoiling. "That's gross. I just watched her for a bit, then left."

If that was the worst of it, Stella thought, then nothing had really changed. She began to let out a breath but quickly realised he wasn't done.

"When I got back to the house, I was so mad," Jackson continued. "It was like my mind just wouldn't stop spinning. I kept thinking about all the things I should have done. I should have confronted them. I should have said something. It was like all this anger was bottled up inside me and I couldn't get it out." He stood up as though something had pulled him out of his seat by his shirt. "I couldn't just leave it, so I messaged her again. I called her a slut and a whore and said she was..."

"She was what?"

"Going to get what she deserved."

The words sent Stella reeling. Her son had sent a threatening message to a woman who days later turned up in pieces on the beach just metres from their home. "Did she answer?"

He paced the length of the kitchen for what felt like forever, then came back to face her. "Yeah, a few hours later. She said we had to talk."

"And did you?"

"That's when she came to the house the next morning. I know I said she came to see Dad, but she came to see me, Mum. I should have told you. I fucked up."

Stella nodded and concentrated on her breathing. In and out. In and out. "Jackson, you need to tell me exactly what happened when she was here."

"Well, it started out like I told you. We got into a shouting match at the door. Levi came out and tried to get involved, but I didn't want him knowing what was going on, so I told him to piss off."

As he explained what happened, Jackson's chest began to heave. When Stella glanced down, she saw that his hands were trembling, and she wanted to scream. No matter what happened between her son and Lauren, this was Andrew's doing. Andrew's fault—and once it was all over, one way or another, Andrew was going to pay for it.

"Lauren kept trying to say I had it all wrong and shouting that I shouldn't have been watching her," Jackson continued. "She wouldn't stop talking over me and making out like the whole thing was my fault for liking her." He pulled at the neck of his T-shirt and tiny beads of sweat glistened across the top of his forehead. "All her talking was making me feel like I couldn't breathe. I just wanted her to go."

"And then?"

"I told her to leave, but she wouldn't, so I started pulling her down the path by the arm. I didn't mean to pull her so hard, but I guess I did without realising it."

Stella got up from her seat and filled a glass with water from the tap. She swallowed the entire thing in one mouthful, then motioned to Jackson with the glass, but he shook his head. "Jackson, regardless of how I feel about your dad and this woman being together, you shouldn't have grabbed at her like that. I need you to know that's not okay. Not ever."

"I know," he sighed. "I didn't mean to. I tried messaging her to apologise. She wrote back once, saying to never contact her again. She said the only reason she didn't call the police was because of Dad."

"And this was a couple of days before she was found on the beach?"

He nodded and pulled at the neck of his shirt.

"Jackson, I'm not going to let you get the blame for what inevitably happened to Lauren, but we also can't let Dad be accused. You do understand that, don't you?" she said. "If Dad really was *involved* with her, then he's going to be their main suspect."

Jackson shifted his weight from one foot to the other and Stella could tell there was something else her son wanted to say.

"Do you think..." he paused, then took a deep breath. "Dad actually did it?"

Stella let her mind drift back to Andrew standing by the fire burning documents and apologising to the night sky, but what she thought didn't matter. What mattered was making sure her son didn't end up getting himself or his father charged with murder.

"No, Jackson, I don't think Dad did it," she told him calmly. "But there is something I need to ask you. When you sent that message to Lauren saying you saw her in the dunes, did you write anything about her being there with Dad?"

He shook his head, and Stella placed both her hands on his shoulders. "Jackson, listen to me carefully. When the police come to question you, and they will, you can't tell them this had anything to do with Dad. Do you understand? You need to tell them you liked Lauren a lot and got upset seeing her with someone else in the dunes, but you didn't see who he was."

"But—"

"No buts. You have to trust me, Jackson. I will not let anything happen to you, I promise."

"You want me to lie to the police?"

"Jackson, if Dad goes to jail, we have nothing. I know you're mad at him, and I am too, but right now we have to stick together. We're a family and that's what families do. They have each other's back."

"Yeah, well, what happened to him having our backs?" he spat.

"Sweetheart, people make mistakes. Dad did, but so did you. The only thing that matters now is neither of you killed that woman."

Eventually, he nodded, and Stella squeezed his arm. "This will all work out. You'll see."

Jackson nodded, got up from his seat, and shuffled slowly up the hall toward his room. He was a good kid. He always had been, and Stella knew there was no way he could have killed someone.

She glanced down at the angry scar on her forearm, the one she told everyone she got from a nasty accident the first and only time she tried using the oven. It was a lie that seemed to amuse all who heard it. The truth, however, was far from funny. Andrew had hurt her. Until that day, she never thought it possible. He was sorry after. He said he had been overcome with jealousy that she spent the afternoon having drinks with a male friend. When he realised it was her hairdresser who had wanted to talk about relationship problems with his boyfriend, Andrew was mortified at what he had done. He never raised his voice to her again, and Stella had put it behind them.

But as she walked over to the window and stared out over the beach, her mind instantly filled with images of Lauren's body parts scattered along the sand. Once upon a time, she told herself that Andrew wasn't the type to deliberately hurt a woman. That what happened between them had just been a misunderstanding. But what if she was wrong?

Chapter Twenty
ANDREW

Across the road, the media scrum was assembling outside City Hall. In a few minutes, Andrew would stand alongside police as they provided an update on Lauren's case, not that there was any new information to reveal. They just felt his presence would give some weight to their pleas for more information.

Andrew had no doubt Willamina Fraser would be there. She'd throw a few curve balls, but Chris would have his back, at least for the time being. That woman, though, Senior Sergeant Dickson—she was a concern.

He tore his eyes away from the gathering reporters and leaned back against the wooden bench. Sometimes he liked to sneak away from the office and come over to Civic Park. The sprawling green space was directly across the road and sitting beneath the towering Morton Bay Fig trees, listening to the splashing water of the fountain, often calmed his nerves. It also helped him remember what was important. Long before the internet and digital books, Marjorie would bring him to Civic Library on Laman Street up behind the park. They would enter through the lobby that housed the famous three-metre statue of a man and woman, their gaze cast skyward. As a child, they soared over him and he would look up at them and think of his birth parents and how they must have been enthralled with things so much bigger than him that they never took the time to look down. When those thoughts filled his mind, Andrew would squeeze Majorie's hand a little tighter and thank God that on the day they met, she not only took the time to look down, but to also lift him up.

Andrew gathered himself and then stood, and glanced over at the library. The statue remained just inside the door and while all the towering trees that once formed a canopy over the narrow street had been removed, much to the ire of local residents, it buoyed him that some things still remained the same. While everyone else was racing forward and living their lives online, Andrew wanted to salvage the contentment of standing still, of smelling the ocean air and greeting people by name. In a world of cities that never sleep, he longed to salvage Newcastle from the arms of insomnia and provide the community with a place where they could close their eyes and not wake up in a world they no longer recognised.

The phone vibrated in his pocket. A text message from his executive assistant telling him he had five minutes before the presser started. The media scrum would no doubt want to know if there were more gory details about Lauren's death, and whether there were any new leads on who killed her and fed her body to the sea. Andrew knew they were out for blood, and in a few minutes, he would be the one getting attacked by sharks—Willamina Fraser, no doubt leading the frenzy.

Chapter Twenty-One
LUCY

O utside City Hall, Lucy snuck a glance at Yieldon and wondered how he would handle the morning media briefing. There were shadows beneath his eyes and he seemed on edge. He was getting pressure from the top to put this case to bed and it wouldn't have surprised her if politics were becoming a factor. The Lord Mayor had been elected as a fiercely independent candidate bound by neither the Labor nor the Liberal party. Add to that his dislike for progress and it undoubtedly made for enemies. There were factions out there, politicians and developers alike, who saw Newcastle as a coastal city on the cusp of becoming a booming market. She was just a local cop, but in Lucy's opinion, those individuals had to be gunning for Andrew's removal from office—and it was no secret that people in high places always had a way of getting what they wanted. Whether Andrew was innocent or not would make no difference to them. In politics, optics alone were often enough to end a career like his. If it even *looked* like Andrew killed Lauren, the truth wouldn't matter. His career would die right along with her.

For Yieldon, who had been friends with Andrew since high school, that meant a choice—his career or his mate. If he believed in his heart of hearts that Andrew was innocent, then he was up against it. Being forced to choose between your head and heart was no easy feat, and no one understood that better than Lucy. The only problem was, it looked like Yieldon was going to choose his heart, and that meant taking her down with the ship.

Lucy nodded at Andrew as he took his place beside Yieldon. She usually got a good read on people, but this morning, Andrew was a fortress. He stood tall. His suit was impeccable, and his face gave nothing away. As they stood side by side, Lucy thought about how narcissists had the ability to almost completely repress their emotions. Andrew fitted the mould. High achieving, handsome, always impeccably presented. She knew from her criminal behaviour studies at university that narcissists were often known to act out in rage and that some of the most famous murderers in history were believed to have been afflicted with the condition, including Charles Manson, and it was thought Ted Bundy. Then again, Madonna, Kim Kardashian, and Tom Cruise had also been called narcissists, so anything was possible.

"Good morning," Yieldon began as he addressed the media. "Thanks for coming today."

The pack of hungry reporters leaned in as one, clearly hoping for a significant announcement. Lucy understood they were a necessary evil, but deep down, it bothered her how much they enjoyed the chase.

"Unfortunately, we don't have a lot to share today in regard to the Lauren Ellis case," Yieldon continued. "In fact, at this time, we are appealing for witnesses to come forward with any information that might help lead to an arrest."

He paused, just long enough for a reporter Lucy recognised as Willamina Fraser from the Newcastle Tribune, to butt in with a question.

"Inspector Yieldon, are police following up suggestions that Lord Mayor Andrew Ashely did, in fact, have a personal relationship with the victim before she was killed?"

Yieldon stiffened, and along with everyone else, Lucy waited for his response.

"Lauren Ellis worked at council and frequently met with the Lord Mayor to advise on environmental matters as part of her job," Yieldon told Willamina calmly. "She was a senior environmental officer, which meant she was best placed to work alongside the Lord Mayor as well as the directorship at council on matters relating to coastal erosion and developmental impacts on the environment."

Clearly unsatisfied, the raven-haired reporter pushed her way to the front of the scrum. "Inspector, how do you explain the two of them being seen leaving the Crowne Plaza Hotel on several occasions at early hours of the morning?"

A buzz of excitement hummed through the pack, and Andrew cleared his throat.

"I'll take that one if you don't mind," he announced, stepping toward the lectern. "Willamina, the truth is what matters. People need to be held accountable for their actions. As a city, we are fortunate to have a newspaper which has always held that sentiment in high regard, and as a reporter working at the Tribune, I appreciate that it's your job to follow all leads no matter how outrageous they may seem." He took a beat and gave her a tight smile before continuing. "I understand you have been questioning council staff about my so-called relationship with Ms Ellis, so let me make it very clear to you here today that at no point did Lauren Ellis and I have an intimate relationship. Like everyone at Newcastle City Council, I valued her commitment and contribution to the city and she is a greatly missed member of our team. What happened to her was a deplorable act carried out by a person who must be found and punished."

He pulled his eyes away from the reporter and stared straight down the barrel of the local NBN Television News camera. "I implore anyone who has information or who may have seen or heard from Lauren in the days leading up to her death to please contact Crime Stoppers and help us find the person who did this. We owe it to Lauren and her family to provide closure and a sense of peace at this most trying of times. Thank you."

Andrew stepped back from the lectern, and visions of the famous mike drop moment from President Obama's 2016 final State of the Union address came to mind. Direct, heartfelt, and purposeful, the Lord Mayor had managed to respectfully belittle and undermine Willamina Fraser, while also conveying a heartfelt plea to help find Lauren's killer. Was it narcissistic behaviour 101, or was he a genuinely nice guy? That was the trouble with psychopaths, Lucy thought, as the media scrum dispersed. It was often hard to tell the difference.

Chapter Twenty-Two
ELLE

David was convinced that Andrew killed Lauren Ellis.

As the lead investigator in the search and rescue effort to locate her remains, he was well placed to make an educated assessment. But as I walked to work, my mind pulled me in a hundred different directions.

Andrew couldn't have killed Lauren in a crime of passion, I told myself. He wasn't romantically involved with her. *Or was he?* He didn't have it in him to hurt someone. When we were together, his touch had been so gentle, so loving. *But how well did I really know him?* To do something like that and carry on each day going to work and living your life would have to mean he was nothing less than a psychopath and it would be impossible not to notice the signs. *Or would it?*

I crossed over King Street where, just metres to the left, stood City Hall. I gazed up at the first-floor windows and wondered if Andrew was already back at his desk after the presser. Willamina would have grilled him over the rumours of an affair with Lauren, and I wondered how he handled it. As I kept walking, just thinking about him caused a tug in my chest. Before I realised what I was doing, I reached into my satchel, rummaging for my phone. I just wanted to hear his voice, I told myself. Just to see if he was alright. But as I scrolled through my recent calls looking for his name, I realised quickly I had no idea what I would say when he answered. Would I ask straight out if he killed Lauren or would I pretend David had never accused him? It was beyond me to keep something like that a secret, and so instead of calling, I slipped my phone back into my satchel, shoved my hands deep inside the pockets of my denim jacket, and kept walking.

Last night, David had seemed so sure. He was basing his conclusion on a number of factors, including rumours from colleagues and council employees who claimed Andrew and Lauren were having an affair. It had been a waning crescent moon that night, and he thought whoever managed to navigate hauling her body down to the water under the cover of darkness must have been familiar with the rise and fall of the landscape. But for David, the most telling factor was Andrew's admission to his wife that he had seen a woman up on the dunes that afternoon. Confused, I asked the obvious question—if he killed her, would he tell his wife he saw anyone at all? To me, it made no sense, but David just smirked, took a long mouthful of Peroni, and said, "Exactly. Telling her immediately distances him from the victim. Don't you see, Elle?" he asked. "That's the genius of it. She has to think he's innocent *because* of the admission."

I couldn't help thinking, though, what if he really had just seen a woman? And what if that woman hadn't even been Lauren?

I stopped at the pedestrian lights on Hunter Street and waited while a bright-red light rail car snaked its way along the tracks.

When the light rail project was first proposed, there had been much community debate over the cost, with one report estimating it had blown out to more than $600-million including repurposing the heavy rail corridor and ongoing operational costs. It had been the subject of my first interview with Andrew when two years ago, I walked into his office for the first time after being taken off general news and awarded my own round to cover—local government.

At the time, Andrew had been a close ally of the community lead organisation Save Our Rail, a vocal group of residents lobbying to keep the original train line that connected services from the wider Hunter into the city and Newcastle Beach. The State Government, on the other hand, was already married to the idea of ripping up the heavy rail line and there was a lot of talk about the project helping Newcastle to reach its potential as an economic, social and cultural centre.

Determined to make a splash my first day on the new round, Andrew and I inevitably found ourselves pulled into a heated debate over the pros and cons of the project which ended only when Walters called asking why my fifteen-minute interview had already seen me out of the office for almost an hour. Despite our clash of opinion, I had been attracted to him right away. Not just to his appearance, but his vision and passion. There was no denying Andrew Ashley was a force to be reckoned with. As it turned out, he felt the same way about me.

From the main street of Newcastle, the Tribune office was a short walk along the Honeysuckle precinct, past restaurants, cafes and government offices. It was tucked in beside the local water utilities office and a child care centre created for the office workers who spent the days torn between getting their work done and watching the city's tug boats as they guided gargantuan coal ships in and out of the port. In the lobby, I swiped my security pass and took the elevator to the tenth floor where, to my disappointment, Willamina was waiting at my desk.

"I've been texting you," she snapped, not even waiting for me to put my bag down. "What gives, Nolan?"

"My phone must still be on vibrate," I told her. "Why, what's up?"

"Our debrief?" she said, as though I was stupid. "I want to know what happened in your interview with Ashley."

Like David, Willamina had already decided Andrew was guilty. Now she was just looking for ammunition to write as much, and despite what David said last night, I still wasn't ready to help make that happen.

"Nothing really," I shrugged. "He just gave me the typical response about any re-zoning or development application having to be assessed on its merits. Then, like I said, someone called up and all he cared about was getting you out of the building."

"Typical," she snarled. "Political bullshit."

"Maybe there's just nothing more to it," I said. "Not everything is a conspiracy, as much as we'd like it to be."

She eyed me carefully and rubbed her chin like a doctor assessing a patient. "You don't think he did it, do you?"

"I don't know, Willamina." I busied myself turning on the computer, so we didn't have to make eye contact.

"You think he's innocent."

"What I think is that you're getting ahead of yourself," I told her. "Everyone has an opinion, but opinions aren't proof."

She rolled a chair over from the empty desk beside me, straddled it, and planted herself down. "Who else thinks he did it?"

She was sharp. I had to give her that. "What are you talking about?"

"You said *everyone* has an opinion. Who else thinks he killed Lauren?"

"No one. I don't know," I muttered. "Just, whoever."

"No... no," she said, leaning in. "You know something, Nolan. Who else thinks he killed her?"

"Willamina, you're making something out of nothing. I didn't mean anything by it." I shrugged my jacket off as the temperature around me started to rise.

"Bullshit, Nolan," she snapped. "You just called me by my first name. I've never heard you call me by my first name, not once. You know something."

"I really don't."

"You know," she began, finally getting up from the chair, "I can't believe you're still trying to steal this story from me."

"What?" I looked up at her in genuine surprise.

"After all I've done to include you, you're still trying to take this story from me. You obviously have a source. So, what's the angle?"

"There's no angle, *Fraser*," I said, emphasising her last name. "I'm not angling for your story. I just don't think he killed her, that's all."

She glared at me and shook her head. "The fact you won't tell me your source means you're either protecting him or your story. But either way, I'm going to find out which one."

"There is no source," I said. "And no one else thinks he killed her. So, if you don't mind, I have work to do."

She stood staring at me a moment longer, then strode off, her high-heel boots clicking against the hardwood floor. Making an enemy of Willamina Fraser was not a good idea, but being her ally meant helping her make Andrew into a murderer, and that was something I wasn't ready to do.

Chapter Twenty-Three
LAUREN

I ordered a coffee, then glanced around the room and chose a table in the back. With a gorgeous view over the working harbour, the café, despite being in the lobby of the Crowne Plaza Hotel, was not an unusual place for a work meeting. But as I waited for Andrew Ashley, I wondered again what I was doing there.

When he finally arrived, he took a seat across from me and gave me a warm and unassuming smile.

Almost immediately, a neatly dressed blonde woman from behind the counter was at his side, pad and pen in hand, ready to take his order. I smiled when he ordered a black coffee, no sugar. "A fellow purist," I said with a grin.

He returned my smile, and for a fleeting moment, held my gaze. "I apologise for calling you after hours, Lauren, really. I hope you don't feel uncomfortable about meeting me here, away from the office."

"Oh, it's fine," I said with a wave of my hand. "I was more than happy to take your call. I am intrigued though and have to admit, I spent the rest of my evening wondering what this is all about."

He looked away and to my surprise, seemed almost embarrassed. "I'm sorry for that. It wasn't my intention to be mysterious."

"Don't be." I flicked my hair over my shoulder and leaned across the table. "I love a good mystery."

Once again, he shifted in his seat and leaned further back, clearly uncomfortable. I glanced down at his hand and noticed he wasn't wearing a wedding band.

"Lauren, I understand you're working on a report that could potentially prove the existence of a rare species of bird on the old Stockton Centre site."

"That's right. The Gemini Birds," I told him. "They're incredibly rare ground-nesting birds usually found only in coastal areas further south."

His coffee arrived, and he took a sip. "And how certain are you of their presence?"

I had to admit I was disappointed Andrew Ashley only wanted to talk about the birds. It was exciting, sure, and as an environmentalist the presence of a rare bird species, and potentially breeding pairs no less, was worth getting worked up about, but he had my attention and while ever I didn't have his it only served to make me want it more. "There's not a strong case for it. Not yet, anyway."

"But you intend to investigate further."

"I'd like to," I replied. "I have submitted a report requesting additional hours be allocated to the project."

He nodded and looked out across the shimmering harbour. I didn't miss the quick smile of appreciation that pulled at his lips.

"Lord Mayor, can I ask what this is all about?"

"When will you know whether the study will be broadened?" he asked, ignoring my question.

"When the Director of Development makes a decision on my application."

"Right, Tony Mansfield," he said. "How's your working relationship with him, if you don't mind my asking?"

I suppressed a laugh. "Ah, strained would probably be the best description. He's not exactly pro-conservation."

"No, he's not." Andrew drained the rest of his coffee and pushed the cup away. "Let me know how you go, and I'd appreciate it if we could keep this conversation between the two of us for now."

"Sure," I smiled. "But do you mind if I ask why you're so interested in the Gemini Birds?"

He thought for a moment, then gazed out over the water one last time before answering. "If you find the birds, Lauren, you also find a reason to stop the development application that will inevitably be lodged by Ridgemont Capitol."

I nodded slowly. "And I take it you haven't changed your stance on keeping Stockton a coastal village?"

"I have not."

I wasn't certain if it was the light reflecting off the harbour or his passion for saving the area from development, but his eyes shone just a little brighter as he declared his opinion had not changed. "You're passionate," I said. "That's rare in a politician."

"Well, yes," he replied. "I suppose it is. I don't like to confuse politics with what's best for the community."

I didn't answer right away and instead let my eyes linger on his. He was older than me but still young for someone in his position. "Would you like to come?" I asked eventually.

"Excuse me?"

"To the site," I smiled innocently. "Would you like to come and see my work at the Stockton Centre site? I could show you what evidence I have so far that Gemini Birds may be present."

He smiled and dropped his gaze. "Yes, I'd like that. But could we do it out of hours? I think it's best I don't take a public interest in this, given my stance on developing Stockton. Any application process lodged by Ridgemont Capitol will have to be judged on its merits. I'd hate to give them any claim of negative bias."

"Of course," I smiled. "Just tell me when and I'm all yours."

Chapter Twenty-Four
ANDREW

Andrew knew that Chris would only be able to hold the upper echelons of power off for so long. This was the moment they had been waiting for. They finally had a reason to get him out of office and they would take every opportunity to remove the one obstacle that had been holding Stockton, and Newcastle for that matter, back from being sold off to the highest bidder. He and the State Government had bad blood, not just from his previous opposition of the light rail project, but from so many development plans over the years. Now they had a chance to get rid of him, not just from office, but maybe all together if the Police Commissioner decided to make it his mission. Once the order came from that high up, there would be nothing Chris or anyone else could do to stop it.

And it wouldn't be long now.

Andrew knew those who walked the corridors of power would be pushing hard for local police to find anything they could use to issue a warrant for his arrest. From there he would be taken in and put through the rigours of being charged, bail would probably be denied given the violent nature of the murder, and then he would be subjected to the rigours of the legal system and eventually tried in a court of law. But the trial, regardless of what evidence or testimony was presented, would be nothing compared to the public trial waged by the Tribune and other media. It was no secret the world of digital communication was taking over, and the local paper had been struggling. But his arrest would breathe new life into the ageing rag. They would splash the front page with headlines and print enough *alleged* accusations to float them for at least a full financial quarter. Advertising companies would be lining up to buy space and they would be cashing in, caring little for the actual truth.

At least there was Elle, Andrew thought. But she had stormed out of his office yesterday, and he couldn't really blame her. She wanted to know about the Ridgemont Development, but there were things he just couldn't share. Not yet. But he had to make it right with her. Time was running out.

Andrew got out of the car and started up the path to her front door. He hadn't called ahead and turning up unannounced on a woman's doorstep on a Saturday afternoon was not something he would usually do, but these weren't usual circumstances. He needed her on-side—more than she could imagine.

"Andrew," she exclaimed, when she opened the door. "What are you doing here?"

"I owe you an apology," he said, short and straight to the point. "I know I haven't been forthcoming with you about Ridgemont Capitol and I blamed you for Willamina Fraser asking questions. That was wrong of me and I apologise."

She looked him over, then stepped back so he could go inside. "She does have it out for you, Willamina, I mean," Elle told him, as he came to a stop in the middle of her living room. "She's determined to find something on you."

"It's her job," he said. "Would be nice if she was a little open-minded, though."

"Well, she's not," Elle said, her tone leaving no room for confusion. "You want a drink?"

When he declined, Elle padded over and sat down on the couch. She gestured for him to join her.

"I wasn't sure where we stood after what happened in your office," she said as he sat down.

Her hair was piled high in a loose bun. She was wearing simple cotton pants and a white T-shirt that read *Be Kind* on the front. On the coffee table alongside her reading glasses was a book about serial killers and an empty pizza box.

"Pizza and serial killers," he grinned. "That's quite an afternoon."

She shrugged and gave him a look something along the lines of, *what can you do,* then stared at him expectantly.

"There is another reason I came over," Andrew began. "Other than to tell you, I'm sorry."

"And that is?"

He moved in closer and let his breath fall over her neck. "To show you that I'm sorry."

When she smiled and leaned in, a wave of relief rushed through him. She was still on his side. Today they would make love, reconnect, and then later, when the time was right, Andrew would make his move. It was the only shot he had.

Chapter Twenty-Five
LUCY

The news an arrest warrant had been issued for Andrew Ashley came just after three o'clock on a Monday afternoon. For the past two weeks, the team had been poring over Lauren's phone and email records. There were several calls between her and the Lord Mayor, as well as numerous text messages, many of which indicated a personal relationship.

With no other suspects, his familiarity with the location, and the text messages, there hadn't been a great deal Yieldon could do to persuade the commissioner to focus police enquiries anywhere but firmly on Andrew. And eventually they hit pay dirt. A text message on Lauren's mobile, left by Andrew just days before she was killed.

While the message wasn't directly threatening in nature, it confirmed an intimate connection between the two of them. Andrew directing Lauren to delete a video police assumed was of the two of them together, and that she was under no circumstances to contact him again. Despite his warning, they found one more call made to his number from Lauren's mobile phone the day before she went missing and he had taken the call. It was enough. They were bringing him in.

Given his public status as Lord Mayor, it was agreed they would arrest Andrew at his home just after 5:30 p.m. Yieldon was adamant they would not use cuffs unless, for some reason, Andrew resisted. Once he was in custody, forensic teams would sweep the house.

When they arrived outside Andrew's home in an unmarked car, Lucy's stomach somersaulted. "You sure you're ready for this?" she asked Yieldon.

"Not even a little bit," he answered, his tone grim. "I still don't believe Andrew did this. Was he fucking her? Maybe. I don't know. But murder? There's no way."

"At least the media hasn't caught wind," Lucy said. "Last thing this needs to be is a circus."

Yieldon nodded and closed his eyes. "Won't be long, though. This will be all over social media in under fifteen minutes."

Lucy thought back to the fanfare that had accompanied the Marshall arrest compared to she and Yieldon arriving quietly outside Andrew's home in an unmarked car. On that day there had been sirens, a K9 unit, and at least four uniform cars. It was true that a man like Coban Marshall, a known dealer, was capable of anything, but the stark contrast of executing that warrant compared to this one said a lot about wealth and reputation.

Yieldon pounded the wheel with his fist, cursed, and then shook his head. "Fuck it. Let's get this shit show over with."

When Andrew answered the door, he was still dressed in the suit he had on at the morning's press conference. "Lord Mayor Andrew Ashley?" Lucy stated.

He looked past her to Yieldon. "You've got to be kidding?"

When he didn't answer, Lucy repeated, "Lord Mayor Andrew Ashley?"

"Well, yes, obviously," he snapped.

"Andrew, who is it?" Stella called from the living room.

"Get Giovanni on the phone," he called back. "I need a lawyer. Now!"

"Andrew Ashley, you are under arrest for the murder of Lauren Ellis," Lucy began, praying her voice would not waver. "You have the right to remain silent. Do not resist. Do you understand?"

Andrew nodded and turned, allowing her to handcuff him. As he turned back, he looked Yieldon right in the eye. "You're making a mistake, Chris. You know me."

"Don't say anything," Yieldon warned. "Wait for your lawyer."

"Jesus Christ!" Stella gasped, as she appeared in the hallway. "What the hell is happening?"

"Call Giovanni," Andrew repeated. "Tell him to come to the station."

She nodded and rushed off as, together, Lucy and Yieldon escorted the Lord Mayor out of his front door and down toward the car.

Lucy wasn't sure what she had expected from Andrew once he was put into the backseat. Perhaps she thought he would implore Yieldon to listen to reason. Maybe his cool, calm and collected act would falter and he would be emotionally distraught. But of all the reactions he could have had, his silence made her the most uncomfortable.

As they drove back through the city, shadows already swallowing up the buildings, Lucy tried to exchange a look with Yieldon, but his eyes remained trained on the road. She ached to turn and take in Andrew's expression, to get a read on him, but instead forced herself to keep facing the front. She tried to imagine what he might be thinking. If Yieldon ever made the decision to turn her in for planting evidence at the Marshall house, it would be her in the backseat, suffocating in silence, and fearing she would never see her family again. She wondered if it was her in the same situation, would she sit quietly like Andrew or be screaming bloody murder? Knowing her fear of confined spaces and how much she'd miss her family, Lucy quickly settled on the latter and hoped like hell she would never have to find out.

Chapter Twenty-Six

ELLE

I had been staring at the page in front of me for the past twenty-five minutes and it was still blank. I had taken the afternoon off and was at home, tucked up on the couch, my favourite fluffy socks warming my feet. I was trying to take the advice of Dr Simms and include journaling as part of my therapy, but so far, it was proving to be a challenge.

I'd used my lunch break to go back for a second appointment, this time making sure I looked as put together as possible, so I didn't feel like a dishevelled crazy person in Dr Simms' polished presence. While I was there, she explained that journal therapy was a proven, therapeutic way to access your inner emotions. Being a writer, she also thought I might enjoy it. Over the years, the closest I'd ever come to journaling was keeping a teenage diary and I couldn't say writing those angst-filled pages ever brought me closer to achieving self-awareness. But I was a journalist, not a doctor, so if that was her advice and I paid for it, then it seemed stupid not to at least give it a go.

I took another look at the list of journaling prompts and chose the one I thought seemed easiest to answer.

What do I know to be true that I didn't know a year ago?

I started with the obvious. I knew now that my binge eating stemmed from the sense of comfort it gave me as a child whenever I felt a sense of loss or fear. I also knew what it was like to make love to Andrew. I knew how it felt when he was at home with his wife and I wished he were with me instead. I begrudgingly knew that no time soon was I ever getting the crime round from Willamina, and I knew that until I wrote something significant,

I was always going to live in the shadow of my award-winning father. *But I'd known that my whole life.*

As I began to write, the floodgates opened and suddenly there were a thousand different things I realised I had learned just in the past few months, not to mention a year.

I understood why I binge ate, but I also realised constantly moving as a child was the reason I worked two jobs all the way through university and saved every dollar I could from my first few years at the Tribune to buy the townhouse. Because even though I struggled to pay the mortgage at times, it was my home. It was my safe place. I knew every leak, creak, and crack and embraced them all. I loved the scent of the old wooden floorboards and the lotus patterned tiles by the fireplace. I loved the chipped cement frog that sat by the front stairs and the collection of doves that gathered every morning in my tiny courtyard.

I found myself smiling as I wrote the list of things I loved about the home I had no intention of ever walking away from. Then, my fingers paused over the keys as another idea came to mind. Over the years, in all the houses we'd lived in, my father had always been more like a visitor than a resident. He had been a shadow. A whisper. A man who was in my sights but who never stayed still long enough to embrace. All my life, he had been just out of reach—much like Andrew. His distance, coupled with his charm and talent as a writer, had only ever served to make me work harder for his attention. I thought maybe if I was more like him, if I could dazzle him with my own writing skills, he would be blinded long enough to stay in one place. But it never worked. I hadn't seen my father in what was quickly creeping up to two years. He and my mother were still married, but in name only, and last I heard, he was in Los Angeles working as a consultant on a serial killer doco-series coming out on Netflix. Still, I thought, as I continued writing, maybe he'd come back if I penned my own best-seller someday. *Then again, maybe he wouldn't.*

I took a break, stood up, and stretched. Maybe Dr Simms was right about journal therapy. I did feel a whole lot lighter, despite the weight of better understanding what a fuck up I really was.

Outside, the sun was fading, and I flicked on the kitchen light. What I really wanted to do was eat, but instead I found my phone and started writing a text to David just to see what he was up to.

It was easy with him. I knew he enjoyed my company and heading out for a drink or a bite to eat together wasn't off limits. Next to him, I could relax and just be myself. I sent the text and found myself hoping he would be free. He didn't excite me the way Andrew did. I didn't feel the electric pull that came from just being near him, but I was happy in his company. He made me feel safe and sometimes that was good enough.

My phone buzzed, and I smiled when I read his reply. He was free for dinner and I caught myself wondering if maybe it was time to let go of old habits and find room in my heart for someone who was actually able to be there. I text David that I would be ready in half an hour and started up the stairs to take a shower. But before my foot hit the third step, the phone rang and when I went back to pick it up, I saw that it was Walters.

"Walters?" I answered. "What is it? Is everything alright?"

"Get in here, Nolan," he barked. "They've just arrested Andrew Ashely for murder."

Chapter Twenty-Seven
LAUREN

*I*n the end, I decided on a simple outfit of jeans and a white T-shirt to meet Andrew Ashley at the Stockton Centre. I knew he was apprehensive about coming out to the site and my goal was to put him at ease in my company. I had always been good at building relationships, especially with men. It was finding one worth keeping that always seemed to be the trouble. Deep down, I knew I was setting out on another road to nowhere. He was married, and the Lord Mayor of Newcastle, but that's also what made it so exciting. When I saw him walking up the winding road toward me, I smiled and waved.

Once a disability home housing some of the area's most vulnerable residents, the now deserted Stockton Centre was a myriad of old brick two-storey buildings nestled between towering pine trees and expansive green lawns with a view of both the adjacent estuary and Stockton Bight sand dunes. It had been a beautiful space once—until it was abandoned.

"Lauren, thank you for meeting me. Certainly a good day for it," he called, gesturing up at the endless blue sky.

He was wearing tan cargo pants and a black T-shirt. It was the first time I had ever seen him in casual clothes, and it struck me that despite how well he wore a suit, he looked just as good without one.

"It's a perfect day," I smiled. "Glad you could make it."

"Of course," he said. "These birds might be the answer to my prayers. If you can find them."

I was an ecologist, not a miracle worker. I wanted to find the birds as much as he did, but the truth was, I was yet to actually see one at the site. "Well, there's every indication they nested here recently," I said. "But it's getting late in the season. Whether there will be more nesting pairs is hard to say."

He fell into step beside me as we made our way toward the back of the property, where the lawn flowed out and disappeared into the dunes.

"And there's not enough solid evidence to prove they frequent the area?" he asked.

"Not yet, but with any luck, you never know."

We walked in silence for a couple of moments before he spoke again. "So, these Gemini Birds. What's so special about them, anyway?"

"What star sign are you?" I asked.

He cast a confused look in my direction.

"When's your birthday?"

"I'm a Capricorn," he said. "But what does that have to do with birds?"

"You ever met a Gemini? Someone who you swear has two personalities living inside them?"

He thought for a moment and then grinned. "My wife can be unpredictable at times, but she's a Leo."

"Makes sense," I laughed. "But no, Gemini Birds get their name from the distinct markings on the back of their head that look a lot like another face. It's a form of natural deception, a way to ward off predation when they're ground nesting. I'm not sure how efficient it is, but that's how they got the name."

"I see," he nodded. "Interesting."

"But the thing that makes their presence here so important," I continued, "is their scarcity. Gemini birds are very few in numbers, mainly due to land clearing and introduced species likes foxes. They are extremely protective and will try to fight off anything that threatens the nest, even if it costs them their life."

I could see he was taking everything in, so I kept going. "There's only about twenty breeding pairs thought to exist along the NSW coast and they've never been documented further north than Jervis Bay. That's what makes finding evidence of them here so important."

"And they nest in the dunes?"

"No, not in the dunes," I told him. "I think it's more of a coincidence this site happens to be near the ocean because they are not shore birds. The female likes to make nests under small trees or shrubs. She uses things like pine needles, which, as you can see, are in vast supply here, along with tiny pieces of wood and mud to form the outside of the nest. Then the male flies off, searching for soft down-like materials to bring back for the lining to make sure she's comfortable. It's all very romantic."

"Sounds it."

We shared a lingering gaze, which I held until he looked away. "So, over here is where I found the first evidence that Gemini Birds were nesting."

We walked over to a small row of shrubs behind the last building before the dunes rolled in toward the grass. "The reason I knew it was a Gemini nest was this..." I scrolled through my phone and found the picture I had snapped of a discarded bird egg. It was small and speckled with a tinge of green on the outer shell. "There is no doubt in my mind that this is an unhatched Gemini egg. It must have been unviable for them to leave it."

He peered in at the picture. "And that's not enough proof?"

"Not for want you want," I said. "To disallow a development application based on the presence of an endangered species, they have to be present, I'm afraid. And one discarded egg isn't going to cut it."

"So, what do we do next?"

"We keep looking. If Tony approves the extra hours, I'll do all I can to find your birds, Lord Mayor."

He shook his head as a shadow of frustration clouded his face. "No. Forget Tony. I want you to spend as much time here as you can. In fact, if you'd be willing to work weekends, keep a logbook of your hours and expenses and invoice me directly. I have a discretionary fund I can use. But we must keep this between us, and from hereon out, please call me Andrew."

I smiled and looked around at the site that would undoubtedly come to feel like my new home. "I'm good at keeping secrets," I said. "And for what it's worth, I understand why you don't want this site developed. I'll do everything I can to help you, Andrew. You have my word."

Chapter Twenty-Eight
STELLA

When Stella called their lawyer Giovanni Russo, the first thing he told her was not to talk to the media. So, when they descended upon the house like a pack of ravenous hyenas, she pulled all the curtains across and instructed the boys to keep their mouths firmly shut.

Outside, she could hear the car horns of neighbours trying to get to their driveways. There were so many media vehicles and television vans they had blocked the entire road. At any moment she expected, or at least hoped, the police would come and move them on. After all, it was their fault this media circus was taking place at all. Arresting Andrew for murder. How dare they!

So far, he had been allowed one phone call to her, and it felt like she had been talking to a stranger. What he said made no sense, and despite Giovanni's strict instructions, the only thing he seemed to care about was making sure some reporter, Elle Nolan, was allowed access to see him in the police lockup. When she questioned him about it, he said was that he was innocent, and Elle was the only one who could help him prove it. The thing that infuriated Stella the most was that he wouldn't tell the police, or her for that matter, where he was on the afternoon and evening of Lauren's demise. He flatly refused. Andrew Ashley, the Lord Mayor of Newcastle, was charged with murder and he was refusing to provide his whereabouts or any information that would assist the police with their investigation. It made no sense, and if he wasn't going to be forthcoming with the information she needed, then maybe Elle Nolan would be.

"Boys, I'm heading out for a bit," Stella called through the house. "Stay inside. Do not go out. Do you understand me?"

She picked up her handbag and turned to find them both standing sheepishly in the hallway. "It's going to be okay. I'm going to see someone who might be able to help Dad, but I need you two to stay put. Got it?"

"Is Dad going to jail?" Levi asked, his lip trembling.

"No Levi, Dad is not going to jail. They're just asking him some questions."

"But the news said—"

"Forget the news," she snapped. "You only listen to what I tell you. I've spoken with Dad and our lawyer and it's going to be fine, alright?"

"Where will we live if Dad goes to jail?" Jackson asked, completely ignoring what she said and clearly scaring the life out of his younger brother.

"Jackson—"

"You said the other day if Dad goes to jail, we'll lose the house."

Levi turned and stared at his brother, his eyes wide with fear.

"Jackson, we are not losing the house. Dad is not going to jail." Stella glared at Jackson and gave an obvious sideways glance at his younger brother. "Be a bit responsible."

He dropped his eyes and nodded, clearly doing nothing to convince Levi that they weren't about to become homeless.

"This is going to be okay," she told them again. "Dad did not kill that woman and the police will figure that out. Now, I'm going to talk to someone who Dad thinks can help. Just find something to do in the house that doesn't involve talking to anyone, especially online. Got it?"

They both nodded and stood watching as she made her way toward the door. "Everything will be okay," Stella told them, as she stepped through the internal door to the garage. "Dad will be home in no time."

In the car, she pulled the seatbelt over and clicked the garage door remote. It was going to be a shit fight of cameras flashing and reporters yelling as she reversed out of the driveway. The irony of trying to escape a horde of journalists to go and see another one was not lost on Stella, but what choice did she have? If Andrew was right and this Elle Nolan person was the only one who could prove his innocence, then they needed her help.

Stella slammed her palm against the horn and planted her foot on the accelerator as she tore backward down the driveway, giving the reporters no choice but to leap out of the way. Screw them, she thought as one man tripped and fell backward onto the front lawn. Screw them and their stories. The only one that mattered was Andrew's and until Stella knew what it was, no one was going to hear a peep out of her.

Chapter Twenty-Nine
ANDREW

After four hours of questioning, it was obvious to Andrew that all the evidence held by the police was circumstantial. Out of hours meetings he had with Lauren, the fact he lived adjacent to the crime scene, and a message he left asking Lauren not to contact him again. None of it accumulated to a murder charge that would stick, despite the fact one neighbour reported seeing him out on the dunes that afternoon, and another having seen his car leave just after dark and not return until a few hours later. But there were powerful people who wanted him gone, and he was afraid that somehow all that circumstantial evidence would inevitably be enough to see him locked away for the rest of his life.

Based on what they had, the narrative police were sticking to was that Andrew walked to meet Lauren in the dunes that afternoon to tell her that the affair was over and to stop calling him. When she refused, and maybe threatened to go public, he killed her and hid the body in adjacent scrubland. After that they would allege he returned home and waited until after dark, and then drove along a waterboard service road to access the body, drag it out into the tide, and weigh it down.

But they had found nothing to substantiate the story and without a confession, it was their word against his. The problem was, Andrew had failed to provide an alibi for the afternoon Lauren went missing and refused to tell them where he was in the hours that followed. On the day in question, Stella left for Sydney in the morning and the boys were wherever teenage boys go when their mother goes away for the night, so no one could account for his whereabouts.

"Andrew Ashley," an officer he had never met before called out as he approached the cell. "You have a date with forensics."

He got to his feet, pleased to at least get a break from the four walls of the cell that every hour seemed to draw closer and closer together.

"Turn around, please," the officer ordered.

Not looking to make a scene, Andrew turned and placed both hands behind his back for cuffing. The steel was freezing as it curled around his wrists, a stark reminder that creature comforts were a luxury he was no longer privy to.

"An examiner will take a mandatory buccal swab and blood test," the officer continued. "Because you are under arrest, your consent is not required. Is that clear?"

"Understood," he said.

In the brief time they had to talk, Giovanni had advised that when they read out the charges, Andrew should refuse the right to comment and prepare himself to be remanded in custody until he could appear for a Committal Proceeding in the Magistrate's Court. The lawyer also thought the process would be swift given Andrew's standing in the community and heightened media interest in the case.

The forensic collection room reminded Andrew of a tiny, barren doctor's surgery. There was a gurney covered in plastic and a stainless-steel cabinet that he assumed housed the equipment needed for swabs and other similarly invasive procedures. But unlike a doctor's surgery, there was no curtain for privacy or place to leave your things should you be required to get undressed.

"Mr Ashley," a woman dressed in plain clothes said, as she came into the room. "I am Amanda Keegan and I'll be taking a buccal and blood sample from you today."

"Alright," he replied. There was no point arguing and the last thing Andrew needed was a story leaked about the Lord Mayor causing a scene in police lockup.

He sat on the edge of the gurney as the technician worked quickly, arranging swabs, syringes and sample vials on the cabinet. She was efficient and detached, and he wondered how many times she had been through the process with people accused of a crime.

"Roll up your sleeve, please."

Andrew did as he was asked, and she attached a tourniquet just above his elbow.

"You doing okay?" she asked as she inserted the needle.

"Needles never bothered me," he told her. "I'm fine."

"How about aside from the needle?"

The question caught him off guard, and he turned to look at her. She appeared to be in her thirties with dark hair and honest-looking eyes. "Well, hard to say," he began. "I've definitely been better."

She nodded and attached another collection vial to the canula drawing blood from his arm. "I always liked you," she said. "Voted for you, too. Hope I wasn't wrong to."

She glanced up, and Andrew considered his response. He had no idea if she was being genuine or if she was sent in to try and strike up the beginnings of a confession. Either way, Giovanni's words rang in his ear. *Do not comment.*

"I appreciate that," he told her, eventually. "I hope not too."

She looked held his gaze a moment, then nodded and stepped away to drop the vials of blood into a plastic pouch.

"We'll do the buccal swap next, then you'll be taken back to your holding cell."

"Until they charge me?" he asked.

"I'm just here to take your samples, sir," she replied. "And to see if you're holding up okay?"

Whether she confirmed the impending charges made little difference. Andrew knew what was coming and what it would take for him to be released. Right now, although she didn't know it yet, Elle held his life in the palm of her hand. What she would choose to do with it was anyone's guess.

Chapter Thirty

ELLE

It was 6:34 p.m. when I arrived at my desk. My face was windblown and stinging from running through the cold air all the way from my house to the office, but I had little time to feel it. The moment the elevator door opened, I could hear Walters' booming voice shouting orders at people.

"Fraser, get down to the police station. Take a clicker, you never know. And how the fuck did you miss this one? We should have been out front when they picked him up."

When I didn't hear a response from Willamina, I guessed it was because she didn't have one. Obviously, her contact at Newcastle Police had declined to give her the heads up on Andrew's impending arrest.

"Nolan!" he shouted as I came into view of the bullpen. "Jesus Christ, where have you been? What's the word from council?"

"I came straight here as soon as I heard," I managed, bent over and out of breath. "I'll get on it now."

"What a shit show," he raged. "Metro will be all over this. There's already vision coming in from outside the Ashley house and *Sydney Morning Herald* reporters are on their way up by chopper. If they scoop us on this, you're all out of a job. Am I making myself clear?"

"Yes, boss," I told him, already at my desk. "I'm all over it."

How could this be happening? I wondered as the computer powered on and I clicked opened my contacts list. What evidence had they found? Was David right? Could Andrew have really murdered Lauren? My mind flashed back to the last time he came over to my house. The way he held my gaze as we made love. The way he gently pushed the hair back from my face. It couldn't be true. It just couldn't.

"See if you can get his wife on the phone," Walters boomed. "You'll never get her at the house, but if you can get her on the phone, tell her you had a close relationship with the Lord Mayor, that you were his go-to for publicity."

If only he knew the irony of what he was asking me to say. "Sure thing, boss," I called without turning around. "But I'll have to try and find a direct contact for her."

"Ah, Nolan?" I turned to find Maxine Mitchell, one of the general news reporters, clutching the office phone between her shoulder and ear.

"What is it, Maxine?"

"Finding her number won't be necessary," she told me. "Stella Ashely is in the lobby. And she's asking for you."

"I'm sorry, what?"

"Andrew Ashley's wife is in the lobby," she repeated. "And she's asking for you."

"Tell her she's on the way down," Walters beamed. "Nolan, get down there and bring her up to the conference room. And no one, I mean no one, goes into that room while they are talking. Has everyone got that?"

No one had to reply. They got it because when Walters gave an order in that tone, it went without saying that you followed his direction or suffered the consequences.

"Go, Nolan," he shouted, red-faced and with his chest puffed out like a boxer about to enter the ring. "What the hell are you waiting for?"

In truth, I was waiting for my head to catch up with my heart. The world was spinning. Andrew was being charged with murder. Stella was downstairs waiting to talk to me. I had no idea what she wanted or what to say to her. Did she know about Andrew and me? Is that what she wanted to talk about? Or was it something as simple as asking me not to write anything derogatory about her husband?

I took the elevator down to reception, my heart in my throat and the skin along my arms prickling. I felt sure the moment she looked at me, no matter what I said or did, she would know I had slept with her husband.

Over the past six months of Andrew and I's ever-growing relationship, I had somehow found a way to put Stella and his marriage away inside a tiny box in the far reaches of my mind. I knew she existed, but in a world where it was always he and I alone together, it proved easier than I thought to pretend she didn't exist. But as the elevator door opened, and I saw her standing there, I had no idea how I had ever managed to tell myself that lie. She was older than me, but despite the years between us, she was completely intimidating. Tall and blonde, Stella Ashley's elegant presence filled the small lobby, and I caught my breath. She was graceful, with fine features, a delicate neck, and impeccable attire. Despite the drama unfolding around us, she stood tall, her posture almost regal.

"Mrs Ashley," I managed, my voice shaking. "How can I help you?"

"You're Elle Nolan?" she asked, looking me up and down.

"That's right."

"Can we go somewhere and talk?"

Once again, I took in her appearance. Perfectly cut dark denim jeans, a cream cowlneck jumper under what looked to be a pastel pink Chanel coat that fell to her ankles, and an unmistakable Louis Vuitton tote bag over her shoulder. It was beyond me how a woman whose husband had just been arrested for murder could look so elegantly put together. Her eyes weren't red from crying and her demeanour was calm and assertive. Beside her, I felt like a child all messed up from playing in the sandpit.

"You're the council reporter, right?" she asked as we stepped into the lift.

She was so much taller than me that I had to look up to meet her eye. "I am."

"You report for my husband?"

"I report for the Tribune," I found the confidence to tell her. "But council is my round."

"Same thing," she said with a wave of her hand.

I nodded and let my eyes drop to the floor. If she knew about Andrew and me, she seemed like the type of woman who would have said something the moment we got into the lift. Maybe this was about something else, I hoped.

When we got upstairs, I led her to the conference room and closed the glass door behind us. "Can I get you a coffee or water?"

"No, I need to ask you some questions," she said, getting right to the point.

"Alright." I sat down across from her and forced myself to meet her eye. Usually I was the one asking questions, and the role reversal, especially under the circumstances, was making me anxious.

"I have spoken briefly with my husband since he was taken from our home by the police this evening," she began. "And the one thing he cared about was making sure you were added to his remand visitor list as soon as possible. I want you to tell me why."

Hot tingles prickled against the skin of my cheeks. "Um, I..."

"Yes?"

"Maybe he wants me to tell his side of the story," I tried. "You know... write what really happened."

She stared at me, and I felt as though she was looking into my soul. "I don't think so," she replied. "He said you were the only one who could prove his innocence."

"He what?" I breathed, not taking the time to think my response through. "That makes no sense... unless he means by telling his story?"

"That wasn't the feeling I got."

"Then I'm sorry, but I can't help you," I told her. "I have no idea what he could have meant by that."

Stella paused a moment, then re-crossed her legs and looked away. "He won't say where he was that night."

"The night Lauren's body was put into the ocean?"

"Yes. He won't tell the police and he won't tell me."

It was the first time since she arrived that I saw a hairline crack in Stella's demeanour. "Do you know why not?"

"I have no idea, Elle," she said, finally turning back to face me. "I was hoping you could tell me. That's why I'm here."

I searched my mind for any reason Andrew would refuse to tell the police where he was that night. He wasn't with me, and it didn't make sense—unless he was guilty.

"I wish I had an answer for you, Mrs Ashley," I told her truthfully. "I'd be happy to see him if it can be organised, but beyond that I really don't know."

I couldn't deny that despite the question hanging over Andrew's innocence, there was a part of me that hoped in his darkest hour he longed to see me because he loved me. *Because he needed me.*

"I'll see what I can arrange," she said flatly. "I'll be in touch."

"Mrs Ashley, before you go, could I ask you a few questions about all of this? Reporters are going to write stories no matter what, and I have a good relationship with your husband. I would be fair and transparent."

She thought for a moment, then shook her head. "No. Not until I know why he wants to see you."

Chapter Thirty-One
LAUREN

A few days after I met Andrew onsite at Stockton, Tony Mansfield called me into his office. I hoped it was because he had approved my request to devote more time to the Gemini Bird project. But unfortunately, it wasn't.

"Sit down, Lauren," he ordered in a tone that sounded ominous. "I'm denying your request for more time to be allocated to the Gemini Bird project. In fact, I'd like you to wrap it up by the end of the week. Submit your report to me by close of business Monday."

"With all due respect," I began, "the evidence remains inconclusive, but with more time—"

"Then put that in the report and have it on my desk by close of business Monday."

Tony was a brick building of a man who wore a permanent five o'clock shadow and the scowl of someone who hadn't had sex in a very long time. "Gemini Birds are an endangered species," I told him. "If they are there—"

"You know what else is an endangered species, Lauren? You, if you don't finish the report this week."

I leaned in and placed my hands on the edge of his desk. "Are you threatening me, Tony?"

"No," he said, getting to his feet. "I'm telling you. File the damned report."

"And if it turns out the birds are present?"

He walked over to the door and pulled it open for me. "Then they can fly away when the machines start demolishing the site."

"They nest on the ground."

"Then they can go nest somewhere else," he said flatly. "They're birds. Who gives a shit?"

I stared him in the eye and tried as hard as I could to convey my wish that he was the one who would be demolished.

"You got something else to add?" he asked.

Without answering, I turned and strode back to my desk, my heart racing with anger.

"You okay, Lauren?" my co-worker Angela Everett asked as I sat back in my seat with so much force it swivelled to the left. "Tony being a pain in the arse again?"

"He denied my application to extend the Gemini Bird survey," I huffed. "It's so much bullshit."

"Well, that doesn't surprise me," she said, lowering her voice. "Before he came to council, he had a history of working with development companies. He's not exactly environmentally friendly."

"Yeah I know," I sighed. "But this is important. It's the difference between..." I was almost going to say Andrew being able to save Stockton, but caught myself in time.

"You do know about his connection to Ridgemont Capitol, don't you?" Angela whispered. "It's quite the scandal."

I swivelled my chair back to face her, then cautiously glanced over my shoulder toward his office. When I was sure he wasn't looking in our direction, I leaned in close. "No, tell me."

"Well, there's nothing concrete, meaning nothing that can be classed as a pecuniary interest, but Tony's best mate from university is one of the managing directors at Ridgemont Capitol."

"Bullshit," I breathed in disbelief. "Is Tony getting a cut on the side?"

Angela shrugged and turned back toward her computer. "I don't know, but you didn't hear it from me."

I glanced back at Tony's glass-walled office. His head was down, and he was typing. If he was being cut in on the deal, it could amount to hundreds of thousands of dollars. Likewise, if his department was responsible for the *application not getting through, it would mean a loss for Ridgemont Capitol that could exceed more than a hundred million dollars. Suddenly Tony's lack of care for a flock of ground-nesting birds had become a multi-million-dollar question. Was he on the take or was he just an arsehole who didn't give a shit about saving an endangered species?*

Chapter Thirty-Two
LUCY

Andrew Ashley's arrest was dominating the media. For the past two days, it had been on the front page of every newspaper in NSW. Talk-back radio hosts discussed it relentlessly with listeners, and so-called experts from every corner of Australia had an opinion on the case. It seemed like everyone wanted their fifteen minutes of fame, from lawyers to psychiatrists and even psychics who claimed Lauren had made contact to tell them who killed her. It was a circus, and right in the middle of it all was Lucy.

As the arresting officer, there were pictures of her splashed across the internet and suddenly everyone wanted to know who she was and on what authority she had arrested Newcastle's beloved Lord Mayor. Facebook groups had been created to discuss her credentials and experience. Yieldon was copping his own fair share as well, but he was an inspector—and a man. For some reason, people didn't seem as interested in questioning his presence at the arrest as they were of hers.

Lucy hated the idea of people discussing her. More than that, she was scared, because trying to keep a secret between even two people was hard enough. Bring in the entire internet and it was a witch hunt waiting to happen.

"Dicks, phone call for you," someone shouted across the station. "Line three."

Lucy sighed and picked up the phone. The calls had been coming in all morning. Savvy journalists from Newcastle, the Central Coast, Mid-North Coast and even Sydney wanting the inside scoop on Andrew's arrest and somehow, they were managing to dodge the police media team and get her directly. It was wearing thin. "Senior Sergeant Dickson," I answered.

"It's Elle Nolan."

"From the Tribune?"

Lucy knew that Elle had filled in on the crime round when Willamina Fraser was away. She spoke with her a few times when Isabelle Summers went missing. She was young but seemed like she knew was she was doing.

"Yes, from the Tribune, but that's not exactly why I'm calling. Well, it is, but it isn't..."

But her rambling was starting to change Lucy's mind. "How can I help you, Ms Nolan?"

"Andrew Ashley asked that I be added to his visitor list. Is that possible?"

The request surprised her, and she wondered if Elle Nolan was trying to pull one over on her just to get an interview. "No, not at this time. He has no visitor list at this stage. He's still being questioned."

Met with silence, Lucy figured Elle was deciding how to rephrase the question. But no matter how she asked, the answer was always going to be no.

"Senior Sergeant Dickson, it's imperative that I speak to Andrew," she said calmly.

"Well, I'm sorry, but that's not possible. Not until he's been before the magistrate."

"Why is it taking so long?" she asked. "You've had him there for almost forty-eight hours. Has he been formally charged?"

"That's none of your concern, Ms Nolan. Now if there's nothing else..."

"There is something else," she began. "I did a follow up on the Coban Marshall case a few months back. Do you remember?"

Lucy immediately stiffened and wondered where this was going. "Yes, I remember."

"The story was about his appeal, but there were additional reports made from a source. Reports I didn't publish."

Lucy looked around the station to see if anyone was paying attention to her phone call, then lowered her voice. "I'm not sure what you're alluding to, Ms Nolan, but I would like to remind you that you are speaking to a police officer."

"Yes, I am aware of that, Senior Sergeant Dickson," she said. "But it's imperative that I see Andrew as soon as possible. As the arresting officer, I'm sure you can find a way to make that happen."

"I already told you that's not possible."

"I see."

"Now if that will be all..."

She cleared her throat, and Lucy held her breath. "Senior Sergeant, I have a source who believes you personally purchased and planted a large amount of methamphetamine at the Marshall residence to ensure Coban's arrest. What is your response to such claims? And by the way, we are now on the record."

Jesus Christ. Internal Affairs were already investigating. If the media ran a story, even hinted at the idea of planting evidence, the internet trolls throwing in on Andrew's arrest would be the least of her concerns. "My response is that's a load of bullshit and if you print anything like that, your career will be over."

"So might yours, Senior Sergeant Dickson."

"Are you actually threatening me, Ms Nolan?"

"No, I'm not," she said with a sigh. "But please, I need to see Andrew. I can't tell you how important this is."

It suddenly hit Lucy that throughout the entire conversation, not once had she referred to him as the Lord Mayor. Only Andrew. "This isn't about getting a story, is it?"

"No, Senior Sergeant Dickson," she said quietly. "It's not."

Lucy sat back in my chair and shook her head in wonder. Either Andrew Ashley had been sleeping with two different women behind his wife's back or they were barking up the wrong tree in regard to an affair with Lauren Ellis because there was no doubt in her mind that he and Elle Nolan were intimately involved. "Alright," she relented. "Come by tonight. Ten o'clock. I'll take you down to lock up myself under one condition."

"What's that?"

"You tell me what the hell is going on."

Chapter Thirty-Three
LAUREN

*T*he day I saw a pair of Gemini Birds, with their bright yellow chest and chocolate wings, fluttering around the foot of a pine tree at the Stockton Centre site, felt like Christmas morning. Not only did it prove I was right, but now I could in no uncertain terms tell Tony Mansfeld to go fuck himself. Well, maybe not in those words, but in sentiment, at least. Not to mention how happy Andrew would be. This tiny pair of brown and yellow birds might single-handedly save Stockton.

The first thing I did was pull out my phone and record a video of them. I smiled as the male strutted his stuff, prancing and fanning his tail to impress the female. She was doing a good job of acting disinterested, but there was no doubt in my mind they would become a mating pair. Birds weren't all that different from humans when it came to dating. The male would chase while the female feigned indifference, making sure he worked for it. That's how it was supposed to go, apparently. But as far as I was concerned, there was no time for games like that. Once I knew what I wanted, I did everything in my power to make it happen. I wasn't the type of woman to make a man dance for my attention.

Certain I had enough footage, I called Andrew, but when he didn't answer I left a voicemail telling him I had found the birds and had a video of them as proof. I hung up and smiled to myself. Thanks to these precious little birds, saving Stockton was all but a done deal. Their presence, coupled with the possibility that Tony Mansfield may be corrupt, was all it would take to declare the application unsuitable. We had done it.

Unable to help myself, I also sent a text Tony Mansfield. I knew I shouldn't, but the thought of his face screwing up when he saw it was too delicious to resist.

Me: Looks like the development might have hit a roadblock. I found the birds.

While I waited for them to reply, I took out my SLR camera and began photographing the birds. They were no bigger than my hand, but so pretty, the fragility of their feathers a stark reminder of how few of them were actually left. When I was confident I had enough evidence that the birds were not only present, but conducting a mating ritual, I packed up and started back toward the car. Behind me, the sun was falling in the sky and I was surprised to realise I had been at the site for four hours.

When I was inside, I pulled my phone out of my pocket, wondering if somehow I'd missed a reply from Andrew, or even Mansfield, but my screen was still blank.

It was unusual for hours to go by without a reply from Andrew, so against my better judgement, I started the car and headed toward his place, just to see if it looked like anyone was home. I couldn't deny that my thoughts of him were getting the better of me lately and on more than one occasion, I had found myself imagining a life with him. He was yet to show any romantic interest, save for the odd occasion I'd catch him holding my gaze a little longer than necessary, but that was hardly grounds for starting a relationship. But this might be the catalyst for him to step in closer.

As I slowed down outside his house, I saw a black sedan in the driveway. It looked like Andrew's car, but it was hard to tell for sure. I couldn't see if anyone was inside because the windows were tinted, but just in case, I quickly pulled over, did a U-turn and drove away. The last thing I wanted was for Andrew to think I was stalking him. Feeling stupid, I chastised myself for acting so immature. What the hell had come over me? I wondered. Was I really stalking the Lord Mayor? The idea was outrageous and just for a moment I laughed to myself at how ridiculous was I acting.

When my phone finally buzzed with a message, I pressed my car's Google play to listen to it. "You have a message from Andrew Ashley."

"Play message," I instructed with a smile.

"Delete the video, Lauren, and don't call me on this number again."

I slowed the car and pulled over to the side of the road. There must be some mistake. All Andrew wanted was for me to find the birds. Now that I had, he wanted me to delete the evidence? It made no sense. I rummaged through my tote bag until I found the phone and when I read the message for myself, there was no mistake. Andrew wanted me to delete the video. I scrolled through my contacts until I found his name and let my finger hover over the call button. He specifically said not to call him again, but not knowing why he wouldn't want evidence of the Gemini Birds was killing me. While I was deliberating over what to do, a second message notification popped up on my phone, this time from Instagram.

Yeah_itsJackowants to send you a message

I had no idea who the user was, but just to distract myself from calling Andrew, I clicked the alert and read the message.

Yeah_itsJacko: *Hey Lauren, it was great meeting you at the beach the other day. It was interesting what you said about the birds you're looking for. Would be cool to catch up some time. If you want to?*

I realised right away who the message was from. When I was looking for the birds last week, I ended up walking down into the dunes following what I thought might have been a Gemini Bird overhead. Instead, all I found was an awkward kid no older than 18, who seemed to develop an instant crush on me.

Me: *It was nice to meet you too. If you want to learn more about Gemini Birds or conservation, you're welcome to follow my Insta. Take care.*

It was polite, but straight to the point. The last thing I needed was some kid with a crush following me around. I dropped the phone back into my bag and pulled the car out onto the road, instantly forgetting about the Instagram message. All I could think about was Andrew and why he wanted me to delete the video we worked so hard to get.

Chapter Thirty-Four
ELLE

At 9:55 p.m. I arrived outside Newcastle Police Station and messaged Senior Sergeant Lucy Dickson. It had taken all my courage to threaten her about writing a follow-up story on the Marshall case, but I hadn't known what else to do. The truth was, I had no evidence whatsoever that Senior Sergeant Dickson, or Dicks as they called her at the station, had planted evidence. All I had was the word of Coban Marshall's best meth customer, who was extremely put out that his drug dealer was no longer available. According to him, Senior Sergeant Dickson had bought meth from a rival dealer who was more than happy to help get his competition off the street. It was hearsay and nothing I could ever print. At the time, I had chalked it up to the ramblings of a meth addict, but the fact I was standing out the front of the station spoke volumes. Maybe Senior Sergeant Dickson wasn't as clean cut as she seemed.

A green light flashed on the glass door, indicating she had buzzed me in. It was 10 p.m. on a weeknight and there was only a skeleton crew at the station. I had no doubt letting me in was a risk she would rather not take, but given the alternative, I figured letting a journalist talk to a man under arrest was a less reprehensible offence than being found to have planted meth at a crime scene.

I made my way through the lobby and waited outside the elevator. When the doors opened, Senior Sergeant Dickson stood there, glaring at me. "Make this quick," she snapped. "No phone. No recordings."

"Understood. I'm not here to interview him."

It was true, although if Walters ever found out I had seen Andrew in custody and not interviewed him, I would be the one who lost their job. If I were honest, the journo in me was dying to snap a photo and get him on record. The woman in me, however, had the last word. Andrew needed me, and that was more important than writing a story—no matter how frustrating it might feel.

When the elevator spat us out on the sub-ground floor, I followed Senior Sergeant Dickson to the end of a cold, dim corridor.

"What are you doing here, Ms Nolan?" Senior Sergeant Dickson asked as she unlocked the metal door. "Are you having an affair with Andrew Ashley?"

I caught my breath and didn't dare meet her eye. "No, of course not."

"Then why the urgent need to see him?"

"He asked for me. He's a friend."

She nodded and pushed the door open. "Don't let your feelings for him get in the way of your judgement, Ms Nolan. Now you have ten minutes. No more. And make the most of it because you won't be coming back."

I nodded and made my way down the corridor. In the cell to my left, Andrew was slumped on the edge of a cot that had seen better days, his back curled over like a question mark. "Andrew?"

When he saw me, he immediately rushed toward the bars. "Elle, Jesus Christ. You came."

I reached in through the bars and held him as best I could. His hair was askew and the smell of two days sitting in the cell had wrapped around him. "Andrew, what can I do?" I asked. "How can I help you?"

"Elle," he managed. "I didn't do this. You have to believe me."

My heart leapt. He wanted me to know he didn't do it. "Of course, I believe you," I assured him, my hand stroking the back of his neck through the bars. "What can I do to help?"

He pulled back and looked me deep in the eye. "If there was any other way, I would never ask you this, Elle, but I have no choice. I need you to tell them I was with you the night Lauren's body was put in the ocean."

"Andrew…" I immediately dropped my arms and stepped away from the bars, the words drying in my throat. "I can't do that."

"Elle, you have to," he pleaded. "It's my only way out of this."

His eyes were wide with desperation. As I watched him, my entire body tightened. "But I wasn't with you, Andrew," I whispered. "Why can't you just tell them where you really were? I don't understand."

His shoulders dropped, and he looked more defeated than I thought anyone could look. "I can't."

"But why not?"

He shuffled back over to the edge of the cot and dropped his head back into his hands. "I can't tell you."

"This doesn't make any sense," I tried again. "Whatever it is, just tell them, Andrew. It can't be worse than them thinking you murdered someone."

"I can't, Elle."

"Well, you have to tell me something. Everyone thinks you did it."

"They do?" He looked over at me and, for a moment, I wondered if he was about to cry.

"It certainly feels that way," I said, my voice sounding as weary as I felt. "I'm not saying I think that too, but you have to explain why you need me to do this. Where were you, Andrew?"

He let out a long breath. "I know how this is going to sound, Elle, but you have to believe me when I tell you there is a reason I can't say where I was. If I do, there's every chance my children might be in danger."

"What kind of danger?"

"I can't say more than that."

"If I were to do this, Stella would know about us."

He looked up at me, the first spark of hope in his eyes. "If you don't, I'll be charged and could get a minimum of twenty years without parole."

"Maybe you'll be found innocent?"

"Elle… come on."

I reached up and rubbed at a headache starting to form behind my eyes.

"Elle, please," he whispered, coming back toward the bars. "I know you care about me. I know you do. Please, I would never ever put you in this position, you know that, but I have no choice. This is my life we're talking about."

"Did you do it?"

"What?" he asked, clearly taken aback. "You can't really think I'm capable of killing someone?"

"Did you do it?" I repeated. "Did you kill her?"

"Elle..."

"I need to know, Andrew. I need to know what I'm getting myself into."

He reached through the bars and wrapped his fingers around my arm. "Elle, you know me. You know I could never do something like that."

"But you were sleeping with her, Andrew. Maybe—"

"No, I wasn't. I swear to you I wasn't."

I felt my shoulders sag under the weight of what he was asking me to do. "Then what the hell? You have to tell me something. You can't just ask me to lie to the police and not tell me anything about what's going on."

"I want to," he said. "Please believe me, Elle. I'd tell you everything if I could."

"Andrew—"

"Times up," Senior Sergeant Dickson called from the end of the hallway. "Let's go, Nolan."

"Elle, please do this for me," he whispered frantically. "I'm begging you. You're the only hope I have."

Chapter Thirty-Five
ANDREW

On Andrew's fourth morning in police lockup, Elle came through.

"Looks like your lucky day," Chris grinned as he approached the cell. "Your girl vouched for you."

Andrew got to his feet, too scared to believe it was true. "You're serious?"

"This morning Elle Nolan swore under oath you stayed at her house the night Lauren Ellis was dragged into the ocean. The nights either side, you were home with Stella. The neighbours confirmed it, so it's pretty straight-forward as far as we're concerned. You have a rock solid alibi."

"So, you're not charging me?" he dared.

"Nope. You're free to go." Chris rubbed at his chin. "You will have to deal with Stella, though."

Andrew held his breath as Chris unlocked the door, and he could finally step out into the hall. "That's not going to be easy."

"No," Chris agreed. "I can't say she ever struck me as the most forgiving woman."

"True, but that said, I'd rather deal with my wife than a jury."

"Exactly."

Andrew grinned with relief. He wasn't going to face a murder charge. Even the hall felt like freedom. "I made a mistake with Elle, that's a given," he told Chris as he stretched his arms back behind him. "But my hope is that Stella will be so relieved I didn't kill anyone that if I put in enough time grovelling, she might find a way to get past my indiscretion."

"You know it will be all over the papers, and Elle's a journo, for Christ's sakes. It will probably end her career."

Andrew nodded and felt his shoulders slump. Elle would likely pay the ultimate price for her loyalty. She would face public scrutiny and judgement. Crossing the line professionally, sleeping with another woman's husband. He had no doubt all the anger people had cast in his direction would now be redirected at her. And there was nothing he could do to help her.

Chris' radio crackled with a call from upstairs. "Shit, the reception is so bad down here," he swore. "Just hold on a minute, would you?"

Andrew nodded and watched as Chris once again closed the door and left him locked in the sub-ground level of the police station. At least this time, he was out of the cell.

While Chris was gone, Andrew pulled his shirt up to his face and winced at the odour of four days locked inside a cage. He had never felt more uncivilised. He was unwashed, unshaven, and still wearing the same suit he had on the day of the arrest. But all that was about to change. In just a few hours, he could shower, put on clean clothes, and take a nap in his own bed. Chris was right, Stella would be furious, but Elle's alibi had all but saved his life.

When Chris made his way back into the room, the colour had drained from his face. "What is it?" Andrew asked, immediately fearing the worst. Maybe Elle had thought twice and withdrawn her story.

"Andrew, I'm going to need to you stick around a while longer," he managed.

"Why? Am I still under arrest?"

Chris swallowed hard and finally looked him in the eye. "No, it's something else. And Andrew... you should prepare yourself. It's bad."

Chapter Thirty-Six
STELLA

S alty air whipped through Stella's hair as the yellow and green ferry cut through the water on its way from Stockton to Newcastle. Going to see Elle Nolan provided no answers, and Andrew was still refusing to tell her where he was the night Lauren Ellis' dead body was dragged into the ocean.

Stella glanced at her phone. 11:25 a.m. She had a meeting with their lawyer to discuss what to do next. On the phone he had suggested the *Newcastle Club*, an exclusive, members only venue that would save her the humiliation of being chased in her car by reporters to his Hamilton office.

When Stella left the house, she'd been careful to slip out the back, her head covered with a scarf so the reporters wouldn't hound her. She needed something. Fresh air. Salt water. Anything to distract her from the disaster unfolding around them. So, she had decided to take the ferry.

Stella had no idea what Giovanni would suggest they do once Andrew was charged. He'd told her not to expect bail given the nature of the crime, and that once Andrew was officially charged with Lauren's murder, he would likely be remanded in custody until his first court date. That meant at some point her husband would be transferred to Cessnock Correctional Centre, a maximum-security prison about forty minutes west of Newcastle, until the conclusion of his case.

She stared out over the harbour and tried to imagine Andrew in a maximum-security prison, but the very idea was incomprehensible. He was a man who wore slippers and used soap-free body wash in the shower. He liked to watch re-runs of *Friends* before falling asleep and was pedantic about rolling the towels instead of folding them the way she liked to. He wore expensive suits and fought like hell for the city he loved. For all the things he did that drove her crazy, thinking of him in prison broke Stella's heart. But it was a roller coaster. Whenever she felt tears burning at the idea of him being found guilty, she wondered again why he wouldn't tell her where he was that night. She thought about their son having to see him have sex with Lauren in the sand dunes just metres from their home. She thought about him kissing and caressing a woman far younger and more beautiful than her. And then she hated him and relished the idea of him going to prison, of him suffering for what he had done to her. And the ride would start all over again. Unless he was willing to tell her the truth, it was impossible to know what to do or how to feel. Until he did, their lives hung in the balance and there was absolutely nothing she could do to stop it all from coming crashing down.

The ferry docked, and Stella waited until everyone else disembarked before making her way across the walkway and onto dry land. As she crossed the road and headed toward Hunter Street, the cityscape stretched its arms out wide. She hitched up her bag and walked by the old Signal Box that used to service the heavy rail line, now an eclectic café frequented mostly by office workers ordering chai lattes. The city was so different from what it was like when she was a kid. Things were changing. It was coming of age. Stella never said it to Andrew, but she thought he was wrong to try and hold back the tide. Everything evolved. People, cultures, and especially cities. She knew he loved the simplicity of what he found here as a child, and how he was drawn to the comfort and safety in it, but nothing lasts forever. People wanted change, especially those in the upper legions of power. If he was innocent, she thought, there was every chance her husband's inability to let Newcastle spread its wings may soon result in his being permanently clipped.

The ring of her phone snapped Stella out of her thoughts, and she reached for it in her bag. Usually she wouldn't answer a private number, but with everything going on, she didn't want to miss anything that might be important. "This is Stella Ashley."

"Stella, it's Chris Yieldon."

It had been two days since Andrew was arrested, and this was the first time Chris had called her. Stella's first thought was that something had changed with the case. Maybe they were letting Andrew go home. "Chris," she breathed, "tell me you have good news."

"Stella, Andrew is being released. He has an alibi for the night of Lauren's murder."

Relief rushed through Stella. It was over.

"But there's been a development," he continued. "I don't know how to say this, Stella, but we have your son Jackson here at the station."

"Jackson?" she instantly stopped walking. Her breath caught in her throat and her neck stiffened. "Why? What's wrong?"

"Where are you at the moment?"

He was hedging, and her heart began to race. There was only so much she could take, and if Jackson had lashed out or done something wrong, she needed to know exactly how bad it was. "I'm in the city. I'm about to meet with our lawyer, but just tell me what's going on, Chris. Is Jackson alright?"

"He's fine. He's not hurt."

"Then what?"

"You need to come to the station. And bring your lawyer."

"Bring Giovanni? Why?"

"Because Stella, Jackson has just confessed to killing Lauren Ellis."

Chapter Thirty-Seven
LUCY

When Jackson Ashley walked into the station, Lucy had no idea what was about to unfold. At first, she thought he had come to try and see his father or advocate on his behalf. She and Yieldon had taken him into an interview room and were about to tell him the good news, that his father was being released, but before they had the chance, he stunned them by confessing to the murder.

Right from the start, it didn't feel right. As a police officer, Lucy was good at reading people and her read on the kid was that he was lying. But when someone confesses to an active murder case, there's a process to follow. So, the first thing they did was have him start at the beginning.

"Just tell us again. Why kill her?" she asked Jackson, who had been sitting across from them for the past hour, his head hanging low.

"I told you already," he huffed. "She was trying to ruin our family."

"And she rejected you," Yieldon added.

"That's not why," he snapped. "She was trying to make Dad leave us."

Jackson was wearing ripped jeans and a yellow T-shirt emblazoned with some kind of surfing logo. Lucy searched his face and was saddened to see the first hint of soft facial hair across his top lip. He was eighteen, technically an adult, but far too young to have so much at stake.

Yieldon sat back in his chair, clearly unconvinced. "Jackson, I've known you since you were born and I'm sorry, but I'm just not buying it."

"But I'm telling you the truth," he said, this time more agitated. "She was a slut and deserved what she got."

Lucy exchanged a glance with Yieldon. Something was definitely off.

"Jackson, tell me again how you killed her," she tried, keeping her tone calm and even. "We just need to make sense of what you're telling us."

He pushed out a frustrated breath and looked at her. "Like I already said, we got into an argument in the dunes. I didn't mean to kill her, but it was her own fault. I was asking her to stop seeing my dad, but she just wouldn't listen. She came up on me and started yelling, calling me names. Then before I could say anything back, she turned like she was just going to walk away and I don't know, man, something just came over me."

He tugged at the back of his hair and there was a tightness to his jaw that Lucy attributed to high levels of stress and anxiety. An angry red rash crept along his neck.

"And then?"

"Then I grabbed her arm and pulled her back. I started choking her. It kinda freaked me out that I was hurting her so bad, but it was like I just couldn't let go or something."

"And that's what killed her?"

"I guess. After that, she was dead."

"Then what? You hid her body and went back later that night and dragged her into the water?"

He nodded but wouldn't look at us.

"Jackson," Yieldon began. "Is there any chance you're telling us this to try and help your dad?"

"What? No," he spat. "I killed her, alright? Why can't you just believe me?"

"Jackson, I want you to take a look at something," Yieldon said. "Can you do that?"

Jackson nodded and leaned in as Yieldon pulled out a folder and placed it on the table. When he opened it up and pushed the crime scene photos across the desk, Jackson recoiled.

"Fuck, get those away from me!" he shouted. "Get them away."

Lucy and Yieldon exchanged another glance, and she was confident they were both of the same opinion—Jackson did not kill Lauren Ellis.

Yieldon gathered up the photos and placed them back in the folder. "Jackson, your dad has an alibi for the night we believe Lauren's body was dragged into the water. There is a chance forensics are slightly off with the date due to the temperature of the water and the state of her remains, but he was at home with you and your mum for three consecutive nights either side of the evening in question. We're letting him go home in a couple of hours."

Jackson sat up straight and looked from Lucy to Yieldon and back again. "For real?"

"Yes," Yieldon told him. "But now we have a problem. You've confessed to her murder and claimed to have left threatening messages on her social media account. We didn't find those in our initial investigation. Maybe she deleted them, but now we're required to follow up on what you've told us. Have a tech expert take another look. So, if that's true and we do find them, we'll have to continue our investigation into your confession."

Jackson dropped his head into his hands. "Dad's really coming home?"

"He is."

Jackson looked up, his face panicked. "I lied. I never killed her. I mean, I did have an argument with her, but it was just outside our house, not in the dunes." He pushed out of the seat, got to his feet, and started pacing. "Fuck, I was just trying to get Dad out. Mum said we'd lose the house, and... fuck... I never killed anyone. Do you believe me?" He stopped pacing and stared at them. Lucy first and then Yieldon. "For real," he said. "I didn't do it."

Lucy and Yieldon and exchanged glances. The case was turning into a mess. "Providing a false confession is an offence and also a very stupid thing to do," he told Jackson.

Lucy looked at Yieldon and gave him a discouraging look. Telling an eighteen-year-old boy who had just mistakenly confessed to murder he was stupid wasn't going to help anyone.

"But I'm taking it back," he said, pounding the table with his fists. "I made it up. I recant or whatever."

"You need to sit down and calm down," Lucy told him firmly. "We can talk this through but, Jackson, but if there are incriminating messages or evidence of a confrontation, we will need to look into that as part of our investigation."

"Fuck!" Jackson pounded the edge of his fist on the table. "I fucking hate her. I'm glad someone killed that fucking bitch and—"

"Hey," Yieldon interrupted, reaching out to Jackson. "Sit down. Now. You won't help yourself saying shit like that, mate. You need to calm down."

Jackson clutched at his forehead and reluctantly took a seat.

"I'm going to go get your mum and dad," Lucy told him. "They're both waiting outside."

He nodded, but didn't look up.

Lucy and Yieldon made their way out into the hall where Andrew and Stella Ashley were waiting.

"Is he alright?" Andrew asked, immediately getting to his feet. "What did he say?"

"He didn't do it!" Stella shouted before either of them had time to respond. "Jackson could never do anything like that. You have to know that."

Lucy reached out and rested her hand gently on Mrs Ashley's arm. "We tend to agree with you, and he's withdrawn his confession. The problem is, he claimed to have left threatening messages on Lauren Ellis' social media account. He also claimed to have had an altercation with her outside your home. Do you know anything about that?"

"This is all my fault," Mrs Ashley sighed, rubbing her forehead. "It's my fault he's here."

Andrew turned to his wife. His relief at being released had clearly evaporated. He was red-faced and looked agitated. "What did you do, Stella?" he demanded. "Why is this *your* fault?"

"Because Andrew..." she began. "I told him to lie if the police asked what he knew about you and Lauren."

"You did what?"

"Before Jackson knew about the two of you, he met her in the dunes," she continued. "He liked her, but she rejected him. Then he saw you fucking her on the beach and heard you on the phone to her late at night."

"That's ridiculous," Andrew fumed. "And so you did what? Told him to lie to the police?"

"I didn't know what else to do, Andrew. I didn't mean for him to say he killed her. I just didn't want you to be any more implicated than you already were."

"Jesus Christ," he swore. "Are you a fucking idiot?"

"Okay," Yieldon said, holding his arms out in a calming gesture. "Let's all try to stay calm. You can't help Jackson by attacking each other."

"Well, maybe if he wasn't fucking half the town, we wouldn't be in this mess," Stella spat.

"Me? You told our son to lie to the police and now he's a murder suspect, Stella!"

"Mr and Mrs Ashley, I understand this has been an incredibly stressful time for the both of you," Lucy began. "But if you want to help your son, you need to put your personal issues aside. At least for now. Can you do that for Jackson?"

They both nodded, but it was Andrew who spoke. "What happens now?" he asked.

"For now, you can take Jackson home. We'll follow up on what he told us and take it from there. In the meantime, I think you all need to get some rest."

"Alright, thank you," Mrs Ashley said. "Can I see my son?"

Lucy nodded and asked them to follow her back toward the room where her Jackson was waiting. But when she looked back, Andrew was still in the hall speaking with Yieldon.

When they stopped outside the door, Mrs Ashley turned to her. "Tell me something, Senior Sergeant Dickson. Was it you who took Elle Nolan's confession this morning?"

Lucy had no idea where she was going with her questions, but with a guilty conscience of her own to protect, she didn't want to be dragged into a game of cat and mouse. "I'm really not at liberty to disclose that information, Mrs Ashley."

"It's just that I met with Elle Nolan and she had no idea why Andrew wanted to see her. Then suddenly this morning she's his alibi." Mrs Ashley paused and kept a close watch on Lucy's face. "Were you on duty last night, Senior Sergeant?"

"Again, Mrs Ashley I'm really not—"

"Because it seems odd to me that she just woke up and decided to be his alibi. Don't you find that odd?"

Lucy shrugged and broke her gaze. "People do strange things, Mrs Ashley. I really couldn't say."

She nodded, her eyes never leaving Lucy's face. "Did she speak with my husband last night?"

"Alright, let's get our son home," Andrew stated as he came up behind his wife, interrupting the conversation. "I don't want him in here a moment longer than he has to be."

Lucy looked at Mrs Ashley one last time and it was clear from the intense look on her face that they would be having this conversation again, and probably sooner than she'd like.

Chapter Thirty-Eight
ELLE

I t was one of those decisions you know you shouldn't make. Andrew had begged me, pleaded with me, to be his alibi for the night police believed Lauren's body was dragged into the water. At first, it seemed like one of those things you automatically say no to. It was lying to the police. It was publicly admitting to having an affair with a married man. But mostly, it was vouching for someone accused of murder who refused to tell you where they were on the night in question. But he was desperate. I could see it in his eyes and when he reached for me through the bars, I knew it was a turning point in my life. I was being handed an opportunity to cast aside the ordinary girl I had always been and instead, do something extraordinary. I could single-handedly save the man I loved, the most important man in the city—all I had to do was say yes.

After providing my statement, I expected to be the first call Andrew made the moment he was released. I imagined the moment over and over again as I counted down the hours waiting for his call. What he would say. How grateful he would be. How this would cement our relationship. I even let myself go one step further, thinking maybe he would forgo the call and instead come straight to my house. I was so certain that he would arrive on my doorstep that as soon as I got home from the station, I spent the rest of the morning cleaning the house. I had lied for him after he was arrested for murder. The bond between us would be stronger than any two people could ever have.

But it was getting late and afternoon shadows were beginning to creep across my freshly washed living room floor. I glanced at my phone again. No calls. No messages. It had been five hours since I left the station. Discouraged, I glanced around the house, the scent of lemon surface spray still lingering in the air. How long did it take for a person to be set free after someone provided an alibi? I wondered. An hour? A day?

They were questions my father would know by heart. He spent his life surrounded by those who lived in the dark corners of society, who committed atrocities, hoping someone would be willing to vouch for them when it was crunch time. What was it, I wondered, that drew my father and me toward the same shadows? He was so addicted to exploring the murky world of murder that he let his own family slip through his fingers. And me, I was protecting a man who, for all I knew, killed a woman and weighed her body down in the ocean.

I shrugged off the voice that whispered in my ear. It was unimaginable. Impossible. The need to be like my father wasn't so strong that I would inject myself into a murder case. I longed to match his literary success, to have him recognise himself in me, but that was not the reason. That would mean I was crazy. No, I loved Andrew, and he needed me. I was the only one who could set him free. My father and his murderous addiction had nothing to do with it. It was all about Andrew. That's all.

But when another hour passed, and I'd still heard nothing, the voices in my head got louder. I needed to see him. I had to know if he was okay. But most of all, I needed to eat.

I glanced at my phone for what felt like the thousandth time and saw that it was four o'clock. There might still be time if it I explained that it was an emergency. I scrolled through my phone contacts and eventually hit *call*. I needed some advice.

"It's Elle Nolan," I said when the phone answered. "I don't have an appointment, but this is a bit of an emergency. Is there any chance I could see Dr Simms before she leaves for the day?"

When I took a seat on her couch thirty minutes later, I realised it was the first time I had allowed myself to breathe out since walking into the police station earlier that morning.

"Elle," Dr Simms smiled, as she sat down across from me. "How can I help?"

"Thank you for seeing me," I managed. "There's a lot going on and I was spiralling. I didn't know what else to do."

She was immaculate as always, but instead of making me feel more out of control in comparison, her togetherness provided a sense of comfort. Of trust.

"Tell me what's happening, Elle."

I took a deep breath and told her what I had done, how I had agreed to be Andrew's alibi.

"So, you publicly admitted to the affair?" she began. "How did that make you feel?"

"Ashamed," I admitted. "Guilty."

"Because people will know?"

"It will hit the media any time now," I told her. "I'll probably lose my job. My family will know."

"I see," she said with a nod. "But by telling the truth, you saved an innocent man, a man you care about, from potentially being found guilty of murder."

I rubbed at my forehead and re-crossed my legs. I couldn't tell her the whole truth. If I admitted I lied for him, she would be legally required to inform the police. Then it would have all been for nothing. The most I could tell her was that I had agreed to confirm he was with me that night. "The thing is, he hasn't reached out. I thought..."

"...that by saving him, the two of you would be closer than ever before?"

"Something like that," I said, feeling stupid. "I mean, I didn't do it for that reason. I just thought I'd at least be his first call."

She placed her notebook down and leaned in toward me. "Elle, you risked a lot today. Your reputation, your career. Are you still comfortable with the decision you made?"

"I'd be a lot more comfortable with a pizza in front of me." I forced a tight smile, but it wasn't returned.

"Elle, you use food as a comfort mechanism. It's a habit closely associated with your father." She took a beat. "I'm sure I don't have to point out the link here?"

I immediately folded my arms across my chest. "I didn't vouch for Andrew because of my father."

She nodded and kept her eyes trained on me.

"My father was never accused of murder. It's not the same."

"But you were fearful he wouldn't be there for you. That he would always be inaccessible. Tell me, Elle, if there had been something you could have done to make sure your father was always available to you, would you have done it, no matter the cost?"

The answer was yes, but it was hard to admit. For the first time, I had to wonder, had my alibi really been to save Andrew, or was I trying to save myself the pain of not having him in my life?

"At first, I thought maybe I subconsciously did it to be more like my father," I sighed. "I know I just said the opposite, but it's hard to admit. These kinds of crimes are his world. I thought maybe without realising it, being a part of something like this would make me feel closer to him."

"Alright. So, do you agree it's possible the reason you did this has a lot to do with feeling closer to your father and making sure the person you consider most like him remains a part of your life?"

"But that's so fucked up," I sighed.

She stifled a grin, and her eyes were warm. "Don't be so hard on yourself, Elle. It took a lot of courage to do what you did today. You were very brave."

Or very stupid. "And the fact Andrew hasn't called?"

"Builds on the abandonment you feel from your father. The silence is twice as painful for you. It makes sense you're feeling out of control or spiralling as you put it."

"I didn't eat," I told her. "I wanted to. But I didn't."

"Then there's hope for you yet, Elle Nolan," she smiled. "Lean on your journal. Let it help you and if you can find a trusted friend, reach out. These are big issues, so it has to be someone you feel safe with. If you can confide in them, let them help you to feel supported. The worst thing you can do is allow yourself to feel alone right now."

I thanked Dr Simms and made my way out onto the street. Six o'clock and still no word from Andrew. What I did have, however, was twenty-three missed calls from Walters. Apparently, word was out.

Chapter Thirty-Nine
ANDREW

Andrew knew he should call Elle. If it hadn't been for her alibi, God knows where he would be. Still in the holding cell. Appearing before a magistrate. It was anyone's guess, but thanks to her loyalty, he was at home and about to take a long-awaited shower.

As the hot water fell over his body, Andrew leaned against the tiles and let the past few days wash away. Since escaping his childhood in Sydney, freedom was a luxury he had come to take for granted. Like most people, he didn't think twice about coming home at night or being able to sleep in his own bed. To have it taken away was a stark reminder of how fortunate he was, and what he had come so close to losing.

After dressing in a clean, comfortable pair of running pants and a T-shirt, Andrew paused in the hallway. His family was together out in the living room. There was none of the usual laughter or banter that came from living with two teenage boys, but he could hear them talking. It wasn't more than a low murmur, but from their tone, he could tell they were afraid, probably angry, and definitely in need of someone to lead the way.

"Family huddle?" he suggested, as he braced myself and entered the room. "Let's get a few things out in the open. I think it's important for all of us."

The look on Stella's face made it clear that it would be a long time before she'd warm to him again — if ever. He had betrayed her. Worse, he had made her feel foolish.

On the way home from the station, they had agreed there would be no television news and no internet until they had the chance to talk as a family.

The last thing Andrew needed was the media filling his family's heads with lies before he had a chance to tell them the truth. Some of it, at least.

"Alright," he began, taking a seat in the middle of the sofa. "Here's what's true. I did not kill Lauren, and neither did Jackson. But I did have an affair with a journalist from the Tribune and I feel horrible about it." He took a beat and looked at each of them closely. "It's something that I regret and something I will be doing everything I can to make right, not just with Mum, but with all of you. I made a mistake, but that doesn't mean I don't love Mum and it doesn't mean that I ever want to be anywhere but right here with you guys. You are my family and I love you. I will never, ever, put that at risk again."

"What do you think they'll say?" Jackson asked. "The media, I mean."

Imagining the headlines boggled Andrew's mind. It was a journalist's dream. An affair, an arrest, the Lord Mayor's son confessing to murder and then being allowed to go free just to top things off.

"Whatever they can," he told him. "The media pack outside our house isn't going anywhere, anytime soon, and there are two things we need to do. One is we need to ignore what they say, and two, is we never talk to them. Not ever. Does everyone understand?"

Stella and both the boys nodded, but it was impossible for Andrew to ignore the fact that none of them met his eye. "Look guys, I know I've let everyone down and I'm sorry."

"But what about Jackson?" Levi asked, shooting a worried glance over at his brother. "What's going to happen to him?"

Andrew reached out and rested his hand on his eldest son's shoulder. "Jackson was just trying to help. They'll look into it and when they see he's innocent, he'll be fine. We all will be if we stick together."

For a moment, they sat together in silence, each of them lost in our own thoughts.

"So where to from here?" Stella asked, eventually.

"We keep our heads down. I've taken a leave of absence from work. The Deputy Mayor can handle things for a while, and we wait. We wait until they exclude Jackson from the investigation and find Lauren's real killer. In the meantime, we get back to trying to be a family. I know it won't be easy, but that's all we can do."

"So, ordering pizza would be part of that?" Levi grinned.

It was the mood lightener they all needed. "Sure, mate, pizza sounds like a great idea," he said with a smile. "As many as you want."

Later in the evening, when the boys disappeared into their rooms and he and Stella were alone, Andrew tried to start a conversation, but it was obvious she didn't want to hear it. "Do you think you can ever forgive me, Stell?" he tried anyway, as she climbed into bed.

She gently tied her hair up and smoothed cream under her eyes. "What matters is keeping Jackson as calm as possible," she replied, without looking at him. "The last thing I want is him thinking he needs to help us again. For his sake, we need to act as normal as possible."

"So, does that mean I can sleep here in our room?"

"As long as you don't touch me."

"Stell..." he sighed, sitting down on the side of the bed. "I'm sorry. You know things have been hard between us for a long time and that's not an excuse but—"

Her head snapped up, and her eyes bored into his. He could see how angry, how hurt, she really was. "You're actually going to try and blame this on me? You've humiliated me, Andrew. The whole city, the whole state, is going to know you were sleeping with two different women behind my back and they're just the ones I know about. I look like an idiot."

"It wasn't like that and I'm the one who looks like an idiot, Stella, not you," he told her. "I'm the one who fucked up."

"Yes, you did," she spat. "Now stay on your side and do not touch me."

Reluctantly, Andrew climbed into bed and rested his head down on the pillow. He had been dreaming of this moment for days and yet somehow the beautiful bed felt more uncomfortable than the stiff, aging cot in the police cell. Stella wanted nothing to do with him, and somewhere out there Elle was coming to the realisation she wasn't going to hear from him. There in the dark, he quickly found himself wondering what she was doing and how she was feeling. Would she understand, or would she be as furious as his wife? He knew there was always the chance she could withdraw her alibi. Eventually, he would contact her, just to make sure she stayed solid, but the relationship had to be over. Andrew's future was with his family. Even though they didn't know it, everything he had done up until this point had been to protect them. Unfortunately, in the process, Elle, like Lauren, had become collateral damage.

Chapter Forty

LAUREN

*A*s I poured milk into the blender for a morning smoothie, I received a text from Andrew asking me to meet him in his car in the underground parking garage beneath City Hall at 7:15 a.m. The message was from a private number and it all felt very clandestine. Despite the fact I was furious he had asked me to delete the footage of the Gemini Birds, I had to admit there was a certain thrill that came with having secret meetings with Andrew, just the two of us conspiring against the world outside.

I arrived just after seven o'clock and found a space in the back corner of the lot. Without knowing exactly why, I reclined my seat far enough back that I could just see over the door rim. I gazed across the almost empty parking garage, waiting to see Andrew's car, and had to suppress a giggle. I wasn't sure if it was the situation or just nerves making me to laugh, but either way it was certainly a unique way to start the day.

When his car pulled into the lot and snaked its way toward me, I held my breath. I peeked up just far enough to see him motion for me to join him in his car. Wasting no time, I gathered up my bag and hurried around the back of my SUV and climbed into his sleek sedan.

"This is all very X-Files," I grinned as I pulled the door closed.

"I know. I apologise for being so abrupt yesterday," he said. "I had to get this burner phone, just to be safe."

He was freshly showered, dressed in an expensive looking navy-blue suit, and his dark hair was still damp. "Be safe how?" I asked. "And why don't you want the video all of a sudden?"

He sat back against the leather seat and let out a long breath. "It's not that I don't want it, Lauren. You how hard we've worked on this. It's just—"

Before he could complete the sentence, his other phone rang, and I glanced over to see it was a private number.

"Excuse me a moment. I should get this."

I nodded and looked out the window to give him some space.

"Yes?" he answered. "No, that won't be necessary." A pause. "Because I already told you it was under control." From the stern tone of his voice, I could tell Andrew was annoyed by whoever was on the phone. "We spoke about this and I told you I would handle it," he continued. "This is not a good time. I will call you this afternoon." He immediately dropped the phone as though it had stung him and turned to stare out the window.

"Is everything okay?" I asked. The thought of reaching out and gently placing my hand on his leg crossed my mind, but I quickly pushed it away.

"It's fine."

"It's probably none of my business, but did that have anything to do with why you wanted me to delete the bird footage?"

Andrew rubbed at the back of his neck and eventually turned back to the front. "Things have become a little more complicated, Lauren."

"How so?"

He finally turned to face me and, to my surprise, reached out and took my hand in his. "Did you delete the footage?"

"I did. But before I got your message, I already told Tony about the birds. I just wanted to stick it up him for being a jerk, you know? I'm sorry." His hand was warm, and I longed to intertwine my fingers with his.

"That explains a lot," he said. "Look, what's done is done, but just get rid of anything else, alright?"

"Can you at least tell me why?"

He dropped his eyes, and I searched his face for any clue as to what might be going on. When he looked back, he held my gaze. "Because I don't want anyone to get hurt, Lauren, including you."

"Get hurt?"

"I can't say anything more. I'm sorry."

"Andrew, do you need anything? Can I help in some way?"

But he shook his head. "You've been so helpful, Lauren. I can't say I've ever met anyone quite like you before. But this is where we need to part ways, I'm afraid. You won't be able to call me anymore."

He let go of my hand, and the moment between us was lost.

"Part ways?" It was the last thing I was expecting. One moment I felt like he and I were entrenched in a secret mission, the next I was on the outs. "Andrew, I didn't know if I should say this, or if you already know but—"

"I do know," he said softly. "And I'm flattered, but there's just so much going on right now."

"Understood," I said sharply. "I guess I've served my purpose then."

"Lauren, please, it's not like that. And besides, you deserve someone who's free to give you everything, and that's not me. I've already made so many mistakes. I'm not going to pull you into another one."

I nodded quickly and pulled my bag up over my shoulder. "Glad to have been of service then, Lord Mayor Ashley."

I slammed his door and climbed into my car without looking back. I reversed out of the car space way too fast and as the car sped backward, I prayed I wouldn't humiliate myself further by crashing into a pylon in the garage. I needed space. I needed a coffee. I needed anything that would help me recover from the humiliating disaster I had just created.

As I drove through the city, I tried to think of somewhere private I could sit and commiserate over a decent latte. I felt like an idiot. For the past week, I had been flirting and trying my hardest to entice Andrew without making him uncomfortable, only to be rejected, and all before eight o'clock in the morning. A coffee wasn't going to cut it. I needed something stronger. At the corner of Hunter and Union streets, I pulled over and took out my phone. It was early, but I knew he'd be up. He answered on the second ring.

"Thought you were sick of me?" he said in a tone dripping with sarcasm.

"Yeah, well, things change."

"I knew you'd be back."

"Oh, shut up," I challenged. "Can I come over?"

"It's early."

"You're still in bed?"

"Want to join me?"

"I'll be there in five minutes."

I dropped the phone back into my bag and pushed the air out of my lungs. Meaningless sex would take my mind off Andrew Ashley, at least for a while.

Chapter Forty-One
LUCY

Lucy rolled over and glanced at the alarm clock on the bedside table. The numbers read 3:32 a.m, and she had already been lying awake for what felt like hours. *Andrew Ashley*. He was all she could think about. She turned again, this time away from the clock, and tried to focus on the gentle rise and fall of her husband's breath. He looked so peaceful lying there beside her, his eyes closed and lips slightly parted, faraway in a world of sleep and dream. What would he think if he knew what she did? How would he feel if he knew her desperate bid to get Coban Marshall away from his wife and daughter may have inevitably allowed someone else to get away with murder? It was karmic, really. A man who was technically innocent had been put behind bars and, in return, a potentially guilty man had walked free. All thanks to her.

Eventually, Lucy gave up trying to fall asleep. Instead, she would use the time to quietly sort things through in her mind and come up with a way to disprove Elle Nolan's alibi, otherwise Andrew Ashley may never be held accountable.

Why would she do it? Lucy wondered as she lay there in the dark. She was a good journalist and had always seemed like a bright, decent young woman. She'd heard things about a fractured relationship with her famous father, but that aside, providing a false alibi and publicly outing yourself for having an affair with a married man was a lot to take on. Could she be that in love with him? Did she do it because she thought it would make him leave his wife?

Stella was a tough woman. Beautiful. Elegant. And tough. Lucy didn't know her personally, but in Newcastle if you lived a high-profile life, it was hard to keep anything private for too long. It was no secret that Stella had grown up poor. There were stories she and her mother had lived in a car on and off for much of her childhood. There were also other not so nice stories of how a nubile, teenage Stella had managed to support the two of them. Lucy hoped that wasn't the case. Perhaps what people said was true and perhaps it wasn't, but there was no denying Stella Ashley took shit from no one. She had made that clear on more than one occasion and if Elle Nolan thought the Lord Mayor's wife would just fade into obscurity while her husband moved on with a woman ten years her junior, she was in for a rude shock.

Beside her, James twitched, his leg softly pushing back against hers. There was a part of Lucy that longed to confide in him. Before the Marshall case, there had never been any secrets between them. They didn't have a grand love story. They hadn't been childhood sweethearts or met in a way that could be attributed to something as fancy as fate, but the love that grew between them was real. He had been a friend of Lucy's housemate's boyfriend back when she first joined the police force and they hit it off. Friends first, then lovers. Two years later, husband and wife, then inevitably mother and father. She knew he was frustrated. More than that, she knew it hurt James that she refused to confide in him. It killed Lucy to keep a secret, but opening up about the Marshall case and how it was bleeding into this investigation would implicate him. She had too much love and respect for him to do that just to ease her own burden. For now, she would have to carry it alone.

Once again, Lucy turned over, putting her back to James. If she could figure out what motivated Elle to provide the alibi, then maybe she could get her to withdraw it. It was her guess the Ashley family's arrogance had them believing that just because Jackson had officially withdrawn his confession, all would be forgotten. But if what he told them about the threatening messages was true, there was a decent chance they would have to arrest him, especially now that Andrew was no longer a suspect. But that wasn't the worst of it for Jackson. There had been a physical altercation between him and Lauren. He had stalked her in the dunes, or so a prosecutor would say.

He had harassed her on social media. With no other suspects, and pressure from above to close the case, there was a very real chance Jackson could be found guilty.

Even though the room was dark, Lucy squeezed her eyes closed, trying to escape the thought. How could she have ever guessed that framing Coban Marshall would lead to Andrew Ashley potentially getting away with murder and his teenage son becoming the main suspect?

Elle was the key, Lucy reminded herself as her mind began to spiral. All she had to do was get her to admit she provided a false alibi and not only was Jackson off the hook, but Andrew would be back on it where he belonged—and hopefully squirming like hell.

Chapter Forty-Two
STELLA

The girl had given a false alibi. There was no doubt in Stella's mind. When she approached her at the newspaper, Elle Nolan said she had no idea why Andrew asked to see her. He had been fucking her. Clearly that much was true, but having a side hustle hardly warranted asking your wife to organise a conjugal visit in the police lockup. Even Andrew wasn't that stupid. *So, what then?* Stella wondered. Did Elle know something she didn't? Had Andrew confided in her about his whereabouts the night in question? It was driving her crazy that he wouldn't say where he was, and yet somehow Elle Nolan seemed to know. Even more infuriating was the fact her son was now in harm's way because a false alibi had made sure Andrew was no longer a suspect.

Before Jackson got involved, Stella's greatest concern had been the financial fallout of Andrew being tied to a murder case. Without his income and status, their lives would be completely different, but now her son was in danger and that trumped everything. No matter what happened, Jackson was not going to take the fall. Not for Andrew and not for anyone. Even if that meant losing everything.

It was just before sunrise, and Stella pushed herself to keep walking. She wouldn't usually be alone out on the beach this early, especially after what happened, but there was every chance the killer was sharing her bed. Perhaps the beach was the safest place she could be. Over the ocean, golden sunlight began to flood the horizon, and she felt the first tingle of its warm rays. It was a new day, and she had two choices. She could let everything become overwhelming or she could put her shoulders back and face it head on.

Elle Nolan had provided a false alibi. If she could find out why, then maybe she could figure out whether her husband was a murderer. And more importantly, how to help her son.

Stella finally allowed herself to stop walking. She took a moment and stared out at the sunrise. She had known Andrew her whole life. Deep down in her heart of hearts, she didn't believe he killed Lauren. Did he sleep with her? *Yes.* Was he a liar? *Definitely.* But a murderer?

As the sun rose higher in the sky, Stella sat down on the sand and thought back to that night. She had been in Sydney at a rooftop bar drinking cocktails with women she pretended to like, but in truth merely tolerated. The boys were both out with friends, Levi staying with mates and Jackson wherever 18-year-olds go when their mother was away. Andrew would have had the whole night free. But when she told Elle Nolan that Andrew believed she was the only one who could prove his innocence, her response had been that it made no sense. So, if he wasn't with her, then where was he? And why did she lie for him?

The golden rays began to fade, and the sky became a brilliant blue. Stella got to her feet and headed back toward the house. Andrew had one last chance to come clean before she took her questions back to Elle Nolan. And one way or another, Stella was getting answers.

When she stepped inside, the kitchen was filled with the aroma of freshly roasted coffee. It had been a long time since Andrew was home late enough on a weekday morning to make coffee, and for the tiniest moment she closed her eyes and tried to pretend that none of this had happened.

"You went out walking," he said, causing her to jump. "Did the media follow you?"

"No," she told him flatly, her memory of better times instantly shattered. "It's not like I went parading out the front door. I took the private access path."

He padded over and looked out the side window. She assumed to check no journalists had found their way onto our beach access path.

"There's no one there, Andrew," she said. "You're being paranoid."

"Paranoid?" He turned and looked at her, his eyes wide. "I was just arrested for a murder I didn't commit. I think being a bit paranoid is par for the course, don't you?"

Stella shrugged and walked over to the kitchen bench. "Is there still coffee?"

He nodded and gestured toward the urn.

"Andrew, where were you the night Lauren's body was put in the ocean?" Stella poured the coffee to distract herself while she waited for his response.

"Stella, I was with Elle. You know that. I don't—"

"So she says, but it makes no sense. Just tell me the truth, Andrew. Where were you?" She took a sip and allowed herself to meet his eye. It was painful watching her husband lie right to her face. Harder still knowing that whatever he was hiding must be worse than having an affair.

"I don't know what you want me to say, Stella. The boys were out. You were in Sydney. I know it was wrong, but that's where I was."

Stella took another sip, let the coffee warm her, then placed the mug down on the island bench. She had to try and stay calm. "You're lying to me and I won't take it much longer," she began slowly. "I've been humiliated. Our son is under investigation for murder. Just tell me where you were. I'm not going to ask you again." Her hands were trembling with a mix of rage, frustration, and betrayal. She had known this man her entire life and yet as she watched him stand there lying, he felt like a stranger.

"Stella, I can't keep saying the same thing over and over," he told her, throwing up his hands. "That's where I was. Would you prefer I was out there on the beach dragging Lauren's body..."

When he trailed off and turned away, Stella took a deep breath. He wasn't going to tell her the truth, that much was obvious. As she waited for him to turn back, she noticed a small tremor in his shoulders and wondered if he was crying.

"Andrew?" She came out from the bench and walked toward him.

Eventually, he turned, and she saw that his eyes were wet. "I didn't kill her, alright? I would never..."

His voice broke, and Stella suddenly didn't know how to feel. Her first thought was to console him, but the questions found their way in first. Why was he crying? Was it because their family was being torn apart? Was it because his career was forever tarnished? Or was it because despite his affair with Elle, he was in love with Lauren and someone had killed her?

Stella quickly let her arm fall back by her side. Whatever the reason, this was his doing and his mess. She was not going to make the same mistake as Elle and be pulled into his whirlwind of lies.

"I didn't say you killed her," she said flatly, her voice portraying none of the emotion she felt. "I asked where you were that night."

His head pulled up, and he stared at her in surprise. He finally understood that she wasn't asking if he killed her. She just wanted to know here he really was.

"Stella…"

"Where were you?" Harsher this time. He rubbed at his forehead and she knew she was getting close. "Tell me, Andrew. Your son is going to be arrested for murder. Now tell me. Where the fuck were you?"

"I can't, alright!" he shouted before storming across the room. "I can't."

"Andrew, that's not good enough," she shouted back, following after him. "You have to tell me."

"No, Stella, I don't!"

"Andrew, you owe me that much!" she yelled. "You've humiliated and destroyed this family. Now you fucking tell me where you were, or I swear to God…"

But without looking back, he grabbed the car keys off the hook in the hallway and headed toward the garage door.

"Don't you dare leave this house, Andrew," she shouted. "If you don't tell me, I'm going to be the one murdering someone and it might just be you!"

He stopped abruptly, paused, then turned his head just enough that she could see the profile of his face. "I can't tell you, Stella," he said, his tone hushed. "Now drop it before you get us killed as well."

Chapter Forty-Three
ELLE

When two days passed with no word from Andrew, I felt sick. A white-hot pain was creeping further and further up my neck and my body ached. My eyes burned, red-raw from crying, and there was a heavy knot in the pit of my stomach. Andrew had used me. He made me believe we meant something to each other, because he knew he'd need an alibi—and I had been stupid enough to fall for it.

I leaned against the weathered wooden rail, the only thing standing between me and a fifty-metre plunge to the bottom of the jagged cliffs overlooking Bar Beach. Not that I was considering ending it all. Far from it. My tears had dried hours ago and now I was furious.

There was still a small part of me that wanted to throw myself on the ground and cry, and with good reason. I had been indefinitely stood down from my job at The Tribune, *just till things settle down*', according to Walters. My affair with Andrew had been splashed across every newspaper and television news broadcast in the state, possibly the country, along with a series of unflattering images dug up by other journos keen to make me look as bad as possible. I felt like an idiot and my mother was humiliated. Suffice it to say, if I did take a flying leap, there would be no need to leave a note. My reasons for ending it all would be pretty obvious.

I took one last look at the waves smashing against the rocks below and pushed back from the rail. I had already taken one leap of faith and fell into nothing more than a pool of grief and regret. I wasn't about to take another. Instead, I walked back to my car and climbed inside. Dr Simms had encouraged me to reach out to someone who would understand. Only one person came to mind, but I wondered if he would be able to understand something like this? Realising it was either him or the drive-through, I scrolled through my contacts, found his name and hit call. When he answered, it was with a tone laden with a mix of disappointment and confusion.

"I can explain." It was the best opening I could come up with, even though I had no idea how to make him understand what I had done.

"Alright, I'm listening," David said.

I paused and tried to come up with something, anything, that made sense. "Shit, actually I can't explain," I muttered eventually. "I'm an idiot. That's about the best I can come up with."

I thought I heard the first hint of a chuckle and hoped it meant he was going to take it easy on me. "So when I told you I thought he was guilty, you two were already *together*?" he asked.

"I thought we were," I said.

"You thought?"

"David..." I needed to tell someone the truth. It was eating me alive. "Can you meet me? I need to talk."

"I'm no therapist, Elle, but I'm happy to listen. The thing is though, if Andrew's gone to ground, there's not much I can do to help."

"Gone to ground?"

"Hasn't been in touch with you. I'm assuming that's why you're feeling, in your words, *like an idiot*."

"No, well, yes, but there's something else."

"What is it? Are you okay?"

"Not on the phone. Can you meet me at my place?"

After he agreed to come over, I dropped the phone back into my bag, started the engine of my tiny red hatchback and felt the familiar flutter of tormented butterflies fill my stomach. There was no telling how David might react when I told him the truth. All I knew was that I had to.

When I opened the front door half an hour later, the first thing I saw was the pizza box in his arms. The second was the family-sized block of chocolate sitting on top. I swallowed hard and tried to push down the butterfly wings caught in my throat. "What's all this?"

"Well, it's lunchtime, and you sounded like you needed comfort food," he shrugged.

"Right. Makes sense," I nodded, terrified at the idea of trying to stop myself once I started eating that pizza. I had been cold turkey since my last visit with Dr Simms. None of the usual suspects had found their way in. Now he held two of them in his arms. "Come in."

As he stepped past, the rich smell of tomato, bread, and mozzarella wrapped its arms around me and squeezed. It wasn't his fault. No one knew about my eating. Not anyone who didn't sell McDonalds, KFC, or pizza, that is.

"Which cupboard for plates?" he called from the kitchen as I closed the door.

"Ah... top right."

It surprised me how instantly comfortable he was in my home. He had never been over before, and it struck me how easy it felt compared to the awkwardness I'd felt the first time Andrew came to visit.

"Alright," he smiled, coming back to the living room with plates and paper towel. "Let's dig in."

"David—"

But he shook his head. "Pizza first, then drama. I can't listen to whatever you have to say on an empty stomach. I get the feeling I'm going to need my strength."

I stifled a grin and finally relaxed. We would share the pizza first and then my troubles. After that, I would wait for him to leave and make myself throw the block of chocolate in the bin. Not the kitchen bin, the outdoor bin. Even I wasn't desperate enough to go trawling through a wheelie bin searching for chocolate. *Was I?*

When the pizza hit my tongue, I closed my eyes and savoured the taste. It was a delicious escape from my agony over Andrew and it would have been rude to say no after David had been so thoughtful. Just this one pizza, I told myself. Just this one, then straight back on the wagon. Or was it off the wagon? I was never really sure.

"Alright," he said with a sigh as his hand came to rest across his tummy—a gesture that he was full. "Hit me with it, Nolan. What did you do?"

I closed over the empty box and pushed it toward the end of the coffee table. "I really don't know how to say this..."

"Just say it," he replied. "No judgement."

I clenched my jaw and rubbed at my temple. "There might be."

"Hey, I was wrong about him. I said he did it and clearly he didn't if he was here with you, so we all make mistakes."

"Yeah, about that..." I turned my body to face him and tucked one foot up under me. I wasn't sure why, but it just felt safer somehow. "I know I shouldn't have, but I said he was here when actually—"

"Elle, no," he breathed. "Tell me you didn't."

"I know it was stupid."

Immediately, he was up on his feet. "You gave a false alibi?"

"I regret it now."

"That lying fucker," he swore. "He did it. I knew it." I watched as he paced the length of my living room, then stopped and turned to face me. "Elle, listen to me, please. All the evidence pointed to him. Your alibi was the only thing that set him free."

"I know, David. I said I made a mistake."

"Then what the hell were you thinking?" He threw up his hands and stared at me.

"He asked me to. I can't explain it. I don't know."

He came back, sat on the couch, and leaned in toward me. "Listen to me. You have to make this right, Elle. You have to tell them the truth."

"How can I now? I'll look ridiculous."

"No offense, but you already look ridiculous in the eyes of the public. You slept with someone's husband. The Lord fucking Mayor, who you were supposed to be holding accountable. You're a journalist. People believe what you write."

"Gee thanks."

"I'm just telling you the truth, Elle. Take a leaf out of my book and do the same."

I sat back and took it all in. Saying it out loud and seeing David's reaction brought home the gravity of what I had done. I had lied to the police and potentially let a murderer go free.

"Elle, are you listening to me? Did you hear what I just said?"

"No," I said, realising David had been talking. "I was just thinking."

"I said, I heard they were looking at his son Jackson for it now. You can't let an innocent kid get the blame when you know Ashley has no real alibi."

"What? No, Andrew wouldn't let his son be accused of murder. Not if..."

"...he was the one who really did it?"

I looked away. "I didn't mean that."

"But you don't know that for sure, Elle," he reminded me. "What we do know is that he needed you as an alibi. Did he say why?"

"He said he couldn't tell me."

"Oh, well then..."

"David..."

"Let's just look at the facts. He can't say where he was. We all know he was involved with Lauren. And now he's letting his own son be investigated for murder. Elle, come on."

"I know it looks bad."

"No, Elle, it doesn't just *look* bad. It's much worse than that."

"What do you mean?"

He sat back and fixed me with a gaze. "How it looks, if you don't tell the truth, is a lot like you're an accomplice to murder."

Chapter Forty-Four
LAUREN

I lied to Andrew. I didn't delete the footage. I couldn't. Not after all the work I put in to get it. I took a sip from my glass of pinot, looked back at my phone, and played the video one more time. They were such beautiful birds. I adored the way they danced around each other, beckoning and retreating, over and over, until eventually they were unable to deny each other. I had hoped it would be the same for Andrew and me. But that obviously wasn't going to happen.

Determined to brush off my bad mood, instead of sipping, I drained my glass and placed it down on the outdoor table to pour another. I loved spending afternoons on my home's back deck, looking out over the reserve below. Every morning and afternoon, the air was punctuated with the choral of magpies and the happy chatter of rainbow lorikeets. My home was my happy place, a sanctuary. The time I spent there was always relaxing, and I wasn't going to let Andrew's dismissal of me ruin that.

I finished pouring the glass and lifted it to my lips when beside me the phone buzzed with a text alert. I didn't recognise the number, but was certainly intrigued by the message.

Private Number: *There's something for you on the front step.*

Perhaps Andrew felt bad for what happened between us in the parking garage, I thought. He'd never been to my place, but it would be easy enough for him to get my address from work. With a tiny flutter of excitement, I put down the glass and padded through the house toward the front door. Sure enough, there on the step was a white gift box delicately wrapped with bright blue ribbon.

Thrilled, I picked it up and brought it inside to unwrap. From the kitchen drawer, I took a pair of scissors and carefully clipped the ribbon. When I lifted the lid and peeked inside, I saw the box was lined with soft tissue paper and my mind immediately conjured images of pretty lace, sweets, or something shiny inside. But as I unfolded the wrapping and saw the contents of the box, instead of smiling, I gasped and stumbled back, step after step, until I was up against the fridge. Inside was a dead magpie, its black and white wings mottled and dirty. Its neck was obviously broken.

"Oh my God," I sobbed, horrified that anyone would do such a thing.

After taking a minute to calm myself, I slowly stepped back toward the kitchen table and peered inside the box. There was no note, only the bird, but it spoke volumes. I knew exactly who left it there for me to find—the one person who had the most to lose should the development fall over. I put the lid back on and carried the box out to the garage. In the morning I would bury the bird, but for now the person who organised the morbid delivery was going to hear from me. I picked up my phone and scrolled until I found Tony Mansfield's number.

Me: *I received your package. Just letting you know I'm about to send something of my own.*

I hit send and then clicked over to Facebook. There were dozens of conservation groups with members all over the country who would love nothing more than getting their knickers in a twist over my footage of the Gemini Birds at Stockton. Fuck Tony Mansfield and fuck Andrew Ashley, I thought as I uploaded the video and wrote a caption identifying the date and location. "Let's see you get your development approval now, you piece of shit," I whispered, before hitting send and then proudly downing the rest of my wine.

Chapter Forty-Five
LUCY

Elle Nolan's two-storey washed-brick townhouse was in Parry Street Cooks Hill, just a few doors up from St John's Anglican Church, where Lucy's parents were married forty-two years ago. She had always imagined having her own wedding in the same pretty cobblestone church surrounded by family and friends, but James refused. His inability to have faith in what you cannot see meant their ceremony was held at the beach—much to the ire of her family.

Lucy knocked on the front door and stepped back. She was dressed in plain clothes. This was not an official visit. In fact, she shouldn't even have been there, but she had to know. Why would a seemingly intelligent woman with her whole life ahead of her risk losing it all for a man who was married to someone else?

Elle opened the door, a mug of what smelled like coffee in one hand and a piece of toast balanced between the corner of her lip.

"Mis Nolan... Elle, we need to talk," she said. "Can I come in?"

Without answering, Elle stepped aside, making way for her to go in. Lucy's first thought was that it would have been a lovely home if not for the empty pizza boxes, chocolate wrappers, and take-away burger wrappings littered across the living room.

She could feel Elle follow her gaze and then visibly shift her weight from one foot to the other. "I... had someone over last night. I didn't eat all that myself."

"I'm not here to investigate your diet, Elle," Lucy told her. "Can I sit?"

Elle nodded and motioned to a scarlet-coloured armchair facing the couch. As Lucy sat, Elle shifted two pizza boxes and took a seat.

"Jackson Ashely is being investigated for the murder of Lauren Ellis," Lucy began. "He confessed right before we dropped the charges against his father." She maintained eye contact and quickly noted that Elle didn't seem surprised by the news, even though it was still classified. "But you knew that, didn't you?"

"I heard, yes."

"Can I ask from who?"

"A contact. I can't provide names."

Lucy's gaze lingered over Elle's face as she wondered if Andrew Ashley had told her. *It had to have been him,* she thought quickly. It definitely wasn't Yieldon. There was no way he'd be the leak. "Alright," she said, her voice tight. "The thing is, I don't believe Jackson is the one responsible."

"Well, that's good news, but why are you telling me?" Elle asked. "I'm not at the Tribune right now, so if it's media coverage you're looking for, there's not much I can do to help."

"That's where I disagree," Lucy told her. "In fact, I think you're the one person who can make sure Jackson is never found guilty."

Elle sighed and leaned back in her seat. Her body language said she was defeated, this young woman who only weeks ago must have thought her life was completely on track. "Elle? Are you alright?"

"Not really," she managed. "This whole thing has nothing to do with me and yet it seems I'm always responsible for what happens to everyone. I didn't ask for this."

"I know that," Lucy said, quickly reminding herself not to get emotionally involved. "But by providing an alibi for Andrew, you became extremely involved."

Elle raked her fingers through her hair and looked away. She was clearly stressed. Her agitated demeanour and the obvious signs of her emotional eating meant something wasn't sitting right with Elle Nolan.

"Is this an official visit?" she asked eventually, looking Lucy over. "You're not in uniform."

"No, not official, but I was hoping you would be willing to help Jackson."

"You know, Senior Sergeant Dickson, the last time we saw each other, our conversation was also less than official," she said, quickly regaining her composure. "This is starting to become a pattern."

Lucy took a moment and thought about what she was risking by coming to the house. If Elle reported her, if she told one of her colleagues at the Tribune about her suspicions and they started digging, she had a lot to lose. But so did Jackson Ashley, and Lucy couldn't let an innocent boy go to jail just because she had something to hide.

"Alright, let's be straight with each other, Elle," she said, sitting up straight and getting right to the point. "I'm here because I think you gave a false alibi for Andrew Ashley. I don't believe he was here with you that night. What I believe is that he was in the dunes, dragging Lauren Ellis' dead body into the ocean because earlier that afternoon he killed her in a fit of rage."

Elle visibly held her breath and stared at Lucy for what felt like an eternity. As she waited, Lucy tried to imagine what she must be feeling. Anger? Fear? Sadness? If she was right, Andrew had used her to make sure he could safely return home to his wife.

"Senior Sergeant Dickson," Elle began. "That's a very big accusation to make."

"Yes, I know."

"And you really believe I would lie to police and say he was here when for all I know he was..." Elle trailed off and it struck Lucy that she couldn't say the words out loud. It only reaffirmed her suspicions.

"I think you did what he asked you to do." She made sure Elle noticed her glance toward the food boxes and wrappers. "And I think you're regretting that decision, Elle, but we can make this right. Come to the station and withdraw your alibi. We can move our focus away from Jackson and back to Andrew, where you and I both know it should be. Don't let an innocent boy take the blame for this, Elle, please."

But she was already shaking her head. "Andrew would never let his son take the blame."

"Well, unfortunately there's a lot of circumstantial evidence that doesn't look good for Jackson and while I don't believe he did it, off the record, he did know Lauren and they'd had a previous altercation."

"You don't have to say *off the record*, Senior Sergeant," she said, rolling her eyes. "I'm not a reporter at the moment."

"I'm just covering myself. The point is, if the investigation turns up enough red flags on Jackson, there won't be much Andrew can do other than confessing himself, which seems unlikely."

Elle got up and walked to the kitchen, where she poured herself a glass of what looked like juice from the fridge. She drank the entire glass in one mouthful and didn't offer one to Lucy.

"What makes you so sure Andrew is guilty, even though he has an alibi?" she asked as she came back and sat down. "Is there other evidence?"

"Something Stella Ashely said," Lucy told her. "And a gut feeling."

"A gut feeling?" Elle repeated, her face sceptical. "You came to my house on a Saturday morning asking me to say I gave a false alibi based on a gut feeling?"

"And something Andrew's wife told me." Lucy emphasized the word *wife* to gauge her reaction, but this time she gave away nothing.

"And what was that?"

"That you had no idea why Andrew asked to see you that night in lockup. Tell me, Elle, if he was with you the night in question, why would you be surprised that he'd want to talk? Wouldn't you expect he'd ask you to vouch for his whereabouts?"

"Senior Sergeant Dickson, Andrew is the Lord Mayor, and he's married. I didn't know how he would want to play it, so I acted dumb to his wife. I pretended I had no idea what he wanted. That doesn't mean my alibi was fake. So the way I see it, all you have is a gut feeling, and I'm not sure that's going to cut it."

Technically, what she said made sense, but Lucy wasn't buying it. "You're still going to defend him? Has he been to see you? Has he even called?"

"I think it's time for you to go, Senior Sergeant Dickson," Elle said, standing to drive the message home. "I'd appreciate it if this was the last *unofficial* visit you made."

Lucy nodded and got to her feet, still not willing to give up. "He's a narcissist, Elle. I know he's handsome and charming and powerful, but really think about it. Something's not right with all of this. Deep down you know that and now he's going to let his son potentially spend the next twenty years behind bars for a murder that I believe he committed. You're no fool. You know what will happen to a boy like Jackson in jail."

"Please leave," she stated. "We're done here."

As Lucy walked back to her car, she glanced over her shoulder at the townhouse, where Elle stood watching from the window. The lie was eating her alive, and Lucy had to believe it was only a matter of time before the truth would force its way out.

Chapter Forty-Six
ANDREW

"I told you not to come back here," Elle huffed as she pulled open the door. "I'm not going to withdraw my alibi."

"Elle?"

"Andrew." Her expression changed from anger to relief, and then quickly back to anger. "I wasn't expecting you. I thought it was the police again."

"Can I come in?" he asked. "It's probably not a great idea for me to be standing out here. Media lurking around and all."

She moved aside, but Andrew could tell Elle had considered saying no. It had been three days since he was released and with no word. She had to be thinking the worst. Now it seemed someone from the police was on a mission to have her withdraw her alibi. He had a pretty good idea who.

"Who was here?" he asked. "Who wants you to change your alibi?"

"That's the first thing you want to say to me?" Elle replied, not looking him in the eye. "I haven't heard a word from you since you were released and all you care about is who was here?"

Andrew lowered his head and considered whether he should try to embrace her or keep his distance.

"Andrew, I lied to the police for you and you didn't even call me. Surely I deserved at least that much?"

Her arms were folded across her chest, and her jaw was clenched. "You're right, of course, and I'm sorry, Elle. Stella's been... I don't even know the words to use... and the media has been camped outside the house around the clock. I haven't had the chance to contact you, but I've thought about you every minute. You have to believe that."

"Well, I don't," she said. "You could have at least sent a text."

"You're right," he told her. "I'm sorry."

She slowly let herself look at Andrew, and he did his best to give her a warm smile. He needed her onside. If she withdrew her alibi, he'd be right back where he started.

"Andrew," she sighed. "I don't want to recant my alibi, but what about Jackson? You're not really going to let him be charged with Lauren's murder, are you?"

"Let him?" Andrew repeated. "Elle, I'm going to do everything in my power to make sure Jackson is safe. But confessing to a murder I didn't commit isn't the answer here. You must know that, unless..." As she searched his face, Andrew could tell Elle was having second thoughts. The idea scared the shit out of him. "They haven't brainwashed you into thinking I actually did this, have they?"

When she didn't answer, Andrew could feel the colour drain from his face. Not knowing what else to do, he rushed forward and pulled her into an embrace. "Elle, no," he whispered into her hair. "I didn't kill Lauren, I swear to you. Please, don't let anyone convince you otherwise. I didn't do this."

"I don't know what to think anymore," she sobbed. "Andrew, this is so hard."

"Shh, it's okay," he told her. "It will all work itself out. I promise."

He held Elle until she stopped crying and then stepped back. Her cheeks were flushed, and he could see she was battling to hold herself together. It had never been his intention to get so involved with Elle, nor had he meant to lie to her. It had just been a harmless flirtation. She was sweet and smart, and he loved her sarcasm—when she was feeling confident enough to use it. But he never meant for it to come to this. Everything had got so out of hand. "Elle, I need you to tell me who was here," he pressed. "Who wants you to withdraw your alibi?"

She sniffed and wiped at a stray tear trickling down her cheek. "Your wife came to see me the night you were arrested. When she told me I was the only one who could prove you were innocent, my response was that I didn't understand why. She must have told Senior Sergeant Dickson."

Andrew nodded. He knew it would have been Lucy Dickson. She was a thorn in his side.

"I told Senior Sergeant Dickson I'd said that to Stella in the hope of quelling any suspicions about our relationship. I didn't know what else to say."

"Alright," he said. "I have to go, but I need you to stay strong, Elle, please. Everything will be okay, I promise." She nodded, but he could tell she was rattled. He glanced around her usually neat and tidy house and realised what a mess it was. It almost looked like she had held a party the night before, but he knew that couldn't be true. "Elle, did you have people over last night?"

"No, of course not," she answered quickly.

He looked closer and noticed two wine glasses still on the coffee table. She followed his gaze. "I had a friend over, that's all."

"Can I ask who?"

Elle had never been one for hanging out with girlfriends. She was a loner who usually seemed happiest in her own company, lost in a book or a movie. When she hesitated to answer, his stomach twisted. Someone else had been in her ear. Someone other than Senior Sergeant Dickson.

"David came by," she said eventually. "But he's just a friend."

"David as in SES David?"

"We went to uni together. I told you before, remember?"

"Do you see him a lot?" Andrew asked, suddenly unsure whether the knot in his stomach was made of jealousy or fear.

"Not really," she said with a shrug. "Just now and then. He's a friend."

Andrew took one last look around the room. "Did he say anything about me?"

"Anything like what?"

She seemed uncomfortable. He searched her face, trying to figure out if it was because she was involved with David and didn't want him to know, or if it was because she'd told him about the alibi. "Does he know?"

"Know what?"

"About the alibi, Elle."

"No, he doesn't. I just needed someone to hang out with. I was upset, Andrew. Surely you can understand that."

He nodded, but was not convinced. David had stood right beside him at every press conference and was heavily involved in the case. Now he had the ear of the one person keeping Andrew out of jail.

"Elle, I know I can't tell you who to spend time with," he began, "but I'd prefer it if you didn't see David again."

She stared at him in obvious disbelief. "Andrew, you're at home with your wife. I didn't even hear from you for three days."

"I know and I've asked so much of you already, Elle, but please, can you just do this last thing for me? I have so much on my plate, and the thought of you with someone else is just too much for me to bear. At least until I know my son is safe. Please."

She shook her head and stared out across the room. "You're unbelievable."

"So, you won't see him?"

She shrugged and rolled her eyes. "I guess not."

"Thank you," he breathed, pulling her into one last embrace. "I don't know what I'd do without you."

Chapter Forty-Seven
STELLA

S tella was frantic. The police investigation had ramped up, and it was clear they were closing in on Jackson. In the past two days, they had questioned him again, come to the house with a warrant to confiscate his laptop, tablet, mobile phone, and taken all the clothes from his closet for DNA testing. Now he was refusing to leave his room and had barely eaten. She was at her wit's end. She had to speak to Elle Nolan again, but Stella had no idea how to find her. She had tried stalking her social media accounts, but there was nothing that pointed to where she lived. And then it finally hit her. Their house was surrounded by journalists.

Stella quickly tidied herself and opened the front door. The pack immediately pushed forward, and cameras flashed from every direction. "Is anyone here from the Tribune?"

"I am," a black-haired woman said, pushing her way to the front of the pack.

"Come inside, please."

The woman's face lit up as she gathered her things and stepped past the envious gaze of her colleagues.

"What's your name?" Stella asked, as she closed the door behind them.

"I'm Willamina Fraser. Senior crime reporter at the Tribune."

"Do you know Elle Nolan?"

She laughed and dropped her bag on the floor in the kitchen. "I do. She's a sweet kid, but obviously not too bright."

"You like her," Stella stated. "Are the two of you friends?"

"Can I sit?" Willamina asked, motioning to the stools by the island bench.

"Go ahead."

She glanced around the rest of the home, clearly taking notes with her eyes. It annoyed Stella no end.

"Before this shitshow Elle was on the fast-track," Willamina began. "She was adamant about taking my crime round. On one hand, it pissed me off, but on the other I kinda admired her ambition, you know? Was never going to happen, mind you, but I liked her, so I threw her a bone now and then. That was until she burned me at council."

"Burned you how?"

She paused a moment, then shrugged off whatever she'd been thinking. "She told your husband I was downstairs asking about his relationship with Lauren Ellis. Got me thrown out of the building."

"So she had his back even before the alibi," Stella replied.

"Seems that way."

Stella nodded and let it sink in. Elle was in love with her husband. *Was that why she provided the alibi?* She wondered. Could it really be that simple—and that stupid? "I need to speak to her. Do you have her address?"

"Nope," Willamina said. "But I can get it."

Stella knew a shakedown when she saw one and had expected no less from a journalist. "I'll give you two questions. No photo. Deal?"

"On the record?"

"Yes."

"Deal. I'll get the address to you by tonight."

Willamina pulled out her phone and was about to click on the voice recorder when Stella stopped her. "Address first, then comments."

Willamina smirked and shoved the phone back into her bag. "I like you Stella Ashley," she said. "I'll be in touch."

Chapter Forty-Eight
ELLE

I was ashamed that David's visit last night had sparked an eating episode, but according to Dr Simms, so long as I got right back on track and didn't let it spiral, I was allowed to forgive myself. What felt harder was forgiving myself for shutting David out after he had been nothing but supportive.

It hadn't been fair of Andrew to ask me to stop seeing a friend. I had done as he asked, but it was difficult having no one to talk to. Since the day Andrew came to my house, communication between us had been limited. A text here and there. One phone call. Whenever I tried to initiate contact, it rubbed salt into the wound to see he had blocked my number. I knew because my texts used to have a *delivered* receipt beneath them. Now they just sat there out in the abyss, and he never responded. I questioned him about it the one time he called. He said his incoming calls and texts were set to *favourites* only because he was getting so many calls from media and Stella was monitoring his every move. It seemed to me there was no reason he couldn't save my number under another name. The fact he chose not to, obviously meant I was no longer one of his *favourite* people, despite what I had done for him.

I tried again to text him, but as usual, it didn't go through. Tired of feeling exiled, I called David. I owed him an apology and an explanation, and for once, I was sick of always having Andrew's back.

"Hey," I said timidly when he answered. "You mad?"

"I'd be lying if I said I wasn't at least peeved."

"Peeved." I was already smiling. "That's an interesting choice of words."

"Yeah," he said with a sigh. "It's somewhere between angry and frustrated that someone can't see what's right in front of them."

For the past couple of months, there had been chemistry between us, but with everything going on and my feelings for Andrew, I had pretended not to notice. He had never pushed it, and that suited me, but now he had come right out with it—I assumed because he figured at this point, there was nothing left to lose.

"David—"

"I know you love him, Elle, but Christ, I just think you deserve a hell of a lot better than what he's dishing out."

"I know," I said gently. "It's just hard to accept."

"Yeah... and I get it... but come on. Enough is enough."

"You're right. I need to start getting over him."

"What you need to do, Elle, is go and tell the police the truth. Don't let him getaway with this. He used you."

"You haven't told anyone what I did, have you? Even though I stopped returning your calls."

"No, Elle, I didn't. But you need to fess up. For yourself. For Jackson Ashley. And for Lauren's family. They deserve to know what really happened."

"I know, but I just keep thinking—"

"Wow. You still don't think he did it, do you?"

"I don't know. That's the thing. I don't *know* if he did it."

"Then let the police figure it out, Elle. That's their job, but they can't do it if they don't have all the information."

Between Senior Sergeant Dickson's visit, David's advice—which made perfect sense, and Andrew blocking me I was finally wavering. Maybe it was time to stop protecting him and admit to what I had done.

"Elle? You still there?"

"I'm still here."

"Will you please go and tell the police that Andrew Ashley wasn't with you that night?"

I let out a long, tired breath. "And then what happens?"

"You'll be in the shit. There'll be another media cycle of stories about your perjury, but after that, it will be over, Elle. You'll be free of this. And maybe..."

"...maybe what?"

"Maybe I can finally ask the girl I've liked since uni out on a real date."

I smiled. "You want to ask me out?"

"Elle, for a smart woman, you sure can be stupid sometimes. I've wanted to ask you out since our first class together back in the day. I just never had the guts." He paused a moment. "I get the idea of coming clean is scary, but there's also a lot to look forward to once you find your way out from under Andrew Ashley and his mess."

"No pun intended?"

He laughed, and it made me smile. I missed him.

"Definitely no pun intended."

"Give me a couple of days to work up to it?"

"Sure, Elle," he said. "Trust me, it will be for the best. You'll see."

I put down the phone and felt a weight lift off me. I had no idea what the penalty for providing a false alibi would be, but Senior Sergeant Dickson was so keen for it that maybe there was a deal to be made.

I sat back and let myself remember the good things about Andrew. The way he made me feel, the buzz of electricity that tingled across my skin whenever he touched me. The day he told me about his childhood and how close I felt to him when we were making love. But it had all been a lie. Andrew didn't love me. Maybe it was time I let someone into my life who would.

Chapter Forty-Nine
LAUREN

*"L*auren!" *He was pounding on my front door like a crazy person.* *"Lauren, open up!"*

When I opened the door, I was surprised by Andrew's appearance. I had never seen him look anything but polished, even onsite at the Stockton Centre site, but standing there on my step, his hair was askew and he looked like he'd seen a ghost.

"What the hell were you thinking?" he shouted, pushing past me and into the house uninvited.

"Um... come in?"

"Lauren, why would you post that video online after I specifically told you to delete it?" He raked at his hair and stared at me.

"Because I'm not your lap dog?" I said. "And because someone sent a dead bird to my house."

"Wait, what?"

I picked up my phone and showed him a photo of the dead magpie in the box. "I got a text that there was something on my front step. When I opened it, this is what I found."

"Lauren, listen to me. This is very serious."

"I'm not afraid of Tony Mansfieldand his mates," I told him defiantly. "I have savings. If I get fired, I get fired. It's not like working in local government was my dream job."

But Andrew grabbed my shoulders and shook his head. "You don't understand. This is bigger than Tony."

Part of me was a little shaken by his urgency, but I also thought he was overreacting.

"Lauren, listen to me, please. You need to watch your back. Take extra precautions. Is there somewhere else you can stay?"

I stepped back and looked at him. The fear in his eyes was starting to scare me. "You're afraid," I said. "What's going on?"

"You might be in danger, Lauren. We all might be."

"Let's go and sit out the back. We can talk there."

When I got him settled on the outdoor couch, I went in and pulled two beers from the fridge. I handed him one and sat down. "What's going on?"

"I'm in trouble, Lauren," Andrew began. "It's bad."

I nodded and took a long mouthful. We were surrounded by the melody of birds singing and a gentle breeze washed over my legs. I had imagined this moment so many times, sitting here in my favourite spot alone with Andrew, but now that it was happening, it felt nothing like I thought it would. "Tell me everything," I said. "And don't leave anything out."

He nodded and straightened in his seat. "A couple of months ago, I met with some executives from Ridgemont Capitol about the development. They wanted to discuss the approval process in a 'less official' setting.

"In other words, they wanted to bribe you," I said and shook my head in disgust.

"I thought that maybe if I spoke to them from the heart, if I explained why it was so important that Stockton remain a residential village they would better understand my perspective and why I was so opposed to the creation of a resort being built there."

"And?"

"They made it clear they cared little for sentiment."

"Right," I nodded. "No surprises there."

"They spoke to me so disrespectfully, Lauren, like I was some country hick with no idea. They pissed me off, and I told them in no uncertain terms that I was not interested in their money and that I would find a way to make sure the development approvals were never endorsed by council staff, starting with

their application to rezone the site. The next day, I started looking for a way to do just that."

"And that's when you read my report about the Gemini Birds."

"Correct. I knew we had to keep it private, especially once I found out about Tony's relationship with the Ridgemont Capitol group. When information started leaking that staff were going to postpone a decision on the rezoning application based on the original findings of your environmental study, Tony told you to stop working on it."

"Yeah, arsehole."

"But it didn't stop there. I got a call from an anonymous number that if any reports were filed which caused the application to be denied, there would be consequences."

I put my beer down on the table and looked at him closely. "What kind of consequences?"

"Candid photos of my family started being delivered in envelopes to my office. When my assistant tried to follow up the courier company, it always led to a dead end. Stella started getting strange hang up phone calls and one day Levi came home saying a four-wheel drive had been following him on his scooter."

"Jesus, Andrew..."

"It was all just to scare me, that's what I thought at least, but when you sent that text about finding the birds to Tony, that's when it really ramped up."

I thought back to how determined I had been to piss off Tony. I had no idea what I was really doing.

"They came to the house, Lauren."

"They what?"

"The day you posted the video, I was out walking and when I came home, there were two men in my kitchen. Stella was making them a coffee, for Christ's sake. She had no idea. They said they were colleagues of mine there to pick me up for an executive team building afternoon at the shooting range. They said I must have forgotten about it. I didn't know what else to do, Lauren. They had guns, so I got changed and went with them."

"Andrew, why didn't you call the police?"

"They had guns, Lauren. Did you not hear me?"

I thought back to that afternoon, how I had driven past Andrew's house and seen a black sedan in the driveway. If only I had known what was really going on. "What happened when they took you?"

"They drove me to the Stockton site and stopped the car. They asked if you would still be there."

"They were looking for me?" I breathed. "To hurt me?"

"No," he shook his head. I think they were looking to kill two birds with one stone, so to speak. To make us both clear on what was at stake if we kept pushing it. They held a gun to my head, Lauren. They threatened to hurt my family if I didn't find a way to stop you from making your findings on the Gemini Birds public."

"Oh my God," I managed. "And I posted the video online. Andrew, we have to call the police."

"No, we can't," he said. "No police. These people are powerful Lauren. Their reach extends way past Chris Yieldon or anyone at the local command. We need to figure this out ourselves. How long has the video been up?"

I glanced at my watch. "A couple of hours. But Andrew, the birding community has gone nuts over it. It's too late."

Andrew drained what was left of his beer and got to his feet. "I have to go. I'll contact the Ridgemont Capital guys and try to buy us some time."

I stepped toward him. We were so close. He was just centimetres away. "I'm sorry, Andrew. I had no idea."

"It's not your fault, Lauren. I should have told you. I've put you in danger. I'm the one who should be apologising."

I held his gaze and wondered what would happen if I reached up and touched his cheek. He looked so fraught with fear and regret that I longed to calm him, but didn't know how.

"Lauren..." he began.

Then, without another thought, I leaned in and kissed him. Softly, gently, waiting to see his reaction. His lips moved against mine and within moments, the fire that had been simmering between us was raging. He pushed me against the wall in my kitchen and I felt him hard against me. I grabbed at his chest and he pulled my hair, forcing my head back and exposing the pale skin of my neck.

"I want you so much." I gasped as his lips brushed across the dip of my throat. "I've wanted you for so long."

He kissed me longer, harder, and more forcefully. But then suddenly stepped back, breathless and flushed.

"I can't do this... I'm so sorry. I want to, but I can't." He bent forward and rested his elbows on his knees to catch his breath. "I can't be this guy. My family is in danger, and I already feel like an arsehole. But it's like I can't breathe when you're near me, Lauren. I've been with Stella a long time and we have our issues... but you... you're like a force of nature. If I go down this road, I don't think I'll make it back."

"Andrew—"

"I'll do whatever it takes to protect you, Lauren. You have my word," he said, stepping forward to kiss me gently on the forehead. "No one is going to hurt you. I'll make sure of it."

No, I thought as I watched him walk down the hall and out the door. Because only you can do that.

Chapter Fifty
LUCY

Lucy's heart sank as she listened to Yieldon say they'd be issuing a warrant for the arrest of Jackson Ashley. Even though it came as no surprise, given the amount of circumstantial evidence against him, she knew in her heart that he was innocent.

"Can I talk to you?" she asked Yeildon. "In private."

He nodded, and she followed him into Interview Room Three, the same room where Jackson had falsely confessed to the murder. "You know he didn't do this," she said, once the door was closed. "How can we take that kid into custody knowing he's innocent?"

"I didn't think so at first either, but the evidence says otherwise, Dicks. We can't make decisions based on emotion. You should know that better than anyone."

He didn't elaborate, but they both knew he was referring to the Marshall case. "How can Andrew Ashley just sit there knowing his son is being investigated for a murder that he committed? The arrogance of that man is unbelievable."

"I don't think he figured it would come to this," Yieldon said, perching himself on the edge of the desk. "He believes Jackson is innocent, so I guess he thought it would all come out in the wash and the investigation would be dropped."

"Yeah, of course he believes Jackson didn't do it. Because *he did*."

Yieldon rubbed at the back of his neck and let out a long breath. "We've been through this, Dicks. He has an alibi. He's not our guy."

"Oh, bullshit!" Lucy swore. "You know as well as I do that Elle Nolan is full of shit. He wasn't with her that night any more than I was."

"You can't keep chasing him down. You gotta let this go."

"Let *him* go, you mean."

"I'm not doing this with you again." He stood up from the table and leaned toward her. "Let it be. That's an order."

Lucy's hands were trembling with a mix of rage at Andrew Ashley and guilt that all of this was her fault. Elle Nolan had her over a barrel and Lucy had caved. What she should have done was call her bluff. What did Elle really know about the Marshall case, anyway? It couldn't be more than the word of some drug dealer who claimed Lucy bought product from him.

A headache throbbed from the nape of Lucy's neck, up over her head, and down into her brow. She was at a loss. Elle refused to withdraw her alibi and Andrew Ashley, it seemed, had no intention of confessing to what he did. That left Jackson to take the fall and there was nothing she could do about it.

"You coming?" Yieldon was standing in the doorway, cap in hand, ready to go and arrest Jackson.

She nodded and shuffled back toward the desk to gather her things. What they were about to do was wrong. She could feel it in every part of her body, from her head to her heart, and down into her gut. "Yieldon—" she began, but he cut her off.

"Dicks, if you're not up for it, say the word. But this arrest is happening. Now, are you in or are you out?"

"In," Lucy mumbled. At least if she was there, she could support Jackson until there was a way to prove Andrew Ashley was not with Elle Nolan on the night in question.

"This is going to be a shitshow," she said as they drove toward the Ashley house. "Media is still camped out front."

"Tell me something I don't know. This kid has royally fucked up his life."

She looked over at Yieldon and shook her head. "You can't really think he did this. You were there when we interviewed him."

"Evidence doesn't lie, Dicks."

"There's no DNA. No tangible proof."

"He's a teenage kid, probably spoiled to the shithouse, who got rejected and didn't like it. People have killed for less."

Lucy scoffed and turned to stare out the window. "That's such bullshit. The department wants an arrest and they couldn't get Andrew so the next Ashley inline will do. That's all this is."

"Do you really think I want to arrest my friend's son? And for murder no less?" Yieldon asked. "Jesus, Dicks, I did all I could to keep Andrew from being charged, only to end up taking his son in. It sucks, but it's our job. This is what you signed up for. This is the hard shit."

It was a good speech, but he was wrong. Lucy hadn't signed up to arrest innocent teenagers, and she didn't sign up to let murderers go free. She signed up to make a difference, to help the people who were unable to help themselves. People like Sarah and Minty Marshall and Lauren Ellis. People who deserved for their killer to be held accountable. She stared out the window and thought back to the day her sister was killed. The car had come out of nowhere. One minute they had been walking home from the shops, Libby trailing behind her, ice-cream in hand, and the next she was gone. Her Mum had trusted her to take Libby and look after her. To hold her hand the entire way, but Lucy had let go. She let Libby fall behind and that man, that drunk, had extinguished the brightest star she knew. The day he was sentenced was bittersweet. Lucy was only twelve, but she would never forget the relief on her parent's faces that he had been held accountable, that he would be punished for what he did. It wouldn't bring Libby back, they all knew that, but it meant her sister's life mattered. And it was that thought that drove her the day she purchased drugs to plant at the Marshall house. Minty's life mattered and if no one was going to hold that dirtbag Coban Marshall accountable for what he was doing to her, then Lucy would. Minty deserved that much—and so did Lauren Ellis.

When Lucy and Yieldon arrived outside the Ashley house, even though they were in an unmarked sedan, the media pack instantly pounced. Reporters shoved microphones in her face and camera flashes exploded around them as they made their way toward the front door.

When Stella Ashley saw them, it was as though the entire world instantaneously crumbled around her. "No," she cried. "You're not taking my son. You're not taking Jackson."

"I'm sorry, Stella," Yieldon began. "But we have a warrant for the arrest of Jackson Ashley for the murder of Lauren Ellis."

By now Andrew was by her side and in the background Lucy heard their youngest son start to cry.

"Chris, you can't do this," Andrew stated, stepping in front of his wife and blocking the door with his body. "He didn't do it."

"This is your fault!" Stella shouted at her husband. "You did this! Tell them the truth, Andrew. Tell them it was you who killed her."

"Stella!" Andrew turned and stared at his wife, shock and disbelief obvious on his face.

"I know Elle Nolan lied," Stella shouted, her voice shaking. "I know she covered for you."

Behind them, two uniformed officers glanced at Yieldon looking for direction.

"We need to take Jackson to the station, Andrew," Yieldon said, ignoring Stella's accusations. "We'd prefer you bring him out, if possible."

Andrew nodded and stared back at his wife a moment longer before disappearing down the hall.

"You know she lied," Stella said, her pleading eyes planted firmly on Lucy. "Please, Senior Sergeant Dickson, you *know* she did. Do something!"

"Mrs Ashley—"

"Stella, please," Yieldon said, cutting her off. "You're not helping the situation."

"Not helping? You listen to me, Chris," she shouted, her finger up in his face. "That's my son. That's my son and you're taking him from me. Your partner knows Elle Nolan's alibi was fake. Tell him, Senior Sargent

Dickson, tell him you let that girl come into the station after hours and see my husband."

Yieldon looked over at Lucy, clearly confused, but probably not surprised.

"Mrs Ashley, I understand this is difficult," Lucy told her. "But if Jackson is innocent, it will be proven in court."

"Oh, right," she scoffed. "Because no one was ever found guilty of something they didn't do."

"Mrs Ashley—"

"How can you do this knowing Elle Nolan lied to protect Andrew?"

Before Lucy could respond, Andrew Ashley appeared at the door with his arm wrapped protectively across the shoulders of a terrified looking Jackson.

"It's going to be okay," Lucy told him, as her heart lurched. "I'll take care of you."

Andrew turned to his son, who was almost the same height as him. "Remember, don't say anything. Giovanni will meet you at the station. I'll sort this out. You have my word."

"Jackson," Stella sobbed, pulling him into a desperate embrace. "I'll fix this, sweetheart. I'll fix it."

"Mr and Mrs Ashley, we really need to go," Yieldon told them. "I'll be in touch every step of the way."

Stella held onto the back of Jackson's sweater until she had no choice but to let go. As they walked down the path, two uniforms provided a barricade from the media, and Lucy glanced at Jackson. His jaw was quivering and despite being eighteen, he looked like a child.

"I didn't kill her, you know that, right?" he managed. "I was just saying it to help everyone."

Every part of her longed to tell him that *yes, she knew that,* but she couldn't. But what she could do was silently swear to make sure that one way or another, Andrew Ashley and Elle Nolan, were held accountable for what they had done.

Chapter Fifty-One
STELLA

Any niceties Stella had shown Andrew for Jackson's sake were long gone. She hated him. She was so furious at what he had done to her son that she was having a hard time containing the ferocity of her feelings. She wanted to hurt him. She wanted to crush his stupid shaped skull and peel his skin off with a carving knife. Any love she ever felt for him had been incinerated into ash.

As she roared over the Stockton Bridge, the v8 engine of Andrew's precious Mercedes echoed in her ears, but all Stella could think about was Elle Nolan.

She did this.

Together, she and Andrew had ruined her son's life.

Now she was going to pay.

When Stella left the house, Andrew was lying in a pathetic heap on their bedroom floor. Curled up in a foetal position, the once all-powerful Lord Mayor no longer commanded the leaders of the city, nor did he hold any rank in the house they had once called home. She didn't just want a divorce. She had demanded one. No longer concerned about stature or status, Stella just wanted out. Andrew had broken them. She would sell the house and whatever was left after Jackson's court case would be used to take care of the boys and her mother. Andrew owed them that. They, on the other hand, owed him nothing.

By the time she pulled into the street Willamina Fraser said Elle Nolan lived in, Stella was blinded by rage. When they spoke at the newspaper, Elle was adamant she had no idea why Andrew had wanted to see her. Perhaps she was just covering up their affair, but Stella didn't believe that. She knew something and finding out what it was might be the only way to save Jackson.

Stella pounded on the front door and when Elle opened it, she stormed in, not bothering to close it behind her.

"Tell me why you lied for Andrew," she demanded, purposely not looking at the couch they may have shared or the kitchen they may have cooked in together.

Elle stepped back, clearly shaken by the intrusion. "Mrs Ashely—"

"Oh, quit the *Mrs Ashley* shit," Stella shouted. "My son has been arrested for murder because you lied for my husband. Now tell me why!"

"I—"

Stella watched Elle squirm beneath her stare. Whatever Andrew saw in her was a mystery. She was pudgy and pale, with squinty eyes and lank hair.

"Stella," she began, purposely saying her name this time, "I—"

But before Elle had a chance to finish, the sound of someone at the front door caught both their attention and they turned to find Senior Sergeant Lucy Dickson, in uniform, standing on the stairs.

"Mrs Ashley," she remarked. "You're here too."

"I am," Stella told her sternly. "It's my right to ask why this *person* provided a fake alibi for my husband."

Instead of arguing or trying to make Stella leave, Senior Sergeant Dickson held up her hands in mock surrender. "I'm not here for that," she began. "I came to speak to Elle, off the record, but it might be a good thing that you're here too, Mrs Ashley." She looked over her shoulder at the open street behind us. "Can we go inside and talk?"

Elle nodded and a few moments later Stella strangely found herself taking a seat on the sofa she had tried so hard to avoid looking at.

"Elle," Senior Sergeant Dickson began, "I assume Mrs Ashley is here for the same reason I am. Jackson has been arrested and it's imperative you come forward and admit to falsifying the alibi you provided for Andrew Ashley. The evidence we have against Jackson is circumstantial, but it might just be enough to see him found guilty if we get the wrong judge. The upper echelons of power want this case closed and without Andrew as a suspect, I'm afraid Jackson may end up taking the fall."

"Elle, for God's sake, stop this charade," Stella added, sensing she might be wavering. "My son is being charged with murder. It's his entire life we're talking about."

She and Senior Sergeant Dickson stared at Elle as they waited for her to speak. Stella was more than ready to squeeze the truth out of her with her bare hands if she continued lying, regardless of whether a police officer was in the room, but she hoped Elle would come to her senses without resorting to violence.

"Stella, I am genuinely sorry for the pain I've caused you," Elle began. "Please believe me when I tell you I would do anything to take it all back. I know it was a mistake. All of it."

Stella eyed her cautiously, unsure of where she was going. Clearly, she was not the type of woman you could trust. She had slept with Andrew and lied to the police. Whatever she was going to say next was anyone's guess.

"Are you saying you'll do it?" Senior Sergeant Dickson asked, her entire body leaning in toward Elle. "You'll make a statement that you falsified your alibi?"

Despite Senior Sergeant Dickson's question, Elle continued speaking directly to Stella.

"The truth is, I don't know where Andrew was that night. And you're right, he wasn't here with me, but I don't believe he killed Lauren."

"Of course you don't," Stella scoffed. "You're obviously in love with him. You'd believe whatever he tells you."

"You're right," she nodded, a sad look shadowing her face. "I would. And what he told me was that if he said where he was that night, you and the boys would be in danger."

"Elle, what do you mean by that?" Senior Sergeant Dickson asked. "What kind of danger?"

"I don't know. He wouldn't say any more than that. I just knew that he wouldn't have asked if he wasn't desperate."

Stella took a deep breath and tried to calm the pounding of her heart. Had Andrew been telling the truth, or did he just pull the wool over Elle's eyes to cover his tracks?

"What makes you so sure he was telling the truth?" Senior Sergeant Dickson asked.

Elle closed her eyes and Stella could see she was transporting herself back to that night. "There's no one thing," she said eventually. "It was just the look in his eyes. He was scared, and not for himself, but for you, Stella. You and the boys."

As much as Stella hated to admit it, it was hard not to believe her. And deep down, despite her hatred of Andrew, the idea of him murdering a woman and pulling her body into the ocean was something she still couldn't quite comprehend.

"So, you think he's covering something up?" Senior Sergeant Dickson asked.

"I have no idea. All I know is that he was in over his head, that's for sure."

For a moment, the three women sat in silence, each contemplating their own thoughts. In the end, it was Senior Sergeant Dickson who spoke. "Everything in my gut tells me Andrew did it, but Mrs Ashley, you know him best. What do you think?"

Stella looked from Senior Sergeant Dickson to Elle, and back again. Right now, she hated Andrew with all her heart and wanted him punished for putting them in this mess. But she could see they were at a turning point. She cast her mind back to those cold nights spent in the car, huddled together and shivering. Stella's mother had stuck by her through everything. Sacrificed the clothes off her back to keep her daughter warm. There's nothing a mother won't do for her child, and if trusting Elle Nolan was the risk Stella had to take to save Jackson, then in her heart she knew that's exactly what she was going to do.

Chapter Fifty-Two
ELLE

They were both staring at me. Senior Sergeant Dickson and Andrew's wife. They were desperate. I could see it in their eyes. Stella was frantic at the idea her son might go to jail and Senior Sergeant Dickson knew she was at least partly responsible for Andrew going free. She had allowed me to see him that night. She provided an opportunity for him to convince me that lying to the police was the right thing to do, and maybe it was. But that was before Jackson confessed.

I knew what withdrawing my alibi would mean. At worst, I could be convicted and spend up to two years in jail. At best, it would mean hours of community service, another round of public humiliation, and a debilitating flurry of comments and opinions on social media from strangers who thought they knew me. It would mean potentially putting Andrew back in a cell and knowing he and I would never exchange so much as a civil word ever again. But it also meant doing the right thing. It meant lifting the burden of Stella's fear and Senior Sergeant Dickson's guilt. It also meant giving myself the opportunity to clear my conscience— and maybe start over.

"Elle," Senior Sergeant Dickson began, "I know this is scary and you have my word I'll do everything I can to make sure you are treated with leniency. If you come forward on your own, it will be viewed favourably by police. We can suggest a suspended sentence and a good behaviour bond."

I got up and paced the length of the room. I knew what I had to do, but I was terrified. All the while, Andrew's words in the police lockup kept repeating in my mind—*there's every chance my family might be in danger.* There was also every chance he had been manipulating me, but I just couldn't let go of the feeling he had been telling the truth. What if I admitted to providing a false alibi, only to see Andrew found guilty of a crime he didn't commit?

"What's it going to be, Elle?" Senior Sergeant Dickson asked. "Will you do it?"

I stopped pacing and looked at them. "No, I won't."

Stella was instantly up on her feet and glaring at me. "Like hell you won't!" she shouted. "I don't care if I have to drag you there myself, Elle Nolan, you are going to admit to what you did. My son is not going to jail because of you and my shitrag husband and— "

I held out my hands to try and calm her. "Just wait... I wasn't done. I won't do it until we know for sure what Andrew meant that night in the police lockup. I understand Jackson is in trouble, Stella, believe me I do, but swapping one innocent person sitting in a cell for another is not the answer."

"No, I want my son out. Now," she said, shaking her head. "Andrew made his own mess. Jackson was just being a stupid kid and trying to help. I won't have him spend one minute more in that place than he has to."

I turned my gaze to Senior Sergeant Dickson. "Can we just ask Andrew? See what he says? You're a police officer, you must understand what I'm saying. There's already one innocent person sitting in a cell. Do you really want to be responsible for making it two?"

"Do not listen to this," Stella said, turning to Senior Sergeant Dickson. "At this point, Andrew is incapable of telling the truth. If he said the sky was blue and I was staring right at it, I still wouldn't believe him."

Senior Sergeant Dickson looked thoughtful for a moment, then stood up. "Do we all agree that if police approach Andrew, he may not be forthcoming with the truth?" she asked, looking directly at me.

Stella and I exchanged an awkward glance and nodded.

"Alright then, we do this ourselves, and quickly. In the next twenty-four hours, Jackson will be scheduled to stand before the Magistrates Court for a hearing date. Once that ball starts rolling, it will take moving heaven and earth to stop it."

"How do we do this ourselves?" Stella asked.

"We pool our resources and try to figure out where Andrew was the night Lauren's body was dragged into the water. Elle," she turned and fixed me with an intense gaze, "you're a reporter, you have skills that can help. And Stella, you're his wife. You know him better than anyone and have access to his home computer, his files, everything that might hold the key to figuring this out. If we move quickly, maybe we can find out the truth. All that matters now is making sure the right person is held accountable."

Stella and I looked at each other, longer this time, clearly weighing up our ability to trust each other. We all had good reasons for wanting to the truth. We all had something to lose, and we all had something to gain by knowing where Andrew was that night. Now it seemed the only way we were going to find out was by working together.

"So, how do we do this?" I asked Senior Sergeant Dickson. "I mean, how do we start?"

"How would you start if it was an investigative journalism piece you were writing?" she asked. "What would be your first move?"

I thought for a moment and tried to take my emotions out of it. What if it was just a story, and the stakes didn't involve my potential imprisonment? What would I do first? "I'd find a source, someone who was willing to talk off the record about Andrew's behaviour in the lead up to the event. From there, try to I'd try to find a lead I could follow."

"Perfect," Senior Sergeant Dickson said. "And Stella, you need to comb through all Andrew's private emails, messages, and phone records if you can get them. Police have gone over his files, but there may have been something we missed, something only you know is out of place. Look hard, there may be something that's been there all along."

My mind was already working overtime. Who, other than Stella and I, knew what Andrew's movements and mood were like in the days leading up to Lauren's death? There was only person I could think of. But would she talk to me?

Chapter Fifty-Three
ANDREW

It seemed impossible to Andrew that a single pair of birds, released via video to social media, had caused everyone's world to fall apart. If only he had known what trying to save Stockton from the developers at Ridgemont Capitol would cost, he never would have asked Lauren to find those damned birds. If only she hadn't been so headstrong and just listened. But deep down, he knew it wasn't her fault. It was his. He had risked too much trying to preserve a dream that had been sold to the highest bidder a long time ago. Now everyone around him had paid the price.

Yesterday Levi made the decision to go and stay with friends. Andrew assumed it was because the idea of being anywhere near him made life feel unbearable. Stella had taken off somewhere in his car, but not before demanding a divorce.

So, not knowing what else to do, he wandered around the home he had once been so proud to provide for his family, that had once been alive with laughter, and cursed the quiet.

He had cheated on his wife. That much was true, but he did not hurt Lauren.

The very idea that anyone thought he could kill her, when in truth he may have loved her, was a crippling weight. And to think his actions caused Jackson to risk his entire future stole the air from Andrew's lungs. What kind of father, what kind of man, had he become when those he loved most thought him so capable of murder they would go to such lengths?

Andrew knew in his heart what had happened to Lauren. Those Ridgemont Capitol thugs who dared to call themselves businessmen killed her.

They warned him many times to leave it alone, to stand down, and stop trying to impede their plans. They had threatened his family and made it clear in no uncertain terms they would stop at nothing to make sure their plans went ahead. They had instructed Tony to pull her off the project, but he was the one who asked her to continue.

He wandered out of the bedroom and along the empty hall, thinking back to the dead bird. While heartbreaking for Lauren to see, it had obviously represented more than the pending annihilation of the Gemini Birds and their habitat. The bird with the broken neck had represented her if she didn't stop her investigation.

If only she had listened.

Chapter Fifty-Four
LUCY

Lucy was so engrossed in combing through the printouts of Andrew Ashley's email records that she didn't hear Yieldon approach her desk.

"What is that? Andrew Ashley's email account?" he asked, leaning over to get a better view.

"Oh, I didn't see you there," she said, closing over the folder. "What's up?"

"Dicks, why are you going through Andrew's file again?"

"Just being thorough," she replied.

He let out a huff and shook his head. "Come with me."

He didn't wait for her to agree. Instead, he stalked off toward the interview room, expecting her to follow. When they got inside, he closed the door and turned to her. "I gave you a direct order to drop this line of enquiry," he barked. "Why are you still pursuing it?"

"Because I think he's guilty and I'm not okay with Jackson taking the wrap for it. He's a good kid. This will destroy his life."

Yieldon folded his arms squarely across his chest and stared down at her. "What is it with you? First the Marshall kid, now this one. You're putting yourself in harm's way, Dicks. Why?"

Lucy took a step back. "What's that supposed to mean?"

"It means I know you planted evidence at the Marshall house and now you're going out of your way to get Jackson Ashley off the hook. The first one I can understand. She was a cute kid. You lost your sister young. I get it. This one has me curious though, so tell me something. If I go through the CCTV of Andrew Ashley's cell, am I going to see you letting Elle Nolan in to speak with him?"

The answer was no. She'd already made sure the video for that night had been erased. "No, you won't."

"But you did do it. You let her in to see him. Now you feel responsible for Jackson taking his place. That it?"

Lucy looked away and silently screamed at herself not to cry. He had her and they both knew it.

"Dicks, you're a good cop, but you're digging yourself a hole here. I've had your back on the Marshall enquiry, but you've gone so far down the rabbit hole now I wouldn't be able to drag you out if I tried. There's only so much I can do."

"No, you can admit Jackson shouldn't be here," she dared. "Help me, Chris. Help me prove Andrew is the one we want. If we can prove he wasn't with Elle that night, which she might be willing to admit, we can put the right person away. That's the job. Getting justice, not closing cases to appease the brass upstairs."

"You're walking on thin ice, Dicks," he warned.

"Help me, Chris, please. I just want to do what's right."

"What's right is doing things by the book. Not going rogue and planting evidence or letting reporters into our lock up in the middle of the night. Christ, Dicks, do I have to spell it out for you? You've broken the law. Do you even get that?"

"Of course I *get that*," she hissed. "But what was I supposed to do? Let a drunken meth head keep beating his daughter to within an inch of her life? Have Elle Nolan report that I planted drugs on scene because I wouldn't let her see Andrew? How was I supposed to know he'd ask her to give a false alibi or that she'd actually be stupid enough to do it?"

"Nolan knows about the plant?"

"She suspects. The dealer I used was a source of hers when she was on the crime round."

"Jesus..." he breathed. "You've really put yourself in it, Dicks."

"You think I don't know that?" Lucy sighed, suddenly feeling like she hadn't slept in a year.

"After the Marshall case, you were a much better cop. Less emotional and by the book to a fault. That's why I let it slide. But now..."

She shifted her weight nervously from one foot to the other and back again. "But now what?"

He took a deep breath. "I think it would be best if you took a step back. Take some leave. Let this one go."

"Let it go?"

"Just for a bit, Dicks. Spend some time with your girls and James."

Lucy was speechless. Right when it mattered most, he wanted me to let it go? "Sir—"

"It's not a request, Dicks. Go home. I'll be in touch." He turned toward the door and then stopped. "Oh, and Dicks...?"

She looked up, hoping he would say it was only for the week.

"Leave your gun and badge. It's not official," he added before she had time to object. "Just as a favour to me. I know you're close to this one, so it might be hard to let it go. Just do us both a favour and leave them in the lockup."

It was clearly not up for discussion. Lucy was off the case and there was nothing she could do about it. When she got home just after eleven in the morning, James couldn't hide his surprise.

"Lucy, what's going on?" he asked, stirring something in the slow cooker.

"That's a good question with an answer you will not like," she sighed, emphasising the word *not*. "I don't even know where to start."

He replaced the glass lid and wiped his hands on a tea towel. "Cup of tea?"

"Please," she smiled. "That would be great."

James busied himself making a pot of tea and as she watched him, Lucy wondered what she had been doing all this time. Why had she been shutting him out? Being a good cop wasn't about turning off her emotions. It was about controlling them, using them to make good decisions. She had overstepped with the Marshall case, that was a given, and looking back, there were other avenues she should have tried. Convincing Sarah Marshall to seek support in moving to a new location, finding her work, getting her therapy. Anything that would have helped them start over without risking her career and putting herself in a position of weakness. Losing control had left her open, exposed, and people like Elle, who were out of options, had taken advantage.

"James, I messed up," she sighed. "Like, really messed up."

He put the steaming mug down in front of her and sat down. "I'm listening."

As Lucy told her husband what she had done, he nodded and listened. It was impossible to miss the clench of his jaw when she spoke about planting evidence, and she worried what he would say once she was done. Would he understand, or would their marriage be over?

But she needn't have worried.

"Luce, I wish you would have trusted me with this sooner," he said with a sigh. "All this time, I thought the problem was that you just didn't love me anymore. You've been alone in this when I could have helped or at least tried talking you out of doing something so stupid."

She nodded and knew from the softness in his tone that he wasn't saying it to start a fight. "I know. I just thought if I pushed my emotions all the way down, put a wall up, I wouldn't make the same mistake again. Trouble was, it stopped me from being a wife to you and a mother to the girls. I'm so ashamed."

Lucy's voice broke, and he pulled her in. After nine months of stopping herself from feeling anything, she finally let her emotions out. She sobbed for what she had put her family through, for what Minty and her mother had experienced, and for Lauren Ellis' family, who were still being denied the opportunity to hold someone accountable for her death. "I'm sorry," she cried, her head buried in James' shoulder. "I don't know what I was thinking."

James stroked her hair and held her close, and when the tears finally subsided, he pulled back and looked at her gently. "I do," he said. "You were trying to honour your sister, and you know what Luce? You never have to apologise for that. Not to me. Not ever."

Chapter Fifty-Five

LAUREN

I *hadn't heard from Andrew in two days, and I was worried. A group of powerful and affluent people had threatened his family, and now I was in their sights as well. But I also needed to go back to the Stockton Centre and collect two motion-activated cameras I had left camouflaged in the brush.*

I dressed and tried calling Andrew, hoping he could get the equipment for me, or at least accompany me onto the site. When he didn't pick up, I felt the familiar stir of anxiety twist in my stomach. Had this project stayed on the books, it would have been council-owned equipment, but since we'd gone rogue, it was my own gear and I needed it back.

Reluctantly, I climbed into the car and made my way over to Stockton. When I pulled up at the site, I got out my phone and tried one last time to call Andrew. Finally, he answered.

"Lauren, are you alright?"

"Andrew," I breathed. "I was worried. I haven't heard from you since you came over."

"I know, I'm sorry," he said. "But I asked you not to call this number. It's not safe."

I glanced down and realised I had called his personal phone by accident. "Shit, sorry."

"We should talk offline," he said. "Are you home?"

"No," I said, then paused. "I actually just pulled up at the Stockton site."

"Jesus, Lauren, do you have a death wish? What were you thinking going back there?"

"Some of my equipment is still here. I'll grab it and get out as fast as I can," I told him, secretly hoping he'd volunteer to come with me.

"Stay where you are," he instructed. "I'll be there in five minutes."

Andrew was already shaking his head as he got out and made his way around the car. "I can't believe you came over here," he said. "We have to be quick. Being onsite is a really bad idea."

I embraced him quickly, then awkwardly stepped back and wished I hadn't. We were out in public and despite our feelings for each other, Andrew had already made it clear he wasn't ready to pursue them.

"It's cold," I said, rubbing at my bare arms as we headed toward the site. "That wind has really picked up."

"Hold on." Andrew jogged back to his car and quickly pulled a council windbreaker out from the backseat. "Here, wear this. It's got a tear on the collar, but it will keep you warm."

I thanked him and put it on, then we headed toward the back of the property, where I left my equipment.

As we walked, I sneaked a sideways glance at him. He looked tired, and I wished there was something I could do to help him. "Did you have a chance to speak to them?" I asked. "The thugs from Ridgemont, I mean."

He nodded stiffly, his gaze focused out in front. "They're not happy."

"What does that mean?"

"It means if council doesn't approve the application..."

He trailed off and I could see the stress weighing heavy on his brow. "I'm sorry, Andrew," I said. "It was rash of me to release that video. I deleted it from social media, obviously, but if the birds are still there, I'm not sure there's any way around it. The watchers will come. I'm surprised they're not here already."

"This is private property," Andrew said, looking over his shoulder. "There'll be surveillance put in any day now, maybe even security guards. No one will be coming onsite."

"It's not just that. This is an environmental issue," I said. "They can't just doze a site that's home to an endangered species."

"They can if there's no sign of the birds."

I stopped walking and looked at him. "What are you suggesting?"

"It's just the one pair, right? Can you move them?"

"Move them?"

"Can you trap and move them? Even if it's back to where you said, the south coast, or wherever it is they come from. Once the development is underway, they won't come back"

"Andrew—"

"This is our lives we're talking about, Lauren. They're just birds."

"They're not just birds, Andrew," I told him. "And besides, what happened to saving Stockton?"

"Lauren, they had a gun to my head.Christ, what am I supposed to do?"

"Fight," I told him. "Fight for what you believe in. I know they threatened us and your family, but go public. Tell the world what they did. I have proof the birds are here. Get these men on record making their threats and then we go to the police and the media—together." I reached out and touched his shoulder. "You're not in this all by yourself, Andrew. I'm right here with you and I'll be damned if I'm going to let a bunch of rich thugs intimate me. If this is what you believe is right, then you have to take a risk. You have to show them they can't tell you what to do. That no one can."

He rubbed at his neck and stared out toward the ocean.

"We can do this, Andrew," I told him. "Together, we can."

Eventually, he turned to face me. "You really think so?"

"Andrew, this place..." I held my arms open and looked at him, "it means everything to you. It's your home. Sometimes you need to be willing to risk it all for the thing you love most."

He held my gaze, and I knew he was also considering what he was willing to risk to be with me.

The wind pulled at my hair as he stepped forward. "I had no idea how empty my life was until I met you, Lauren," he whispered.

"I feel the same way," I told him. "I know you have a whole other life, but, Andrew, you're all I think about."

He nodded quickly, feverishly, his eyes locked on mine. Then, without another word, he stepped in and pressed his lips hard against mine. He pulled me closer, his hands shaking just a little as they tangled in my hair. There was something raw in the way he kissed me—desperate, almost frantic, like he was afraid to let go. It wasn't just a kiss, it was a plea, a question. I felt his heartbeat against my chest, and I had the sudden, inexplicable urge to cry because this was more than passion, more than heat. It was fear. It was hope. It was the kind of kiss that says everything you're too afraid to speak out loud.

"I can't do this anymore," he said when we finally stepped back. "I don't know what will happen or how this is going to work. God knows I'm already in over my head, but I need you."

My heart was racing. When this started, it had just been for fun. I thought he was a handsome guy who seemed like a challenge. What I hadn't anticipated was the chance I might fall in love with him.

"Let's go for a walk," he smiled, nodding toward the dunes. "I think it's just the escape we need."

Chapter Fifty-Six
STELLA

The idea of working with Elle Nolan made Stella's blood boil. Regardless of why she lied, Jackson was in police lockup, and as far as Stella was concerned, Andrew and Elle were the ones to blame. So if finding out where he really was that night was the only way to make Elle tell the truth, then that's what she was going to do.

When Stella pulled into the garage, her SUV was gone. She had taken Andrew's Mercedes out of spite, so he had no choice but to use her car. She had no idea where he was or how long he'd be out, so she made a beeline straight to his office. It was time to uncover the last of her husband's secrets.

Andrew didn't have any locked drawers or secret filing cabinets. The whole time they had been married, both she and Andrew enjoyed a healthy respect for each other's privacy, mostly because she never had reason to question him. *Little did she know.*

Stella started with his laptop. The password was *Stella1994*. Her name and the year they were married. It was things like that. All the little things that had provided such a false sense of security over the years. To think Andrew had cheated with two women and possibly loved one or both of them was something it would take her a long time to come to terms with.

She searched through his folders, word docs, and photos, but there was nothing out of the ordinary. Most of the files were work-related or pictures of them taken with the kids. Their most recent family trip to Hawaii, a driving holiday along the east coast of Australia in 2018. For a moment, she let herself get lost in the memories. Scanning through photo after photo of happy faces and sun-kissed skin, Stella never could have known he craved the affection of another. She reminded herself the images were taken before the affairs, at least the ones she knew of, but everything was tainted now. Every memory, every moment, every word, was stained. So many times, over the years, she had let out a long breath, safe in the knowledge that even though their marriage wasn't perfect, it was built on trust and respect—and was forever. But it had all been a lie.

Unable to look at the images any longer, Stella closed the laptop and moved to his desk drawers. Not knowing how long it would be until he returned home, she quickly rummaged through papers and pens and old council reports, but again, there was nothing that told her where he had been that night or why. She spun around in the old leather desk chair and pulled herself over to the steel grey filing cabinet. She searched one drawer at a time, but again, there was nothing—until she got to the bottom drawer. Inside was a metal lockbox about the size of a shoe box. It had a dial that required a six-digit code to open it.

Stella got down onto the floor and sat cross-legged with the box in her lap. "What would you make the code?" she whispered, staring at the box. "Jackson is too long, and Levi is too short. She tried her own name, but without success. *How about a birthday?* She wondered.

She tried the six digits of her birthday, and then Andrew's, and then the boys, but none of the combinations worked. She considered whether he might have used Elle with some kind a numerical sequence after, but she would never be able to guess what it would be. And then it hit her. She knew what the code was.

L.A.U.R.E.N

The case popped open, and Stella's stomach turned. But her anger was quickly replaced with fear when she saw what was inside. She slid the gun out of its slip bag and held it across her palm. It was heavier than she expected and cold to the touch.

"Stella!" Andrew shouted from behind her. "What are you doing? Put that down. Now."

She immediately got to her feet and glared at him, her gaze a mix of fear and anger. "What the hell, Andrew? Why is there a gun in our house?"

"Stella," he began, his voice calm and even compared to the shrill tone of her question. "Put the gun down. I can explain. But I need you to put it down."

She nodded as a single tear escaped and ran over her cheek. "You did it, didn't you? You killed her."

"Stella, no, I didn't. Now please, give me the gun."

"Then where were you?" she demanded. "Tell me where you were, or I swear to God..."

Andrew took a slow, purposeful breath, clearly trying to calm himself. "Stella, please. We can talk, but not like this."

Visions of her son sitting hunched over in a cold police cell filled Stella's mind. She imagined Andrew naked, entangled with Lauren, then Elle, and wanted to be sick. Her stomach lurched as she swallowed a pool of bile gathering in the back of her throat. "Fuck you, Andrew," she said, her voice breaking. "You ruined us."

"Stella—"

Before he could finish whatever he was going to say, Stella lifted the gun and pointed it at him. "Tell me the truth! Did you kill her?"

"Jesus Christ, Stella," he gasped, stumbling back.

"Tell me!"

"No!" he told her, his voice firm. "I didn't kill Lauren."

"Then where were you? Just fucking tell me! I deserve that much."

"You don't understand," he said, slowly taking one step back toward Stella, his arms stretched out in surrender. "I'm not trying to hide it from you. I'm trying to protect you. All of you."

Stella thought back to what Elle had told them. "Protect us from what?"

He stared at her for a moment. "From ending up like Lauren."

"For all I know, *you* killed Lauren," she spat. "I don't believe you."

"Just give me the gun, Stella, please."

"Why do you even have a gun?"

"I told you. For protection. When I was released, I got it. Just in case."

Stella shook her head, trying to make sense of what Andrew was saying, but her mind was spinning. He wasn't going to tell her where he was. That much was clear. There was only one more thing she could do.

"You're doing all this to protect us?" she spat. "That's what you're saying?"

"Yes. Everything I've done has been for you, for our family. I know I fucked up, Stella, but you have to believe me."

"You care about me that much?"

"Of course. You're my wife."

Stella steeled herself, swallowed hard, then lifted the gun to her temple. The chill of the muzzle stung her skin, and she caught her breath.

"Fuck, Stella," Andrew gasped, his hands flying up to his face. "No!"

"Then tell me the truth or I swear to God I'm ending this right now. I can't take anymore. You've broken my heart and humiliated us. I can't take one more day of this. I need to know who you really are, and if you don't tell me where you were and what happened, I'm pulling this trigger." Her hand trembled as she held the gun to her head. It was do or die.

"Stella, please, stop," he begged, tears streaming over his cheeks. "I'll tell you, okay? I'll tell you. Just please, put it down."

"No. You tell me now."

"Okay, alright," he said. "I was at a meeting that night. The Ridgemont Capitol developers, they're not just into property, Stella, they're part of a Sydney crime syndicate. Lauren had proof that some endangered birds called Gemini Birds were present at the Stockton Centre site and we were trying to use that to stop the development application."

Stella watched him closely as he explained, searching for any sign that he was lying.

"They were threatening us, all of us, including you and the boys. I went to a meeting that night to try and get them on record. I thought if I could record them, Lauren and I could take that and the evidence of the birds to media and the police and we'd be safe if everyone knew what was going on. But Stella, I fucked up. They figured out I was trying to record them. They beat me and cracked my rib. They said if I needed more persuading, it wouldn't be a problem. A day later, they found Lauren."

His voice trembled, and tears coursed down his cheeks. For the first time, Stella saw just how scared he really was. She slowly lowered the gun and let it fall to her side.

"Stella, they killed her. They killed her because of me. I thought if I told anyone what happened that night, they'd come for you and the boys. It already looked like I was the one who killed Lauren. It wouldn't be a stretch to think I'd gone nuts and done something to all of you as well. I couldn't let that happen."

He bent over, his elbows on his knees and his head in his hands. He sobbed openly, his body shaking, and Stella didn't know what to do. She believed him, but what he had done to their family, the lies, the cheating, the danger he put them all in. She was frozen to the spot. They couldn't go back, but how would she ever move forward?

"Goddamnyou, Andrew," she said eventually, her voice quiet. "You always loved this city more than anything else. More than me, more than your family—even more than her. You risked everything for something that couldn't love you back, and look what it got you."

Andrew didn't answer and when Stella's phone buzzed in her pocket, she didn't know if she had the mental strength to answer it. Putting the gun to her head, albeit just to make Andrew tell the truth, had shaken her beyond words. But knowing it could be about Jackson, she pulled the phone out and looked at the screen. It was Senior Sergeant Dickson.

"Hello?" she managed, her voice still shaking.

"It's Lucy. We need to talk. Elle and I have been working on—"

"He didn't do it," she cut in. "I know who did, but I don't think we can ever prove it."

Chapter Fifty-Seven
ELLE

Trying to get information out of Andrew's executive assistant, Jackie had been a bust. In less than five minutes, I realised she was painfully loyal to Andrew, and in less than ten, I'd been be forcibly removed from City Hall.

Now I was back home, sitting cross-legged on the floor. Around me, the entire living room floor was covered in papers, reports, and file photos that Lucy had swiped from the station after being told to stand down.

"Want any snacks?" Senior Sergeant Dickson, or Lucy as she said to call her now that she was officially off duty, was making coffee in my kitchen. When Stella left to go and look through Andrew's things, Lucy stayed and together, we had begun constructing a map of what we knew so far.

I lifted my head from the jigsaw of files and reports and suddenly realised I couldn't remember the last time I thought about food. Usually, this level of stress would incite a binge like no other, but I was so focused on figuring out Andrew's secret that it had totally consumed my mind. "No. I'm good thanks," I called back, a tinge of pride in my voice.

Lucy returned and handed me a mug of coffee. "What do we know so far?"

I sighed and surveyed the sea of papers and reports surrounding me. What we knew was that Andrew wasn't with me the night in question. We also knew, as much as it pained me, that he had some form of relationship with Lauren. We knew Jackson wasn't guilty and that for all the police's searches and questions, there had been no solid proof or motive for Andrew to kill Lauren—other than a romantic relationship gone wrong. But even then, all we had was phone calls and texts. Nothing that really stood out. "Nothing new," I told her. "We need more time. How long do we have before they realise you took these files?"

"Probably not long." She considered the papers spread out across the floor and shrugged. "My career is pretty much over. I didn't have time to make copies, so if the last thing I do as a cop is make sure Jackson goes free, then it's worth it."

"Because of the Marshall case?" I asked.

She looked at me and nodded slowly.

"For what it's worth, I get it," I told her. "Coban was an arsehole. He deserved what he got, regardless of how it came about. You shouldn't beat yourself up about what you did."

"It was the wrong thing to do," she admitted. "There was a flow on effect that reached into my home life, my career, this case—everything. I got too close, and it changed who I was. I should never have let that happen."

"Will you go back? To being a cop, I mean?"

"If I have the chance to," she said. "But if saving Jackson Ashley from spending his life in prison for something he didn't do means losing my career, then so be it. That's what matters most."

The weight of what I had done to Lucy by threatening to go public suddenly wrapped itself around me. At the time, all I cared about was seeing Andrew. I hadn't given any thought to how it would affect her—only how it would help me. "I'm sorry for the situation I put you in," I told her. "Andrew was the first person, the first man, who had ever made me feel *seen*. I thought I was in love with him and maybe I was... God... maybe I still am, but I shouldn't have put you in that situation. I really am sorry, Lucy."

She forced a half-hearted smile. "What's done is done, Elle. What matters now is getting this right and if Stella really does know who killed Lauren and where Andrew was that night, then maybe we can finally put this thing to bed."

I took a sip of coffee and prayed she was right. I was exhausted—emotionally and physically.

"You okay?" she asked.

"Yeah, just worn out, I think. This has been a lot."

"You have someone you can go to?" she asked.

I thought of Dr Simms. She had been a huge help, but this was not something I could talk to her about. Then my mind went to David. He knew what I had done, and even though he was disappointed and angry, he would still be there for me. As I thought of him, it struck me how reassuring it would be to feel his embrace.

"Looks like a yes," she smiled.

"You know him, actually. David Hammond from the SES. He's just a friend, but I enjoy his company."

"Of course," she smiled. "You should reach out when we're done here. Let him comfort you."

When Stella eventually returned, it was the first time I had ever seen her looking anything less than immaculate.

"He didn't do it," was the first thing she said as she burst into the room.

Lucy and I both got to our feet and stared at her, waiting for more information.

"But we're screwed," she continued. "I don't know how we're ever going to bring my son home."

Lucy and I listened as she relayed everything that happened with Andrew. I passed her some kitchen paper to use as a tissue when she broke down, telling us how she had held a gun to her own head, trying desperately to make him tell her the truth.

"He planned to record them threatening him and then he and Lauren were going to take the recording and evidence of the birds to the police and the media." She looked at me. "To both of you, I suppose."

"Wait... he said Lauren found endangered birds?" I asked. "Did he say what kind of birds?"

"Why? Does that matter?"

"It might," I said, thinking back. "Did he say what species they were?"

Stella looked thoughtful and rubbed at the back of her neck. "Oh, yes, Gemini Birds, like the star sign."

My pulse was racing. I had heard about the Gemini Birds before, back when I was filling in for Willamina on the crime round. They were the same birds Isabelle Summer's mother told me she had been looking for right before she went missing.

Chapter Fifty-Eight
LAUREN

I wanted to hold on to that blissful warmth, the kind that lingers in your bones after making love, but the second I walked through my front door, the spell was broken.

There was an Instagram message alert from the kid who approached me in the dunes a couple of weeks back. At the time, I hadn't realized who he was. I should have known—his face was all over Andrew's social media. But in the dunes and out of context, I just hadn't connected the dots. He was Jackson Ashley. Andrew's son.

While Andrew and I had thought we were tucked away in our private world, Jackson had been out on a walk and seen us together. Now, he was flooding my inbox with rage-filled messages, calling me all kinds of names and threatening me.

When I first read them, my instinct was to fix it. To somehow keep him from spilling the truth to Stella. I didn't want to be the reason Andrew's world imploded. I thought maybe I could talk to Jackson, reason with him. Tell him it was all a misunderstanding, that I had no intention of tearing his family apart. But when I got there, it was obvious he was too hurt and too angry, and I left feeling ashamed for what I had done, especially given there was already so much at stake.

Not knowing what else to do, I came home, made a coffee, and sat by the window watching the magpies in the yard. Maybe they would steady my nerves. But my mind kept spinning. Jackson could tell Stella everything—if he hadn't already—and the fallout would be catastrophic. I was imagining the look on Stella's face, when my phone buzzed beside me.

"I'm outside. We need to talk."

It wasn't Andrew. That was the thing about flings, I thought as I sighed out loud. Sometimes it was hard to make them go away.

I text that would be out in five and then tipped the rest of my coffee down the sink. Could this day possibly get any worse? I wondered as I closed the door behind me. Why couldn't anything just go the way it was supposed to?

When I got out to his car, I climbed inside and got right to the point. "I shouldn't have come over the other day and I'm sorry for that," I began. "I was upset and didn't think it through. But I need you to understand this thing between us needs to be over."

"Because of him?" he asked. He was staring straight ahead, his fingers drumming on the steering wheel.

"Because of who?"

"Andrew fucking Ashley."

Hearing him say Andrew's name sent a spasm of shock through my body. How could he possibly know unless... "Have you been following me?"

"Wouldn't matter if you didn't have anything to hide."

"That's not the point," I gasped. "I'm going back inside. Please don't contact me again."

But as I moved to open the latch, he planted his foot on the accelerator, throwing me back against the seat.

"What the hell are you doing?" I shouted as the car tore down my narrow street, leaves and debris flying out from each side. "Stop! Now! I want to get out."

But he didn't answer and stared intently at the road ahead, his fingers still drumming against the wheel.

"Did you hear me, David?" I shouted again. "Stop the car and let me out!"

Chapter Fifty-Nine
LUCY

Lucy and Stella were both staring at Elle.

"Wait, let me get this straight," Lucy said. "Isabelle Summers, who went missing three months ago, was also looking for these particular birds?"

"Yes," Elle said, excitement crackling in her voice. "When I interviewed her mother, Marianne, she told me that Isabelle was an avid birdwatcher, and that she had taken trips all over the country looking for different species. She said in the days leading up to her disappearance, her daughter had been excited because she read online there had been sightings of these rare Gemini Birds further north than they would normally be around coastal bushland. Apparently, she thought land clearing had caused them to relocate north, and that's why she was going to Glenrock Reserve that day—to see if she could sight any."

"And she never came back," Lucy finished.

She thought back to their investigation. There had been emails between Isabelle and others about birds and bird watching, but they had all been dead ends.

"Didn't Marianne tell you that when you interviewed her?" Elle asked.

"She mentioned the bird watching, and that Isabelle had gone to Glenrock for that purpose, but nothing specific about the species. When we followed up leads with the people she chatted to online, there was nothing in it. There were no direct contacts who seemed to have accompanied her that day, so we let that line of questioning go. We figured she met with foul play, pardon the pun, once she was out in the Glenrock Conservation Area."

"It can't be a coincidence, can it?" Elle asked, her journalistic instinct clearly on high alert.

"Doesn't feel like it. Let's go back and talk to the mother again. See if there's anything else she can tell us."

But Elle glanced at her watch and winced. "I can't," she said, shooting a guilty look in Stella's direction. "There's something I have to do. Just for a few hours. But you two go and let me know what she says."

When they arrived outside the home of Isabelle Summers', Lucy turned off the engine and stared out the window. It was a small weatherboard house in the back streets of Whitebridge, not far from where Isabelle had gone missing. Pretty stained-glass windows peeked out from under green shutters and there was a garden that looked like it had once been well tendered to.

Officially, Lucy wasn't there as a police officer, but if she was up front about that, there would be questions that might prove difficult to answer.

"How are you going to play this?" Stella asked as though reading her mind.

"The only way I can," Lucy told her. "By ear."

"Marianne," Lucy said, when Isabelle's mother opened the door.

"Senior Sergeant Dickson." The woman smiled warmly and looked her up and down. "Plain clothes. You must have made detective."

Lucy smiled tightly and side-stepped the comment. "Mrs Summers, this is Stella Ashley. We were—"

"My goodness, Mrs Ashley," she breathed, clasping her hands at her chest. "What a turmoil you've been through."

Marianne Summers was a portly woman who looked like she enjoyed a decent bowl of pasta. She had warm eyes and a round face that reminded Lucy of a warm apple pie. She had made it clear the last time Lucy was there that faith was keeping her positive.

"Marianne, I'm sorry that I don't have any updates on Isabelle, but I was hoping to ask you a couple of further questions, if you don't mind?" Lucy said.

Marianne glanced at Stella once more and then stepped aside, indicating they could go in.

"I know it must seem odd that I'm here," Stella offered once they were inside. "My husband was working with a woman from council on a project about some birds and we just thought—"

Lucy shot Stella a look that was strong enough to stop her mid-sentence. "Marianne," she smiled, starting over. "How are you doing? I know the past few months must have been hard on you."

"I have my faith," she replied, clutching at a crucifix hanging from a chain around her neck. "I have to believe Issy will come home."

Lucy forced a smile and glanced around the room. Despite her bright outlook, Marianne's home was dark. The blinds were drawn and there were unwashed dishes piled up in the sink. Even though Isabelle was twenty-four years old, she had still lived at home and was Marianne's only child. Her absence meant Marianne had been left with no one.

"Have you spoken with someone?" Lucy asked. "It would be helpful for you to have some support."

Marianne let out a breath, the first indication the situation was wearing on her. "I have the congregation at church, and Pastor Adams. He's a Godsend you know."

"Marianne, I'm sorry to intrude on you like this, but I was hoping you could tell us a little more about the birds Isabelle went looking for that day. The Gemini Birds."

She stared out into space, her head tilted slightly back as she thought. "She was so excited about those birds. Apparently, they'd never been seen up here before."

"And had she been talking to anyone else about them? Maybe someone who could have met up with her that day?"

"No, not that I knew of."

Lucy took out her notepad in the hope she would give them something of use. "Did she ever mention anything about the old Stockton Centre site. Maybe about going there?"

"No, not that I can remember."

"And what about a development company called Ridgemont Capitol? Did she know anyone who worked there?"

Again, Marianne shook her head and Lucy's hopes began to fade. They weren't getting anywhere.

Beside her, Stella straightened and leaned in. "Did she ever mention my husband, Andrew Ashley?"

Lucy glared at Stella and wished more than anything she hadn't brought her along.

"Actually, it's funny you should mention that," Marianne said, and Lucy's heart skipped a beat. "The night before she went missing, Issy waitressed at a function he was going to be at. Something at the Newcastle Club."

Lucy inched forward to the edge of the couch. "You didn't mention that when we interviewed you before."

"I'm sure I did," she nodded. "I said she was working at a function that night."

Lucy searched her mind, trying to recall the interview notes. If Andrew Ashley's name had been there, she would have remembered.

"So, she met him?" Stella asked.

"No, he didn't show," Marianne replied. "Issy came home very disappointed. She always liked him."

"Yes, he's very popular," Stella managed through tight lips.

Lucy got to her feet, and beside her, Stella did the same. "I'm sorry to take up your time, Mrs Summers. We'll keep looking for Isabelle. You have my word."

"There was something else..." Marianne said, pulling herself up from the old couch. "About a month ago, I found a piece of paper with a number written on it in the pocket of the pants she wore to work that night. I never washed them, you see. Couldn't bring myself to. I called it, but he said it was the wrong number. Said he'd never even heard of Issy."

Lucy swallowed hard and tried not to react. "Mrs Summers, why didn't you call us?"

"Like I said, I called the number, and he was very polite. He explained he'd just got a new number, you see, and had been receiving a lot of calls from people looking for the previous owner. I thought it was nothing."

When she turned to go and fetch the piece of paper, Lucy and Stella quickly exchanged glances.

"I'm glad you kept it," Lucy said, when Marianne returned and handed her a scrap of paper she immediately recognised as part of a coaster from the Newcastle Club.

"It might have been one of the last things Issy held, other than the things in her room. I couldn't bear to throw it away."

"Well, thank you. You've been very helpful," Lucy said, as they made their way toward the front door. "NSW Police and our local department will continue to do all we can to find your daughter."

The moment Lucy got back into the car, she took out her phone to call the number Marianne had given them. Beside her, Stella leaned in close, peering over her shoulder. She quickly punched in the number, but as Lucy stared at the screen, her stomach somersaulted. She didn't need to make the call to see who would answer. He was already there, saved in her contacts: **David Hammond – SES.**

Chapter Sixty
ANDREW

Seeing Stella hold a gun to her head tore Andrew's soul in two. Knowing he had pushed her to that point, that he created a situation where she would even contemplate taking her own life was a crushing blow.

Outside their house, the media had finally started to disseminate. There were one or two straggler reporters and a couple of news crews, but nothing like before.

He grabbed his car keys and shuffled out to the garage. There was nothing he could do to help his son. No way to prove his innocence without putting Levi and Stella's lives at risk. Andrew knew his wife would never leave her mother, so moving away was out of the question. Without Lauren's bravado, he didn't have the energy or the courage to try and take down the Ridgemont cartel on his own. All he could see ahead was a bitter divorce, the kind that leaves scars you carry forever, and a lifetime of resentment from his sons—one of whom might spend the next twenty years behind bars. The thought of it was like a punch to the gut.

Andrew started the car and eased it into reverse, the tires crunching softly over the gravel. He pulled out slowly, cruising down the road that curved along the beach, the scent of saltwater lingering in the air. The route took him up and over Stockton Bridge, the city skyline coming into view. God, he loved this place. The thought of losing it—of losing everything—was too much to bear.

Not so long ago, Andrew had considered himself responsible for its welfare. Like a third child, he had done his best to nurture its growth and keep it safe from those who didn't have its best interests at heart. When wild weather and king tides eroded its shores, he made sure they had strategies in place to protect the coastline. When fires licked the border, as a volunteer firefighter, he joined the ranks to help push back the flames. He tended to its culture and art and made sure it had a soundtrack to be proud of. He tried to stop development that endangered its soul and fought hard to ensure anyone intent on participating in anti-social behaviour or crime was sufficiently punished. But overtime, it had been stolen from him piece by piece by people who did not share such love or affection for the place he called home.

Andrew swallowed down his tears. Jackson was facing murder charges. Levi had left, and the city had fallen into the hands of strangers. All his children were gone.

He took the long way around, driving up through Merewether past the Beach Hotel and the iconic ocean baths. Out to his right, the sea was sprinkled with surfers, while walkers powered their way along the coastal stretch, some with friends, others with dogs, and some alone, but all enjoying the sunshine.

He travelled past the sprawling King Edward Park with its pretty lace rotunda, down past Newcastle Beach, then to the lighthouse that stood at the end of Nobby's break wall. Out on the harbour, a coal ship was navigating its way into the port, four green and yellow tugboats providing safe passage. It was a sight so unique to Newcastle that, despite his despair, Andrew found himself smiling.

When he finally reached City Hall, Andrew pulled the car to a stop and turned off the engine. The silence that followed felt heavy, almost suffocating. He let out a slow breath, sinking back against the leather seat, and staring up at the building's façade. It was strange, really. He had achieved so much, but somehow lost so much more.

Who would step into his shoes now? He wondered. There were plenty of councillors champing at the bit, eager to slip into the role and soak up the spotlight. But would they fight for the city the way he had? Would they protect it, nurture it? For Andrew, being Lord Mayor had never been about the title or the power—it was a guardianship, and he worried about what the city would become under someone else's leadership.

Eventually, he turned the key and brought the engine back to life. He took one last, lingering look at the office window where he'd spent countless nights working long after the lights of the city had dimmed. And then, pulled away from the curb, and headed toward home. He had fought the good fight. He had given everything he had to give. But it was over.

When Andrew pulled into the garage, he was relieved to see that Stella was still out. He hadn't expected her to come back. She had probably booked herself a suit at the Novotel or Crowne Plaza, at least for tonight.

He pressed the button on the garage door remote, and watched in the rear-view mirror as it swallowed up the last sliver of daylight. The quiet click of the door sealing shut felt like a final breath as Andrew's fingers gripped the gearshift and he slipped the car into park. He carefully placed the remote down on the center console, as if it mattered where it landed and closed his eyes. The engine continued its low hum, a steady thrum that filled the silence, and he tried to imagine her.

Around the car, exhaust fumes thickened, slowly filling the garage, but Andrew paid no mind. He thought back to the bright yellow skirt Majorie had been wearing the day she picked him up in Sydney. He pictured her face and swore he could see her walking toward him. A single tear slipped over his cheek as he felt the warmth of her fingers close around his. She had come. She was there to take him home. He would be alright.

He let out a long breath and moved in closer to Majorie. The yellow fabric brushed his cheek, and he gazed up at her.

"You're here," he whispered. "I missed you."

And then everything faded to black.

Chapter Sixty-One
LAUREN

*W*hen they arrived at the Stockton Centre site, David finally pulled over and turned off the car.

"What the actual fuck, David?" I shouted, pulling frantically at the door handle. "Let me out!"

But the central locking stopped me from being able to get out of the car. My heart and pulse were racing. I wasn't afraid—I was furious.

"Calm down, for Christ's sake," he snapped. "I just want to talk to you."

I spun around in my seat, my face burning. "Talk? You've taken me against my will. Now let me go!"

"Lauren, Christ, don't be so dramatic. I just wanted to get us here so we could go for a walk and talk this through."

"There's nothing to talk about. Now let me out!"

He closed his eyes and took a deep breath in through his nose, then blew the air out through his lips. I watched as he visibly tried to steady himself and, for the first time, a tingle of fear found its way along my neck.

"Lauren..." he began, his voice slow and measured. "Here's what's going to happen. You're going to calm down, then we're going to go for a walk in the dunes and get this all sorted out, alright?"

Overhead, storm clouds were gathering, and my stomach twisted. "Let's just talk here," I said, forcing myself to sound calmer this time. "It looks like it might rain."

He glanced out the window and shook his head. "It'll pass. There's nothing in it. Now, are you calm enough for me to let you out?"

My fear spiked. For me to 'let' you out. I swallowed hard and tried to calm my breathing.

David and I had met a few months back at a police and media briefing when Isabelle Summers first went missing. He was in charge of the investigation, and I was there to brief the searchers on any poisonous plants or dangerous animals, including venomous snakes, to be mindful of when navigating the heavy bush-land of the Glenrock Conservation Area. His leadership and commitment to finding the missing girl had been hard to miss and even harder to resist. When he asked me out for drinks, the next day I immediately said yes. But as the weeks went by, David got too attached too quickly. I made it clear to him on our first date that I wasn't looking for anything serious. I thought he understood, but he began calling every day, sometimes every few hours, just to check in and see what I was up to. I spent a few nights at his place and he a few at mine, but eventually his neediness became claustrophobic and I all but stopped seeing him. I had made the mistake of a quick catch up here and there, just for sex, but every time we saw each other, it just reignited his need to be near me all the time.

"I'm calm," I told him. "You're right. I think we do need to talk. This has all been a misunderstanding."

"Finally," he grinned, completely oblivious to the underlying fear in my voice. "There's my girl. I knew you'd come around. That's why I brought you here, because I knew."

I returned his smile as best I could and felt a wave of relief wash over me as the click of his central locking sounded a chance at freedom.

As he climbed out, I searched desperately for any sign of someone nearby, but the site was empty.

Wind raked through my hair as I followed him toward the dunes. My heart was racing, and a heavy sickness formed in the pit of my stomach.

"Where did you go?" he demanded, as we drew closer to the dunes.

"What? I don't understand?"

"In the dunes. Where did you and Ashley go to..." He squeezed his eyes closed as though his head might be about to explode. "Don't make me say it."

"We were just here researching the birds," I lied. "It wasn't like that."

"Don't lie to me!" he shouted, and I jumped at the sudden volume of his voice.

"I'm not, I—"

"Where was it?"

"David—"

He spun and grabbed me by the arm. "You fucked him in these dunes. I know you did."

I thought back to the day Andrew that and I had made love. His touch had been gentle and reassuring. Just being with him had made me feel safe.

"Show me!" he bellowed again, causing me to flinch.

"Alright, okay," I relented. "It was over there." I pointed to the place we made love and wished more than anything I could be back in that moment, wrapped around Andrew and far away from the man whose fingers were digging deep into my arm.

He looked over to where I was pointing and stepped forward, pulling me along with him. "Let's go."

His strides were long, and it was hard to keep up. I tripped as he pulled me through the deep, soft sand, and gasped when my ankle hit a rock half buried beneath scattered beach reeds.

"Here?" he demanded, when we reached the place I had pointed to.

"Yes, it was here," I nodded. "Now what?"

"We erase that memory and start fresh," he told me.

"We what?"

"We make love, then we start over. If the two of you were together in any other place, we'll deal with that too, but for now, this is the one I know about, so this is where we'll start."

"David, this is ridiculous," I managed. "How could you possibly know that?"

"I saw the change in you. I was right there in the car watching the two of you. You walked in and there was distance between you, but when you came out, things were different. I could sense it in the way you walked next to him, the way your hair was messy."

"You've been spying on me?"

"Not spying, just watching," he said. "I needed to know."

I shook my head, anger starting to replace my fear. "Needed to know what, exactly? I told you I didn't want a relationship."

"I needed to know why you were with him all the time. Meeting him in cafes and parking garages."

David had been stalking me. He had followed me everywhere I went and knew every move I made.

"David, why?" I asked. "Why would you do that?"

"I tried," he said, shaking his head. "I tried to warn you that you were making me upset, but you just ignored it."

"Warn me?" I asked. "Warn me how?"

"I left that bird in the box. I tried to tell you, Lauren. I tried to warn you that I was getting upset, but you didn't even mention it. Stella too. I rang and hung up so many times. I wanted to tell her what you were doing with her husband. I even followed the boy once. Thought about telling him his father was a fraud and a liar. I just... I just had to be sure first."

The air disappeared from my lungs as I realised that aside from the two men who went to Andrew's house, all the other threats and strange goings on had been David. Not the developers.

He paced back and forth, scratching at the back of his head as though a thousand invisible ants were crawling over him. When he looked away, my eyes darted across the dunes, desperate to see anyone I could call out to, but the beach was deserted. I glanced behind me, wondering if I could outrun him, but there was nowhere to go.

Suddenly, he stopped and stared at me. "Get undressed."

A chill ran through me. The thought of him seeing me, touching me, made my skin crawl. I shook my head, instinctively wrapping an arm around myself.

"I said, get undressed!" He lunged forward, and I barely had time to throw my arms up, bracing for impact. "Why? Why do you want him and not me?"

"David," I whispered. "Please, stop."

"I want to know why! You're all the same. You come on all strong like you want something, then none of you ever do. Tell me why!"

My body was shaking with a mix of fear and rage. I wanted to stand tall and scream in his face. I wanted to punch and kick at him. But he was unstable, emotional, and clearly capable of anything.

"What do you mean?" I asked, trying to steady myself. "Did someone else do something to hurt you?"

"Someone else?" He stared at me as though I was insane and then threw up his hands. "How about everyone else? My wife, for a start. Before we could start a family, she left me for some fuckwit from the gym. Then the girl I met after that, she said she didn't want anything but women say that just to pull you in, you know? But the harder I tried to show her how much I wanted to be with her, the more she pulled away."

"David—"

"That's not all," he continued. "It goes all the way back to university. There was Elle, she was the first one. She made out like she wanted something between us, but—

"Elle Nolan? The Tribune reporter?"

"That's right," he spat.

"That was a long time ago," I said, trying to calm him. "I thought the two of you were friends."

"But nothing's changed!" he shouted. "You're all the same. Every time I put myself out there, I risk my pride, my dignity, I give it all. Do you have any idea what that's like? How humiliating it is? How degrading, when every single one of you throws it back in my face? Even fucking Isabelle."

"Isabelle?" I breathed, shock pulsing through my body.

He immediately stopped pacing and stared at me, his eyes wide with panic. "Fuck!" he shouted. "Fucking idiot!" He pounded his fist against the side of his head, and I took two steps back. My mind screamed at me to run, but there was nowhere I could run to.

Slowly, he looked up and fixed his gaze on me. "She made me think we were on a date," he said, the sudden quiet of his voice scaring me even more. "We caught up at Glenrock the morning after a function."

Sensing where the story was going, I tried to stop him. "David, I don't want to know this. Whatever happened is your business. I don't want to get involved."

"I was helping her navigate the area to look for some endangered birds," he continued, ignoring my pleas to stop. "She thought she saw some with a nest but when she got closer, they started swooping, trying to protect it. She stumbled, and I caught her. She was so close. I just wanted to kiss her, but when I tried, she freaked out on me."

"David please—"

"She was so desperate to get away from me that she fell and hit her head."

His eyes were glassy and vacant as he recounted the story. I gently took two more steps back up the dune, finally creating some distance between us. Behind me, the waves were crashing, and I turned to see if anyone had come onto the beach. My heart instantly leapt when up in the distance I saw the shape of a person and a tiny rambling speck that might have been a dog.

"Hey!" he shouted, suddenly noticing I had moved further away. "Come down from there."

"I'm still here," I reassured him, hands outstretched, as I reluctantly moved back down into the gully.

"I didn't do it on purpose. You need to understand that," he said. "But even when I tried to help her, she just kept screaming at me to get away from her like I was some kind of monster."

I nodded and did my best to appear understanding.

"She just kept screaming 'don't touch me, don't touch me'. I don't know what happened, but something just snapped." He tore his eyes away from me and searched the ground.

"David?"

He walked over to the rock I had tripped on and pulled it out of the sand. It was a little larger than his fist, and I felt a tear slip over my cheek.

"Eventually, I picked up a rock just like this one and smashed it into her head. I had to just to shut her up."

My throat was dry, and any words I wanted to say broke apart like brittle leaves.

"I'm sorry, Lauren," he said, stepping toward me. "I already know I can't trust you."

I turned to try and see over the dune to where the person on the beach had been. But before I could run or scream, he raised the rock over his head and brought it down with all his strength.

My last thought was the warmth of Andrew's arms holding me close right there in at that very spot among the dunes.

Chapter Sixty-Two

LUCY

When Lucy looked down, her hands were trembling.

"Okay, let me get this straight," Stella began. "David from the SES who searched for Isabelle Summers, actually gave his number to her the night before she disappeared?"

"Yes, and then pretended not to know her when Marianne called."

Lucy nodded slowly. "So, you think he had something to do with her disappearance?"

"It's looking like a possibility. David..." Lucy breathed. "How did I not see this before?"

"So, what do we do now?"

Lucy turned to answer, and then suddenly it hit her. She was the reason Elle hadn't come to see Marianne. When they'd spoken about the pressure she was feeling, Lucy had encouraged her to reach out to someone for support. That someone had been David.

"Shit!" Lucy swore as she turned the car on. "Elle might be in trouble."

Stella stared wide-eyed as Lucy chose Elle's number from the contacts in her phone and hit *call*. The phone quickly connected to the communications hub in her car and they both leaned toward the speaker and waited for Elle to pick up.

"Shit, do you think we're too late?" Stella asked.

"We don't know anything other than he gave Isabelle his number," Lucy reminded her. "It could be nothing."

But as they exchanged glances, Lucy knew they were both fearful for Elle's safety.

"Try to call her again," Stella urged, as Lucy started the car and headed back toward the city.

When she didn't pick up the second time, Lucy cursed and pushed her foot even harder on the accelerator.

"Do you really think he's capable of doing something to Isabelle Summers and then actually leading a search team to try and find her?" Stella asked, as they flew down the highway.

"I don't know," Lucy replied. "But what better way to lead searchers away from the body?"

For a moment, they were both quiet, and then Stella looked over. "How sure are you that Elle's with him right now?"

"Sure enough," Lucy said.

"Call him."

"What?" She glanced over at Stella, not certain she had heard correctly. "Call David?"

"You know him, right? Call him. Say you're looking for Elle. Say it's something about the case."

Lucy ran the idea over in her mind. It wasn't completely stupid. But could she pull it off without alerting him to why she was really calling? Deciding it was better than pounding on Elle's door with no explanation, Lucy found his number and called.

Once again, they leaned in and waited for an answer.

"Lucy?" a female voice answered.

"Elle? Is that you?"

"I saw your name come up, so I answered. David's in the bathroom. Is everything alright?"

"I was trying to call you," Lucy whispered, not really knowing why. "Can you quickly look through David's phone and see if he called anyone called Isabelle?"

There was a pause on the other end of the line. "You mean Isabelle, as in, Summers?"

"There's no time, Elle. Please, just look. And hurry."

Lucy held her breath as the line went silent, and didn't breathe again until Elle came back on the line.

"No, nothing."

"Social media?"

"I don't have time for that," she said. "He'll be back any minute."

"Photos?"

"Of?"

"Anything that seems out of place."

The line went quiet until Elle caught her breath. "Elle? Elle, what is it?" Lucy urged. "Talk to me."

"There's a selfie of him and Isabelle at the start of the Glenrock track," she managed, her voice trembling. "But that's not all. There's also a heap of pictures of him and Lauren Ellis, like they were *together.*"

Lucy glanced at Stella and tried to comprehend what Elle was saying without veering off the road. "There's pictures of him with *Lauren*?"

"Yes, it's Lauren. Lucy, what the hell?"

"Elle, listen to me very carefully. I think David killed Isabelle and Lauren."

Suddenly there was a noise in the background, and Lucy heard David ask what Elle she was doing. Then a cluttering sound as though the phone dropped onto the floor.

"Elle?" she shouted. "Elle?"

But the line went dead.

"Jesus Christ, he killed both of them. Lauren and Isabelle," Lucy breathed, as she reached down and pulled the car's hand-held CB radio up to her lips. They were only ten minutes out, but there was every chance it might be long enough for Elle to become David's third victim. "All units, this is Senior Sergeant Lucy Dickson. Break and enter at eighteen Parry Street, Newcastle. Occupant is inside. I repeat, female occupant is inside."

"Dicks!" Yieldon's voice boomed back. "Change frequencies to 477.3 Now. This is Inspector Chris Yieldon. Units will disregard. I repeat, all units will disregard."

Lucy screamed out in frustration. Elle was in danger and Yieldon was still acting as though she had lost her mind and couldn't be trusted. She quickly changed frequencies. "Yieldon, it's Lucy. Come in."

"Dicks, what the hell? I told you—"

"It's David Hammond!" she shouted into the receiver. "He killed them both. Isabelle Summers and Lauren Ellis."

"What?"

"He did it. I have evidence. Yieldon, he's at Elle Nolan's house now and I think he knows we're onto him."

"*We*? Who the hell is we?"

"Just get there! Now, Chris. She's in trouble."

Lucy screeched the car to a stop out the front of Elle's without bothering to park. As they leapt from the vehicle and ran toward the door, something in Stella's hand caught her eye.

"Stella!" she gasped. "Where did you get a gun?"

"It's Andrew's. I thought—"

"Give it to me."

Stella had been about to hand it over when the sound of Elle screaming echoed from inside the house. Lucy instinctively turned and kicked at the door, over and over, until the wood of the door frame splintered. With the door hanging from its hinges, Lucy turned to take the gun, but before she could act, Stella ran right past her and into the house.

Chapter Sixty-Three
ELLE

"**S**top!" I screamed, as David pounded on the bedroom door trying to get in.

"Elle!" he shouted. "You've got this all wrong. Just let me in so I can explain."

"You killed them," I sobbed, my back against the door. "Isabelle and Lauren. You killed them. Why?"

"Elle, please. Just open the door."

My phone was in the kitchen and when David caught me looking at his photos, the look on his face had been enough to send me running upstairs to lock myself in the bedroom. Now I was trapped. "Lucy is on her way," I shouted. "The police are coming."

When he didn't answer, I waited and dared to hope he had run before Lucy arrived. After a few seconds passed, I slowly and quietly pressed my ear to the door. When I heard nothing, my hopes rose a little higher. He was smart enough to know Lucy would have called it in, that in minutes police would be swarming my house. Very carefully, I knelt on my hands and knees and peered under the door, expecting to see only the empty platform at the top of the stairs. But to my horror, he kicked the door in, the force throwing me back into the corner of the room.

"You pack of bitches," he swore, his lip curling as he stormed toward me. "You all think you're better than me... and you... you're the worst of all."

"What are you talking about?" I cried, cowering on the floor.

"You were the first," he said. "Even back at uni you were a tease, always thinking it was a game to play with my feelings."

I couldn't breathe. I was crumpled in the corner of my bedroom, and no air was getting to my lungs.

"David, please," I tried. "My ribs..."

"Tell me something, Elle," he said, crouching down in front of me. "What's so great about Andrew fucking Ashley, huh? You and Lauren, you both made fools of yourselves running after him. Why?"

"Nothing," I gasped. "He's an arsehole."

David grinned and clicked his tongue. "Didn't stop you fucking him though, did it?"

"David—"

"Oh, that's right," he said with a sneer. "You loved him. My apologies."

"And, Isabelle?" I asked, gasped for air. "What did she do?"

"That was an accident. I told you that already."

"No, David, you didn't."

He thought for a moment, confusion clouding his face.

"Is that why you killed Lauren?" I managed. "She found out about Isabelle?"

"Shut up!" he shouted. "You're confusing me. You're all trying to confuse me."

Behind him, movement on the stairs caught my attention and to my surprise, it was not Lucy but Stella creeping forward, her finger on her lips and a gun in her hand.

I immediately knew what I had to do. I winced and reached to the right side of my ribs. "It hurts so much. I can barely breathe..."

"That's because you have a broken rib," David said, his voice flat and void of any emotion. "It's punctured your lung." He leaned in to look closer, clearly captivated by the pain he had caused me.

As he looked down, I nodded to Stella, and she rushed into the room. "Stand up and back away from her!" she shouted, pointing the gun straight at David. "I mean it. I've had enough and I swear to God, I will shoot you."

David leaned back, his eyes blazing into mine. Then he slowly stood and turned toward Stella. "You," he scoffed, as Lucy strode into the room and quickly took the gun from Stella.

"No. *Us*," Lucy corrected.

David chuckled and rolled his eyes, his attention now focused on Stella and Lucy.

"I've called it in, David. You're done," Lucy said, the gun still pointed at him.

"It's done when I say it's done. And just so you know," he said, gesturing toward the gun. "The lovely Mrs Ashley left the safety on."

In the fraction of a second it took for Lucy to glance at the gun, David dived forward, knocking her to the ground. As they wrestled for the gun, Stella picked up a potted fern from my dresser and smashed the terracotta pot over David's head. Momentarily stunned, he rolled off Lucy, and she grabbed for the gun, but it slid just out of reach.

"Stella," I called. "Kick it to me!"

Stella and David both went for the gun, but she got to it first, kicking it out of his reach. As he and I both stared at it lying on the floor, I knew that despite my pain, I had to try. I launched forward, landing on my stomach as my fingers closed around the barrel. I quickly rolled onto my back and as David lunged forward, I fired and the bullet hit him in the chest. His body slumped over me, and I gasped under his weight. Stella and Lucy worked quickly to roll him off, the gunshot wound covering me in his blood.

"Elle, are you alright?" Lucy gushed. "Talk to me. Can you breathe?"

"I think I have a punctured lung."

"The ambulance is on its way. They'll be here any minute. Just hold on."

"Stella, you came in first," I managed. "Despite everything you—"

Suddenly, to our surprise, David gasped and lunged up from the floor toward Lucy, grabbing her from behind. As his hands wrapped around her throat, without thinking, I lifted the gun and fired. Once, twice, three times until he fell back with a heavy thud.

"Christ," Lucy breathed, clutching at her throat. "Elle, he could have killed me."

I stared down at David's lifeless body covered in blood and swallowed hard. He had been a friend. Someone I trusted.

"Elle..."

"I killed him," I managed. "I..."

Lucy and Stella both flung their arms around me at once. "He was a murderer," Lucy managed. "And what you did just saved my life."

David was dead. I was the one who pulled the trigger. How I would ever get over that, I had no idea, but I wasn't alone. Stella and Lucy were there, their hands reaching for mine, holding me up when I felt like crumbling. Somehow, through this tangled mess of lies and loss, we had found in each other the kind of bond that only the darkest moments can create.

As sirens echoed from the street outside, we all took a moment to look each other deep in the eye. Together, the three of us had risked it all and, despite our differences, betrayals, and mistakes, we had been rewarded with what we needed most.

For Stella, it was knowing her son would go free now that we could prove David killed Lauren.

For Lucy, it was a clear conscience and the chance to start over.

And for me, it was simply knowing that I was strong. That for all my mistakes and feelings of inadequacy, I no longer needed food, or men, or my father's love to define who I was. No matter what I chose to do with my life from that moment forward, whether I met everyone's expectations or chose my own path, I was finally strong enough to cast my own shadow as I flew up toward the sun like a brightly coloured bird.

EPILOGUE

Branches cracked underfoot as Isabelle ran along the bush track. She could feel the sharp edges of loose bark and branches cutting into her skin, but she didn't dare stop. It was raining and it was dark. Wet branches slapped against her cheeks, and she slipped in the loose mud gathering along the track.

The last time she was at Glenrock Conservation Area, she had been looking for the Gemini Birds.

An SES agent she met the night before had offered to show her where he'd seen them only a few days earlier. He was handsome, and he was nice. But when his lips had searched for hers out on the trail, she wasn't ready. She said no, but he kept coming. She had fallen and hit her head, but he still wouldn't stop. When he smashed the rock against her skull, Isabelle felt like the world was caving in around her. The throbbing pain. The blinding light.

But her nightmare hadn't been over.

When he hoisted her up and over his shoulder, Isabelle could only watch as the trees tilted sideways and her world began to spin. As he carried her back to the house, her dreams began to blur. She slipped in and out of consciousness, and the next thing she remembered was waking up on a cot in the dark.

In the days and weeks that followed, David Hammond tendered to the wound and gave her a camper toilet to use. He brought meals and eventually started what would become their *relationship*. He would undress her, touch her, and force himself upon her.

As she ran along the muddy track, Isabelle heard the sound of tyres throwing up water on the road ahead. Not much further now. Her lungs were burning, about to explode, but she had to keep running. When she finally broke the tree line and ran out onto the road, an oncoming car swerved wildly, its headlights flashing into the bush. She screamed as it came to a screeching stop across the centre line.

"Are you fucking crazy?" the driver shouted as he got out and marched around the car. "You could have killed us."

A woman in an evening gown climbed out of the passenger side and shivered against the cold.

Isabelle opened her mouth, but words failed her. The rain had soaked through her torn nightgown, and it clung to her skin. She was freezing and her feet were torn and bleeding.

"She needs help, Jack, the woman shouted as she got closer. "Call an ambulance and the police."

Isabelle took shelter in the couple's car until help arrived, and it was like feeling the sun on her face. Finally, she was safe.

"So, what do you think?" I asked as Isabelle finished reading the opening chapter of my book. "Are you happy with it so far?"

When Isabelle recovered from her injuries, the physical ones at least, I asked if I could write her story. It would be my first book.

As I waited for to her answer, I watched her sitting across from me. Her long dark hair fell loosely around her shoulders, and she had soft, delicate features, like someone who had always felt more like a dream than a reality. She had an air of quiet resilience and something in the way she held herself told me she was stronger than she looked. She must be to have weathered the storm that was David Hammond.

"It's really good, Elle," she said eventually. "I really hope working on this with you helps me to move forward."

I smiled and sat back in my chair. "I hope so too. I always thought... well, from what David said, it sounded like... I'm just glad you got away."

"David." His name hung on her lips. "He was an unbalanced man. So angry and resentful. What he did in the bush that day was out of rage and rejection. I know that now, but what came after was inhumane."

I paused a moment and considered my words. "I thought of him as a friend once. I confided in him," I said eventually. "I just can't get my head around what he did to you, and to Lauren."

"I honestly never thought I'd get out of there," Isabelle said. "But when days passed, and I realised he wasn't coming back, it gave me time. Time to escape. I have you to thank for that, Elle." Isabelle peered down at her hands. Scars had formed where her fingers were sliced open as she desperately tried to unscrew the rusted bars from the windows. "I thought I was going to spend the rest of my life in that room in the dark, with him coming in and..."

Tears welled in her eyes, and my heart ached for her. "Isabelle—"

"I'm sorry," she said, sitting up straighter in her seat. "Hopefully in time..."

"You're doing great," I told her with the best smile I could manage. "There's nothing to be sorry for."

I had hoped writing the book would be cathartic for both of us, but Isabelle clearly needed more. She needed support.

"There was a time when I felt like I was alone too," I told her. "I can never completely understand what it is you're going through, but there was one thing, well, two things, really, that helped me a great deal. I'd be happy to share them with you if you'd like?"

She glanced back at me and, for the first time, I saw a glimmer of hope in her eyes.

"I'd really appreciate that, Elle," she said. "What were they?"

"I think it would be better to show you," I said. "Do you have some time?"

When she nodded, I pulled out my mobile phone and scrolled to the group chat between myself, Stella, and Lucy.

David's actions had irreversibly changed all of our lives. While on the outside, we couldn't be more different, trauma had tangled us in a way that could never be untied. If anyone was going to understand the impact of what David did to Isabelle, it was the three of us.

I began to type, already knowing what their answer would be.

I hit send and my phone wasn't even back in my pocket before they had each sent a reply.

"They're on their way," I said to Isabelle with a smile.

"They?"

"My two friends, Lucy and Stella."

Isabelle looked at me, and I could see she was confused. "You mean Stella Ashley? As in the former Lord Mayor's wife and Lucy Dickson from the police?"

"Yes," I told her. "I know we must seem an odd trio, you know... after everything."

Isabelle raised her brow and took a sip of coffee. "Not really," she said eventually. "People are not so different from birds."

"Birds?"

"All creatures, really. Do you know why the Gemini Birds were so much further north than their natural habitat?"

I shook my head and leaned in closer.

"Because they were dying," she said in a tone that was matter of fact. "Over development was causing the loss of their habitat. For them, the world was changing. If they didn't change with it, they would have all died out. So they started moving north."

I searched her face and understood that she wasn't just talking about the Gemini Birds.

"You're saying the three of us migrated toward each other to survive?"

"Didn't you?"

I thought back to the moment Stella and Lucy burst into my room and saved my life. "I guess we did," I said. "Literally, actually."

Isabelle smiled, and for the first time, it reached her eyes. "I think you know that's not what I meant."

"I know. A lot of things have changed. I've changed."

"We've all changed," she said quietly. "Sometimes, it's hard to see how something so horrible could ever be a good thing, especially when it changes who you are."

I nodded and waited for her to finish.

"But that's the thing about life, Elle," she continued. "Change is inevitable. Trying to stop it is like trying to hold back the tide. You'll drown trying. The only way to survive is by surrendering. By letting life take you to wherever it is you need to go."

"I considered her words and thought about all we had been through, and those we lost along the way.

"Letting go is hard," I managed. "Especially of the things that make us who we are."

From across the road, Stella and Lucy called out and waved.

"Well, the good thing is you don't have to do it alone, Elle, "Isabelle said, looking over at my friends.

I followed her gaze and then looked back and squeezed her hand. "No, I don't. And now neither do you."

Tell The World!

Loved The Alibi?

Your opinion matters! Without readers like you, authors
like me would never have the privilege of doing the
one thing we love most - writing.

If you enjoyed the book please leave a review to let
other readers know that they might enjoy it too.

It only takes a minute and would mean the world to me.

Thank you!

About the Author

Nikki Lee Taylor is a long-time newspaper journalist turned fiction writer.

She is also a dreamer, a doer, a storyteller, a coffee lover, and fur-mum to a little Cocker Spaniel / Tasmanian Devil named Saxon.

She loves to write stories about women finding their inner strength and reminds herself every day that what we often see as flaws, are really just the cracks that allow our light to shine even brighter.

Nikki's previous titles include International Best Selling duology The Secrets We Keep, and The Truth We Tell.

Ready For Your Next Great Read?

One woman who has lost everything. Another with everything to lose.

SOPHIE

Sophie Miller had it all. A loving husband and adorable six-year-old son. They were a perfect family. Until a drunk driver lost control and James and Josh were killed on their way to a soccer game. Five years later, and a mother without a child, she remains a shadow of herself, barely leaving the house and relying on anti-anxiety pills just to get through the day. Working from home as a book editor is safe – or so she thinks, until a manuscript comes across her desk that threatens to turn her world upside down.

Because Sophie has a secret. A child that many years ago she helped to conceive.

The story triggers in her a sudden longing to know. Would the child share Josh's chestnut hair? The same gold and brown flecks of his eyes. She wouldn't interfere. She would watch from a distance. Just to know. Could she see the features of her little boy reflected one last time?

It wouldn't hurt just to look. *Would it?*

MADELYN-MAY

Madelyn-May Marozzi has it all. To her Love, Mommy online community she is the perfect mother. She has a successful husband, perfect twins, and an idyllic life.

What they don't know is that Madelyn-May is not who she says she is.

Certain everyone who knows the truth about her past is long gone, Madelyn-May's world is turned upside down when an anonymous email drops into her inbox threatening to expose a horrific crime she committed as a teenager.

But should she take the threat seriously? Everyone involved is already dead. *Aren't they?*

Let's Stay In Touch

I love to hear from my readers and endeavor to answer all emails personally.

You can reach me at **nikki@nikkileetaylor.com**

- **Website**: nikkileetaylor.com
- **TikTok:** nikkileetaylor_author
- **Insta**: @nikki.leetaylor
- **FB:** Nikki Lee Taylor
- **Goodreads**: Nikki Lee Taylor

Nikki Lee Taylor